HAIL
TO THE
CHEF

JULIE HYZY

BERKLEY PRIME CRIME, NEW YORK

THE BERKLEY PUBLISHING GROUP
Published by the Penguin Group
Penguin Group (USA) LLC
375 Hudson Street, New York, New York 10014

USA • Canada • UK • Ireland • Australia • New Zealand • India • South Africa • China

penguin.com

A Penguin Random House Company

HAIL TO THE CHEF

A Berkley Prime Crime Book / published by arrangement with Tekno Books

Berkley Prime Crime Books are published by The Berkley Publishing Group.
BERKLEY® PRIME CRIME and the PRIME CRIME logo
are trademarks of Penguin Group (USA) LLC.

For information, address: The Berkley Publishing Group,
a division of Penguin Group (USA) LLC,
375 Hudson Street, New York, New York 10014.

ISBN: 978-0-425-22499-1

PUBLISHING HISTORY
Berkley Prime Crime mass-market edition / December 2008

PRINTED IN THE UNITED STATES OF AMERICA

15   14   13   12   11   10   9   8   7   6

Cover illustration by Ben Perini.
Cover design by Annette Fiore Defex.
Interior text design by Laura K. Corless.

For Rene
and
For Karen

ACKNOWLEDGMENTS

I wish I could cook as well as Ollie does, because then I would invite everyone over for a lavish dinner to express my heartfelt gratitude.

Since I can't do that, my sincere thanks here will have to suffice:

To the wonderful people at Berkley Prime Crime, especially my editor, Natalee Rosenstein; Michelle Vega; Catherine Milne; and Erica Rose. I hope you know how much I appreciate your guidance, help, and support. And to the great folks at Tekno Books: Marty Greenberg, John Helfers, and Denise Little, without whom Ollie would never exist.

When I asked my brother, Paul, how to rig up an electrical charge strong enough to kill a person and possibly destroy the White House, he was delighted to help. He even created a mock-up and patiently explained how to make it work. In the book, Stanley does the same for Ollie. Any errors in that scene, or others, are mine alone.

I read and reread former White House chef Walter Scheib's book, *White House Chef*, but there's no substitute for talking with someone who's actually been there. I owe a special debt of gratitude to this kind and gracious man who answered my questions about room locations, staff meetings, and certain protocols. Again, any errors are mine.

Thanks to the Southland Scribes, Mystery Writers of America, Sisters in Crime, and Thriller Writers of America for camaraderie and support, and to readers who e-mail to tell me what they think about the newest book. Means a lot to me.

Special thanks to my writing partner, Michael A. Black, whose wise counsel keeps me going and who always has my back.

And, as always, to my family: Curt, Robyn, Sara, and Biz. You guys are the best.

CHAPTER 1

I STOPPED SHORT AT THE DOORWAY TO THE White House solarium. I knew better than to interrupt the First Lady when she was in such deep discussion with her social secretary and the assistant usher. Particularly today. But when Mrs. Campbell saw me, she beckoned me into the top-floor room.

"Ollie, thank goodness," she said, silencing her two staff members. "Talk to Sean, would you? Persuade him to come to Thanksgiving dinner."

Seated apart from Mrs. Campbell's conference, across the expansive room—I'd missed him at first glance—Sean Baxter sprang to his feet. With his sandy blonde hair and boy-next-door good looks, he could have passed for Matt Damon's younger brother. "Hey," he said. "It's good to see you again."

The two staffers had stopped talking long enough to acknowledge my presence with polite smiles. As soon as

Sean stood, however, they resumed peppering the First Lady with their requests.

"Mrs. Campbell," the social secretary said, her voice strained, "if we don't confirm these last-minute updates today, the final batch of Christmas cards won't be sent until next week."

The assistant usher added, "The press will skewer us for slighting these folks."

Mrs. Campbell nodded. "Then let's not wait a moment longer. How many—"

Sudden, hard footfalls above us halted all conversation. One breathless instant later, a flash—like black lightning—streaked past the room's floor-to-ceiling windows. Though distorted by the sheer curtains, the silhouette was clear. A man. Carrying a high-powered rifle.

Sprinting along the adjacent promenade, the shadow moved at hyper-speed. I barely had time to process his appearance when the gunman burst through the solarium's outside door, ordering us all into the central hall.

"Move!" he shouted, darting around us to take the point position at the doorway. "Come on!"

His all-black garb and bulletproof vest didn't scare me. Neither did the gun.

But the look on his face sent prickles of panic tingling down the back of my neck. This was Dennis, one of our rooftop snipers. His words were terse. "Follow me."

The First Lady stared at him. "But—"

"No time," he said. "Secret Service agents are on their way up. We have to get you out of here. Now."

We had been through drills before, so we knew what to do—but the peculiar energy wrapped around this situation made everything seem louder, brighter, scarier. Dennis tensed. He'd slung the rifle onto his back and now gripped a semiautomatic pistol in one hand, and another weaponlike object I didn't recognize in the other. His head twisted side to side as he walked, the picture of stealth. "Stay close," he whispered as he stopped to peer around the corner. "Stay low."

Two suited Secret Service agents joined us in the central hall, using hand signals to shepherd us toward the stairway nearest the music room. Secret Service agents didn't generally accompany the First Family into the residence. That must be why Dennis had been tagged for getting us out. As one of the many snipers on the rooftop, he was closer to the First Lady's position than an agent would be.

The moment we entered the stairway, Dennis ran back the way we'd come. The five of us from the solarium tried to be quiet, but our shoes clattered down the steps, just loud enough to mask the thunderous pounding of my heart. I watched our escorts, knowing better than to question, knowing better than to say a word. The two suited men spoke into their hands in low, brusque tones as we made our way to the bottom level of the East Wing. The First Lady, Sean, and I were herded by Agent Kevin Martin. The other two were taken by Agent Klein.

I knew where we were headed. The bunker.

This was no drill.

I started back toward the kitchen. "My staff," I said. As the White House executive chef, the safety of my people was of paramount importance to me.

Agent Martin shook his head. "We've got your people covered, Ollie," he said, tension making his blue eyes darken.

He hustled us down, deeper into the fortresslike bunker. The enormous tubelike structure, built back when Franklin Delano Roosevelt was president, was purportedly designed to withstand a nuclear blast. Officially known as the Presidential Emergency Operations Center, it had several meeting rooms and conference areas outfitted with televisions, telephones, and communications systems. Sleeping rooms, too. Agent Martin stopped us in front of the first one on the right.

"Get in there. We'll come back when it's clear."

I couldn't let it go. "Where's my staff now?"

Before he could answer, Mrs. Campbell interrupted. "Where's my husband? Is he safe?"

"He's been evacuated."

"Is he all right?"

Martin nodded. "Please remain here until you're given the all-clear."

"But what—"

"I'm not at liberty to—"

"Agent Martin," Mrs. Campbell said with more than a little snap. "You will tell me exactly where my husband is. And exactly what's going on."

He pursed his lips, shooting a derisive look at Sean. "Only staff members . . ."

"You can talk in front of Sean," Mrs. Campbell said. "He's family. Now, where's my husband?"

Agent Martin's jaw flexed. One of our more handsome Secret Service agents, the man was blessed with Irish good looks and rigid determination. With obvious reluctance, he said, "Marine One evacuated the president to Camp David." He started to move away, but Mrs. Campbell stepped forward, laying her hand on his arm.

"Tell me why."

"The president is safe for now," he said. "But we have reason to suspect an explosive device may be present in the White House."

I couldn't decide whether the loudest gasp came from

me or Mrs. Campbell. She recovered immediately, however, and nodded, surprisingly cool. "Thank you."

I had to know. "Who went to Camp David with him?"

Martin fixed me with a meaningful look. "Everyone you would expect."

I sighed with relief. That meant Tom had been evacuated, too. At least he was safe. "What happens next?" I asked.

He ignored my question. "I'll be back when I can."

The armored door closed behind him with a *thunk* of frightening finality as the three of us turned inward, forming an uncertain triangle. "Where do you think they found a bomb?" I asked.

Mrs. Campbell paced. The room we occupied was small, with a curtained, fake window on its far wall. Lights behind the plastic panes strove for a sunny-day touch, but their cold, blue fluorescence fooled no one. Designed for safety rather than lavish entertaining, the room was nonetheless comfortable with a kitchenette, a set of bunk beds, chairs, recent magazines on the dining table, and cabinets that I assumed were stocked with shelf-stable foods and water. I took a quick peek behind the far door and found a full bathroom. Good. Just in case we were stuck here for a while.

"This may be just a precaution," the First Lady finally said. "I'm sure there's no bomb. Perhaps the Secret Service is running an unusual drill."

Sean asked, "This is an awful lot for just a precaution, isn't it?"

Neither Mrs. Campbell nor I answered. He was right. The White House and its inhabitants received threats on an almost daily basis. Precautions were taken as a matter of course, but rarely to this extent.

Something occurred to me. "Wasn't the president conducting meetings in the West Wing today?"

Mrs. Campbell nodded, the lines between her brows deep with worry. "I was originally scheduled to meet Sean in the dining room outside the Oval Office," she said. "We planned to lunch with Harrison. He hasn't seen Sean in such a long time."

"Did you say lunch?" I asked.

Mrs. Campbell waved away my concerns. "I didn't put it on the schedule, Ollie, because we planned to grab a bite from the White House Mess. But then the president needed to meet with his advisers about this new terrorist threat, and everything shifted. In fact, that's why I called you up to the solarium—to inquire about getting lunch." She smiled, but I could tell it was less for my benefit than for her own. "And here we are."

So they hadn't eaten yet. In an effort to inject normalcy into our bizarre circumstances, I started opening cabinets, assessing what ingredients I had at hand to play with. "If they evacuated the president to Camp David," I said, musing, "then the bomb must be located between the Oval Office and here. Otherwise he'd be in the bunker, too."

Sean pulled a box of cookies from the cabinet's very top shelf. "Thank God they found it. And that they got him out. You're right, Ollie. They wouldn't want to transfer him across the residence. Can you imagine the risk . . . ?" He let the thought linger. I wished he hadn't.

"I'm certain this is just a precaution," Mrs. Campbell said again with unnatural brightness. "Any minute now they'll give us the—"

A high-pitched siren cut off the rest of her words. Loud even through the bunker's thick walls, the danger signal rang clear. Jolts of fear speared my gut. Above the door, a Mars light undulated—its beacons of red shooting across the room, like an ON AIR signal gone haywire.

When the siren silenced, the intercom crackled. "Do not leave your assigned room . . . I repeat . . . do not leave your room. Do not open your door. Wait for further instructions. This is not a drill."

Sean dropped the box of cookies. The shock in his face was no doubt a mirror of my own. Mrs. Campbell collapsed into one of the chairs, her head in prayerful hands. "Dear God," she said, "protect us all."

CHAPTER 2

"I KNOW THAT THIS ISN'T MUCH," I SAID, AS I placed a thrown-together lunch on the small table, "but we don't know how long we'll be here. We need to keep our spirits up."

"Do you need any help?" Sean asked me.

I shook my head. We'd been sequestered for more than an hour. In that time, one of the Secret Service agents had stopped by long enough to let us know that the purported bomb had been located and disabled by the bomb squad. Before allowing any of us to resume our duties, however, the entire residence would be swept for additional explosives. The special agent requested our patience for the duration.

While we waited, I scrounged. In addition to the bottled water and PowerBars, I'd found a supply of interesting ingredients and freeze-dried packets. What used to be called C-rations were now more appealingly known as MRE— meals ready to eat. Augmenting these were canned foods and a few necessary staples. I went to work.

Less than fifteen minutes later I'd pulled together canned chicken chunks, added a bit of soy sauce, peanut butter, a splash of oil, and a dash of pepper flakes, then heated it all in the microwave, and served it on a bed of microwave-cooked rice.

I'd then drained a can of carrots and bamboo shoots. With a little maple syrup and more soy sauce, I had a serviceable side dish. Next up, three-bean salad—again from a can. Drained and tossed with Italian dressing, it wasn't half bad. We were ready to serve.

"This is amazing, Ollie," Mrs. Campbell said as she and Sean sat at the table to enjoy the meal I'd cobbled together. I was used to using fresh vegetables, herbs, and even flowers as garnish. Here I presented a no-frills meal on utilitarian plates. Still, the chicken smelled good. "I can't believe how wonderful this all looks. You are a miracle worker."

I thanked her and began cleaning up.

"Aren't you planning to join us?" she asked.

Just as I opened my mouth to demur, my stomach rumbled its displeasure at the thought of turning down a meal.

Mrs. Campbell laughed. "That settles it. Sit down, Ollie."

I took the chair to the First Lady's left, which set me across from Sean. He smiled at me as he popped a forkful of bean salad into his mouth and said, "This is really good."

Ravenous, I nonetheless managed restraint as I helped myself to some chicken and carrots. Two bites in, I knew I'd done well. In fact, I wished I would've written everything down as I'd put it together. White House chefs were always hounded to create cookbooks. I envisioned my future tome with a chapter titled: "Bounty from the Bunker."

"I wonder when they'll let us out," I said with a glance at the room's digital readout. The White House assistant usher had called a staff meeting for this afternoon. With

Thanksgiving only two days away, and holiday decorations going up the day after that, we were already operating under tight deadlines. Every hour delay squeaked the schedule ever tighter. While we ate, I formulated alternative methods to get everything done on time.

As though reading my mind, Mrs. Campbell said, "How are plans for Thanksgiving dinner progressing?"

"Perfectly," I said. It was true—mostly. I'd taken over the position of executive chef in the spring, and since then I'd come to learn just how difficult it is to manage meals, staff, and administrative responsibilities at the same time. So far, however, plans for Thanksgiving were right on schedule. And they would continue to be, as long as we got out of our bunker prison soon. "Your guests are in for a treat. And Marcel has another spectacular dessert planned." Just to keep conversation going, I asked, "Are we still planning for six guests in addition to you and the president?"

Mrs. Campbell sighed. "Unfortunately, yes. The rest of my husband's family won't be attending this year, so we've invited my Washington, D.C., business partners—they're practically as close to me as cousins. But I have to admit, I was hoping to host a bigger event this year." She directed a pointed look at Sean. "Thanksgiving is a time for families to be together. Isn't that right?"

Sean considered the question. "It may be better for me to skip this one, Aunt Elaine." When he looked up, his eyes were clouded. "You know your partners wouldn't want me there."

She leaned toward him and placed a hand over his. "*I* want you there." Sitting up, she gave a bright smile. "And Ollie does, too. Don't you?"

Startled by the apparent non sequitur, I answered, "Of course."

Sean smiled at me from across the table. "Well, then, maybe I could reconsider."

My brain skip-stepped. Comprehension struck me— and I could only hope my instantaneous panic didn't show. If I was reading this interchange correctly—the First Lady was attempting to play Cupid. But she was obviously un- aware of my relationship with Secret Service Agent Tom MacKenzie. Although the excitement from last spring might have led people to suspect there was more to our companionship than dodging bullets might warrant, Tom and I chose to keep information about our love life quiet. We leaked details of the relationship on a need-to-know- basis only. And until this moment, I'd decided Mrs. Camp- bell didn't need to know.

From the looks on Mrs. Campbell's and Sean's faces, however, it was clear the First Lady had designs to fix me up with her nephew. Here was a wrinkle I hadn't antici- pated. At once I was honored that she thought so highly of me—because I knew the esteem she held for Sean—but at the same time I was quietly horrified.

How, I wondered, could I disentangle myself from this particular dilemma without ruining her image of me—and, just as important, without coming clean about my relation- ship with Tom?

For the moment I could do no better than deflect. I wracked my brain to come up with the Thanksgiving guest list. "The three couples attending are the Volkovs, the Blanchards, and the Hendricksons?"

Mrs. Campbell shook her head. "Helen Hendrickson isn't married. She's bringing a guest."

"Her attorney," Sean said to me. Shaking his head, he again addressed his aunt. "Don't you see? They're plan- ning to surround you with their arguments to convince you to sell your stake in Zendy Industries. Why else would Helen bring Fitzgerald along? I'll bet he's already drawn up all the papers. They'll be pressuring you to sign before the gravy congeals."

She laughed. "Don't be silly. Thanksgiving is a time for being grateful for all our blessings this past year. No one will be talking business."

"I changed my mind," he said. "I'm coming to dinner after all."

"Good."

"Somebody needs to look out for your interests."

As they talked, I realized I was in a peculiar position—although I was most certainly present, I was not part of the conversation. Feeling like the eavesdropping elephant in the room, I desperately wanted to extricate myself.

Although I kept my seat, my right knee twitched with the beat of anxiety. I wanted to be busy in the kitchen. My *real* kitchen.

Questions raced through my brain. And although I tried to maintain a neutral, disinterested demeanor, an errant thought must have skittered across my face because Sean turned to me, explaining the one thing I'd wondered about—why Mrs. Campbell wouldn't have a champion in her husband. "Uncle Harrison—that is, President Campbell—makes it a point to stay as far from decisions like this as possible. At least publicly." Turning to the First Lady, he continued. "He's against you selling the business, Aunt Elaine. We both know that. I also realize that he can't make a big deal out of it. His influence on your decision—if made public—could cause economic repercussions. It's a tough position to be in."

"Which is why Sean is my personal financial consultant,"

she said with obvious pride. "Other than my husband, Sean is the most trustworthy person I know."

Sean's cheeks flushed pink. Though obviously pleased, he waved off her praise. "I'll be there for Thanksgiving dinner. You two talked me into it."

"Great," I said, and then with over-the-top peppiness, I asked, "Will you bring a guest?"

Their twin looks of incredulity cemented my earlier matchmaking assumptions. "No," Sean said, meaningfully. "I'm not seeing anyone right now."

"Well, then," I said, suddenly at a loss for words, "I'll let the staff know to set a place for you."

Whether it was the close quarters, the long wait for an all-clear signal, or the fact that I was being double-teamed in my love-life department, I didn't know. I just suddenly needed to break free. I stood. "Let me clean up," I said, reaching for Mrs. Campbell's plate.

Sean stood, too. "I'll help."

"No." I whisked his plate away before he could touch it. "You visit with your aunt. I've got this."

"But—"

"It sounds as though you have a lot to talk about," I said, effectively cutting off his path to the sink area. To my surprise, he sat back down. In an attempt to guide the conversation back to safe territory, I then turned to Mrs. Campbell. "I didn't realize you were part of Zendy Industries. They're huge."

"They are," she said. "My father started the company with three friends—years ago when I was young and his friends' children weren't even born yet. That's why Nick, Treyton, and Helen are invited for dinner Thursday. We grew up together. Now, they're all my business associates.

I guess you could say I inherited the business and I inherited them, too."

The sudden sadness in her eyes reminded me of her recent loss. Mrs. Campbell's father, Joseph Sinclair, had been killed in a horrific car accident about two months earlier.

"You also inherited your father's good business sense," Sean said. "All I'm suggesting is that you rely on your own instincts now, and not defer to your colleagues' demands. No matter how convincing Volkov and the others might be."

"You're a good boy, Sean," Mrs. Campbell said, patting his arm.

By the time I had the bunker room's kitchen back in order, I'd overheard enough about the Zendy Industries situation to understand why Thursday's dinner had the potential to get ugly. I made a mental note to talk to Jackson, the new head butler, to keep his eye on the alcohol intake. Mrs. Campbell was a social drinker—limiting herself to an occasional glass of wine—but the Blanchards, the Volkovs, and Helen Hendrickson had been our guests only a couple of times in the recent past. I couldn't remember if they'd achieved status on our "Do not serve" list. I made another mental note to check.

While the White House is first and foremost a gracious host, it is also a wise one. Over time, certain guests have proved to be unable to handle liquor in a responsible manner. We would never deign to refuse anyone a drink—but one must not dance on White House tables, literally or figuratively. If someone does, he or she earns an immediate place on our "Do not invite" list. If, to our great disappointment, we find that this person *must* be invited in the future, our sophisticated staff manages to keep the inhibition-loosening beverages just out of the ersatz performer's reach.

With nine diners—including Sean—for dinner on Thursday, Jackson would have a relatively easy time of keeping tabs on the intake.

I continued to listen in, even as I puttered around, trying to tidy up an already Spartan room.

The First Lady stood up and walked over to the fake window. "All discussion about this Zendy situation should be tabled until after the holidays," she said. "How I wish we could get out of here. I have so much to do."

"The deadline for a decision is December fifteenth," Sean said. "That's why I think they'll be pressuring you to agree to the sale of the company."

She turned. "I thought we had until March fifteenth."

Sean shook his head. "The trust was very clear: Ninety days after the death of the final founder—your father—the four of you are required to file a decision as to whether you intend to sell the company or not."

"And if we don't, we have to wait ten years to decide again." Mrs. Campbell sighed. "Such a peculiar requirement."

Sean gave a wry shrug. "Not so peculiar when you think about what the founders intended. They envisioned this company as they would one of their kids. One that they all fathered. The four men who brought Zendy Industries to life were wealthy, successful businessmen in other ventures. They didn't need Zendy's income. They needed to believe they'd made a mark on this world."

The bunker door opened, cutting Sean off. Special Agent Martin gestured us out. "Follow me," he said.

CHAPTER 3

"ALL CLEAR?" MRS. CAMPBELL ASKED. "WHAT A relief. Was it actually a bomb? Or was this all just precaution?"

Kevin Martin licked his lips. "We are confident that the White House is currently safe from any explosive or incendiary device."

We'd made our way into the Center Hall. Mrs. Campbell turned to face Martin. "But earlier you said that a bomb was located on the property," she said. "Is that true? Was it really a bomb?"

He flicked a wary glance at Sean, who clearly understood his cue. "I have to be going anyway," he said. "See you both on Thursday. Take care, Ollie."

Another agent stepped up to escort Sean out, but before I could make my own hasty exit, Kevin Martin answered the First Lady's question. Incurable snoop that I am, I stayed to listen.

"The device we found was not a bomb."

"Thank goodness," the First Lady said. She closed her eyes for a long moment, and I felt as though I could almost read her mind. And, I could totally empathize. The relief washing over me was as powerful as it was sudden. This was Mrs. Campbell's home, and the president's. But in many ways, it was my home, too. A bomb had threatened to destroy the world's symbol of freedom. I'd compartmentalized my fear while we were sequestered—I'd pushed it aside to deal with matters at hand. But now that we were back in the residence, and safe, I felt the full weight of the ordeal we'd been through.

Kevin continued. "The fact that there was never an actual bomb on the premises, coupled with the time crunch the staff is under to prepare for Thanksgiving and Christmas"—he acknowledged me with a look—"has convinced us to allow everyone back into the residence for now. However," he added, arching his brows, "we are at a state of heightened alert. And we are asking the entire staff to be our eyes and ears wherever possible. We'll call a meeting later with further instructions."

"If it wasn't a bomb you found," I asked, "what was it?"

Kevin hated when I poked my nose where it didn't belong—a habit I'd gotten into quite often recently, and one he repeatedly tried to quash.

Before he could tell me to butt out this time, however, Mrs. Campbell chimed in. "Yes, what was it?"

"An apparent prank. We're investigating it now." He fixated on some middle distance with such laser intensity that I almost pitied today's prankster. Knowing Kevin and the rest of the Presidential Protection Detail (PPD) as I did, the guilty party would be found. Very soon. "An alert will be distributed to all departments describing what was discovered, and what to look for in the future. We're bringing in a team of experts to educate the staff."

When the First Lady turned the conversation to the happenings at Camp David, I made a polite excuse and hurried off to the safety of my kitchen.

Marcel met me as I walked in, his dark face tight with concern. "Where 'ave you been?" he asked. His French accent was ladled on heavier than normal. "We 'ave been very worried."

"Long story." I gave my staff a quick rundown of the past several hours.

Bucky frowned. "That's nice. They put you in a bunker with the First Lady, and they make us wait out on the South Lawn in the storm." He shook his head. "And now they tell us it's safe and we're supposed to believe them."

"Outside?" I said. Although we were still in the mid-fifties this late in November, it was pouring rain, and definitely too cold to remain outside for very long. "Kevin Martin told me you were safe."

Cyan, washing dishes, turned off the water and wiped her hands as she came toward me. "We *were* safe, Ollie," she said, glaring at Bucky. Although she was at least fifteen years younger, Cyan was almost as accomplished in the kitchen as our senior chef. And in the past couple of months, I'd watched her confidence grow even more. "We weren't out on the South Lawn; we walked down to E Street, where we sat on buses until they gave the all-clear."

"It was still storming," Bucky said. "And cold."

When I glanced at Marcel, he shrugged. "Eh, the temperature was tolerable. But the boredom was not. We have much to do and this incident has thrown a . . . *flanquer la pagaille* . . . into my plans for the day."

"If Henry was still here, he would've been out in the buses with us. Not cozying up with the First Lady in the bunker."

Arguing with Bucky over this matter served no purpose, so I changed the subject.

"There will be another guest at Thanksgiving dinner," I said. "Sean Baxter is coming after all."

Bucky snorted and headed back to his station, where I could see tonight's dinner preparations were already under way. "That SBA chef was due here over an hour ago. I'll bet she gave up when she couldn't get in."

"I'm sure the bomb scare changed a lot of plans," I said evenly. "But I do hope she shows up. We need another pair of hands here by tomorrow at the latest." The chef in question, Agda, was the first new recruit sent to join our staff. Service-by-Agreement chefs, or SBAs, worked in the White House on a temporary, contractual basis, until a hiring decision was made, or until the SBA chef found another job elsewhere. I'd been an SBA before I accepted a position here. In my opinion, there was no better opportunity anywhere. I hoped this particular chef agreed—after all, we needed the help.

"We're already behind schedule," Bucky said.

I bit back the urge to snarl. Hurling sarcastic retorts at those who reported to me was petty. Worse, it was unprofessional. I was beginning to see why Henry never stooped to fight meaningless battles. It wasn't worth the effort, and it only accomplished the lessening of oneself.

I forced a placid smile. "You're right, Bucky. That means that we need to work faster if we hope to get tonight's dinner together on time. Not to mention all the prep work we need to do for tomorrow and Thursday."

"And Friday," Cyan added.

I sucked in a deep breath. Friday promised to be a media

circus day. Not only was it the last day the White House would be open to the public before the official holiday season began, it was the date of a long-awaited luncheon. Preparations for Thursday's intimate Thanksgiving meal paled in comparison to those for Friday's buffet.

On Friday, Mrs. Campbell would open the White House doors to mothers from all over the country. Her goal was to find commonality among all mothers, whether they be working, single, stay-at-home, or sharing child-care duties with a partner. Almost every state would be represented, and every mom was bringing kids, along with homemade decorations for Christmas, Hanukkah, and Kwanzaa. Each invited child had been sent a template of a gingerbread person on which to base his or her artwork. Continuing the theme of how we are all different, yet we celebrate together, the kids were encouraged to create masterpieces within the template's parameters. Each hand-crafted gingerbread man—or *person*, in these politically correct times—brought to Friday's celebration would be added to the hundreds we received by mail per an open call for participation. I could only imagine how tough this security nightmare would be for our Secret Service personnel.

"And Friday," I finally echoed.

We weren't quite sure what to expect. We only knew it would be fun for the attendees, and that the news folks would be all over this one like ants on spilled sugar. Not that you would ever find ants in my kitchen.

"Ollie!"

I looked up. Gene Sculka, our chief electrician, stood in the kitchen's doorway.

"You heading down?" he asked.

I caught myself before asking, "Down where?" Darn.

He was talking about today's staff meeting. In all the excitement, I'd lost track of time.

"Hang on," I said, grabbing my notebook and pen. "I'll go with you." To Bucky, I said, "If Agda shows up, put her to work."

"Henry would have insisted on a formal interview first."

I swallowed my frustration. If Bucky planned to challenge my every move, we were in for a long holiday season. "She's coming from the Greenbriar, so she's no slouch. She's been screened and cleared." Keeping my tone as nonthreatening as possible, I added, "I'll risk putting her to work right away. We'll worry about the interview later."

He turned his back to me. "Whatever you say."

"That's the spirit, Bucky." Without waiting for a reply, I hurried to catch up as Gene headed toward the elevator.

I would have preferred taking the stairs, but that wasn't an option for our master electrician any longer. Gray-haired and big-boned, he wore his double chin and spare tire with comfort—as though he'd been born with them. He'd joined the White House staff during the Carter administration, and had worked his way up to the top position with his know-how and can-do attitude. "Can't believe they're still holding this meeting, what with all the hullabaloo this morning."

"There's a lot to be coordinated, especially over the next couple of days. This meeting is probably just to make sure we're all on track. I'm sure it'll be quick."

"It better be," he said.

"How's the knee?" I asked, as we rode one floor down to the basement-mezzanine, often referred to as the BM level.

He slapped his right leg. "Good as new," he said. "I told those doctors they had to get me back to work here by Thanksgiving. And they did." With a nod to no one, he added, "Nothing was going to keep me from working on the Christmas decorations. I've been running the electric here for who knows how long and I'm not about to let anybody take over during my favorite time of the year. No way."

"We're all really glad you're back." It was true. During Gene's knee-replacement recuperation, I'd had the misfortune of having to deal with Curly, Gene's second-in-command. Although the two men were close in age, Curly was as unpleasant as Gene was friendly. I only hoped that when Gene retired, Surly Curly did, too.

We were the last two to arrive for the meeting of the dozen or so department heads. I couldn't help but think about how much time I was spending away from the kitchen today—in the bunker this morning, and now here in the lower-level cafeteria, where a few staff members were taking lunch breaks.

Our florist, Kendra, leaned forward to talk to me around Gene's massive form. "No samples for us today?"

I knew what she meant. Today's cafeteria offerings were pretty basic. For our standard staff meetings, I usually made sure to have a new creation available for my colleagues to sample. Not today. "Limited facilities in the bunker," I said as I took my seat. "Unless you'd be interested in a hermetically sealed brownie topped with freeze-dried ice cream." Not an entirely accurate description of MREs, but it garnered a laugh.

"What kind of floral arrangement do you think I should come up with for that little delicacy?" she asked. "Maybe we ought to consider installing silk flowers in the bunker, huh?"

When we both laughed, I started to relax. Sure, this was our busiest time of the year, but now that the morning's excitement was over, we could finally get to the work at hand.

Up at the front of the room, Bradley Clarke took a few

minutes to get himself organized. I seized the opportunity to talk a bit more with Kendra. "Great theme this year," I said.

"Do you like it?" Kendra asked, clearly not expecting me to answer. "We've been working on this since early summer. I think it's a good one, given the nation's climate of fear these days." She shuddered, then went on. "And I like the way it dovetails with President Campbell's peace platform."

The First Lady was always credited with the concept, but the truth was, from start to finish, this was a team effort. It took months for the social secretary, the florist, and a myriad of designers to bring the project to life. Most of the decorations were chosen from a vast collection stored nearby in a Maryland warehouse. Our florist alone had a team of more than twenty-five designers who worked odd hours to assemble wreaths, arrange bouquets, and bring design elements from concept to reality.

"Together We Celebrate—Welcome Home," I recited. "Who came up with the title?"

Kendra blushed. "I did."

"I love it. And I love the way we've used the theme to pay tribute to diversity."

She gave a little self-deprecating shrug, but I knew she was pleased. "My team has been working hard," she said. "They've put in a lot of time."

"It shows. I can't wait to see it all put together."

Bradley Clarke cleared his throat and called the meeting to order. Tall, and with a perpetually friendly smile, Bradley was the kind of man you worked hard to impress. After a few brief announcements, he said, "Let's start with the big-ticket items before we go over this morning's situation. Thanksgiving first. Ollie?"

I brought the staff up-to-date on our menu and made

sure that the waitstaff as well as Marguerite, the social secretary, knew that Sean Baxter would be in attendance. Everyone who needed to scribbled notes, as did I when Marguerite informed me that Mrs. Blanchard had sent her regrets.

"Does the First Lady know?"

"I'm meeting with her right after this."

"Thanks for the heads-up." Mrs. Blanchard had been our only dietary-alert guest invited to dinner Thursday. "That opens up some possible last-minute additions to the menu," I said. As I wrote myself a note, I added, absent-mindedly, "We're going to be heavy on male guests this time. Sean Baxter's coming alone, and now without Mrs. Blanchard . . ."

Marguerite interrupted. "Treyton Blanchard is bringing his assistant instead."

"Bindy?" I asked.

Marguerite nodded. "It will be nice to see her."

"Isn't that a little odd?" I asked. "Shouldn't he be with his wife on Thanksgiving?" I knew I'd blurted my thoughts before corralling them, but this was a staff meeting, after all. It was where we were supposed to air our questions.

"Senator Blanchard's family is hosting dinner at their home later that night for both sides of the family," she said with a sniff. "Mrs. Blanchard appreciates the invitation, but she knows the Thanksgiving luncheon at the White House will be mostly business. She'd rather stay home with the kids and keep their traditions alive." Turning down an invitation to the White House was considered sacrilege. "All of this according to Bindy, that is."

Bindy Gerhardt had been part of the White House staff until she'd accepted a position on Treyton Blanchard's team. She'd fast-tracked her way into his inner circle, and I started to hear Sean Baxter's refrain in my head. These people weren't coming to share a Thanksgiving meal, they *were* intending to conduct business.

As a former colleague and White House staffer, Bindy would be uniquely qualified to secure Mrs. Campbell's ear. I was suddenly glad Sean would be at dinner. And especially glad the president would be there to back up his wife.

Marguerite added, "And you know Helen Hendrickson is bringing Aloysius Fitzgerald, right?"

Her attorney. "Yeah," I said. "And who is Nick Volkov planning to bring? His financier?"

The other department heads looked at me in surprise. Marguerite's brow furrowed. "The last I heard, he's bringing his wife." She tilted her head. "Is there something I should know?"

I waved off her concern. "Sorry. Stressful morning. My mind took a tangent." Smiling brightly at the group, I continued my update before passing the floor to the next person.

We were just finishing the meeting when one of the assistants came in with a note for Bradley. "Gene," he said, after he'd read it. "I thought you said the power to the Map Room had been restored."

Gene rocked back in his chair. "Yep. Last week, just like you asked."

"Not according to the cleaning crew. They were just in there and couldn't get the lights to work."

Gene sat forward, the front chair legs landing with a *whump*. "Curly said he took care of it." Shaking his head, he stood. Like the rest of us in the White House, he knew better than to place blame. "I'll take care of it right now," he said, and started out as the rest of us got up to leave.

Bradley held up a finger. "We're almost done here. Before

you go, I want to let everyone know that the Secret Service has arranged for"—he hesitated—"classes to educate the staff in threat assessment."

From the group: "Does this have to do with the thing they found this morning?"

Someone else asked, "What aren't they telling us?"

Bradley raised both hands. "You guys know the Secret Service. They'll tell us when and what they need to tell us. Just be aware that you'll be contacted soon, and that these classes are mandatory."

Above the disgruntled murmurs, Kendra voiced the concern we all had. "Don't they know we're gearing up for Christmas? Can't this wait till after New Year?"

"Terrorists don't care how much work we have." Bradley said. That reflection sobered us all. "Sorry," he said. "I know the deadlines we're all up against. If everyone cooperates, we'll get through this quickly. Okay?"

Gene had already bolted to the door, muttering something about not being able to depend on his people. Curly was in for an earful when Gene got down to the electrical office. Staff members were rarely caught falling down on the job, and Curly, for all his unpleasantness, was generally quite dependable. I wondered what was wrong.

CHAPTER 4

THE SBA CHEF, AGDA, WAS HARD AT WORK when I returned to the kitchen. Even though I felt I knew her on paper, this was the first time we'd met in person. I didn't know what I'd expected, but it certainly wasn't a six-foot-tall bombshell who chopped carrots faster than a food processor on high speed. Wielding a knife so long she could have used it in battle, she halted her *chunk-chunk-chunk* carrot-hacking and smiled hello.

From Agda's curriculum vitae I was able to determine how old she was—late twenties—right between Cyan's age and mine. But heightwise, she had us both by about a foot.

I was in for another surprise. Her command of English was limited. Severely.

"It's nice to meet you, Agda," I said, reaching up to shake hands with her.

With a supermodel's smile, she nodded down to me. "Hallo," she said, then hesitated. I could practically see her searching her brain before her next words came out, enunciated with care. "You are born France?"

"I was born in the United States," I said, thinking that was a mighty peculiar question to ask the first moment on the job. From the sound of her last name and the natural blond of her chignon, I'd already deduced her to be of Swedish descent.

When she spoke again, haltingly, I smiled at the lilt in her words, even as I worried about communication in an already stressed kitchen. "They tell me you are . . . Paris."

"Oh." Realization dawned. "I get you," I said, knowing she was clearly *not* getting me. Slowing down, I pointed to myself. "Olivia . . . Ollie . . . Paras." I nodded encouragingly. "My name is Ollie Paras."

Her mouth turned downward. "I am to work for French chef."

"Marcel has an assistant," I said. "He's the pastry chef."

"No, no. No pastry," she said, shaking her head in emphasis. "I can be sous-chef. I work here for French chef."

"You speak French?" At least we could have Marcel translate when necessary.

She shook her head apologetically. "Ah . . ." she said as she put her fingers up to indicate, "*un peu.*"

"Well, now that that's cleared up," Bucky said from the far end of the kitchen. "Isn't this great? Even if she's capable, the best we can do is give her tasks we can pantomime." Using exaggerated hand motions, he pretended to stir an imaginary handheld bowl. "Like this. And you wonder why Henry always insisted on an interview first."

Agda's forehead crinkled. She may not have understood him completely, but his manner was distressing her.

"What a laugh," he continued. "We're working short-handed, and instead of sending us someone we've used before, the service expects us to be the United Nations."

"Bucky, that's enough," I said.

He fixed me with a glare, but at least he shut up.

"Come here," I said to Agda, leading her to the side of the room farthest from Bucky. The White House kitchen is surprisingly small. For all the meals that come out of this place, everyone expects a larger area and state-of-the-art equipment. To be fair, some of our stuff is cutting-edge, but because all purchases must come out of a budget supported by the public, we learn to make do with what we have. "When you finish the carrots"—I pointed—"why don't you begin making the soup?" I pulled up the recipe from our online files.

Agda's eyes lit up. "I read," she said with some pride. "I know how"—she searched for the right phrase—"follow recipe."

"Great," I said. As I headed to the computer to update my notes from the staff meeting, she called out to me.

"Ollie," she said, making my name sound like *oily*. "You are kitchen assistant, yes?"

Bucky barked a laugh.

"No," I said, slowly, moving back toward her. "I'm the executive chef." Even now, months after my appointment, I still felt a little thrill anytime I said it. Pointing to myself yet again, I smiled. "I'm the boss."

"You? Boss?" She laughed, not mean-spiritedly. Her voice went up an octave as she hovered her hand, flat, just inches above my head. "You are little for boss, no?"

From the corner, Bucky guffawed. "I like this girl already."

NOT TEN MINUTES LATER, ONE OF THE SECRET Service guys appeared in the kitchen. "Time for the meeting, Ollie," he said.

My hands and attention deep in the floured batter that would become soft biscuits, I looked up. "What meeting?"

"The Emergency Response Team. The ERT guys. They have that department-head meeting going in the East Room."

Bucky and Cyan grumbled. Marcel was out of the room at the moment, and Agda clearly didn't understand.

"Now?" I asked.

He tapped his watch. "Hurry up. The sooner we get in there, the sooner you'll get back."

"But—"

"I know, I know. I've heard it from everybody so far. Too much to do. No time. Today's bomb scare threw everyone off and believe me, we're hearing about it." Pointing upstairs he added, "It's mandatory."

I washed my hands and dried them hastily on my apron as he talked. For the second time that day, I grabbed my notebook and pen and put Bucky in charge of the kitchen. "Get as much done as you can," I said. "I'm sure I won't be long."

"Uh-huh," Bucky said.

Cyan rolled her eyes. Agda smiled and waved her knife.

Measuring about eighty by thirty-seven feet, the East Room is the largest room in the White House, and is generally used for social events, such as when singer Karina Pasian performed here, in celebration of Black Music Month during the George W. Bush administration, or in the 1980s for President Ronald Reagan's seventieth birthday bash. Although the room is also used for more down-to-business purposes, such as bill-signing ceremonies and award presentations, I liked to think of it as the party room. The White House's first architect, James Hoban, probably had a similar idea in mind, because he had dubbed it the "Public Audience Chamber."

Today, in addition to the stunning eagle-leg grand piano that sat beneath a protective dust cloth in the southern corner and the collection of chairs brought in for the staff, the room was lined on two walls by folding tables. Whatever they held was also covered by white cloth, but I didn't imagine their role was to keep away dust. The lumpiness beneath the white fabric led me to believe that whatever was under there was to be kept from the staff's prying eyes.

I took a folding chair toward the back, finding myself seated near Gene again. "How's it going?" I asked, not really expecting much of a reply.

"I can't find Manny or Vince," he said.

I wasn't quite sure what to do with that information. Manny and Vince were journeymen electricians who did a lot of the maintenance work around the grounds. "They're . . . missing?"

"Damned if I know," he said, leaning close enough for me to smell his stale coffee breath. "Curly told them to get the Map Room hot again, but now he's gone for the day and I can't find either of the two young guys."

Vince might be considered youthful. Manny, not so much. Of course, from Gene's point of view, twenty- and thirtysomethings probably did seem like youngsters.

"Curly's gone? With everything we have to do?"

Gene shook his big head. "His wife's in the hospital. They called him out there. What could I do?" he asked rhetorically. "I need to make sure they take care of things. With the Map Room out of juice, I start worrying about the Blue Room and the Red Room. Even though they're on the floor above, they're close, you know."

I knew where the Blue and Red rooms were, but I also knew Gene was just working off stress by explaining it to me. The Christmas tree, due here in just a few days, would be set up in the Blue Room for White House guests to see and admire. The Red Room would host the gingerbread house. Lack of electricity in either location was not an option.

Just then, three men dressed in black marched into the room. All had enormous rifles, solemn expressions, and baseball caps pulled low. Behind them four other men followed. These guys were dressed in camouflage gear. When the procession came to halt before our gathering of department heads, the men pivoted and came to attention. I didn't know whether I should stand, salute, or what.

"Welcome to the first round of educational seminars scheduled for White House personnel." I leaned to see around the people in front of me. A tall, fortyish man stood in front of us on a raised dais. Watching us, he ran both hands through his sandy hair before he leaned forward to grip the sides of a lectern. With a voice like his, he didn't really need the microphone, but that didn't stop him from using it. "I am Special Agent-in-Charge Leonard Gavin. I am in command of this endeavor." He worked his tongue around the inside of his mouth, and tugged his head sideways the way men do when their collars are too tight. "In the course of White House business, you will refer to me as Special Agent Gavin."

Now I really felt like saluting.

Still booming, he continued. "You will be given name tags and asked to sign in so we know you were here. I will attempt to learn all your names. We have a lot to accomplish, so we will begin by passing out a study guide. Nickerson?"

One of the camouflage men stepped forward to begin distributing booklets.

Gene muttered under his breath, "We're never going to get out of here."

"Don't say that." I took one of the handouts and passed the rest to Gene, whispering, "I've got two big events—"

Special Agent Gavin pointed to me, his voice loud and irritated. "Is there a question?"

Startled, I shook my head. "No."

As though I wouldn't be able to hear him, he came around the lectern, his voice still about fifty decibels higher than it needed to be. "What is your name?"

"Ollie," I said. "Ollie Paras."

"What is your position?"

I stood. "I am the White House executive chef." Wow, I got to say that twice in an hour. But would he view me as "too tiny" like Amazon Agda had?

"Come up here," he said.

I started to protest, then thought better of it and decided to comply. Wasn't this great? I'd inadvertently become to-day's troublemaker for talking in class. Just like in school. Years of not knowing when to keep my mouth shut taught me it was better to go along with the teacher's orders and take my lumps right away, than to suffer built-up wrath later. I scooted sideways from my chair and made my way forward. Going with the flow might help things move along faster here, too.

I skipped up the steps to the dais, presenting myself as willing and cooperative. Or at least I hoped that's how I came across.

"Now, Ms. Chef, look out there," Gavin said, pointing to the audience. Department heads and assistants stared back at me from the safety of their folding chairs.

I followed Gavin's direction. "Okay."

Way back, next to where I'd been sitting, Gene squirmed. A half beat later he sat up and twisted, as though someone had called his name. Apparently someone had.

Manny stood in the room's doorway, beckoning to Gene, who needed no further encouragement. Hefting his bulk, he was up and out the door within seconds. I was glad for Gene that Manny had found him. At least one of us was getting something accomplished.

I chanced a look at Special Agent Gavin, who stood next to me—imposingly—looking as unperturbed as I was discomfited by the heavy silence in the room. I opened my mouth to ask a question, but he silenced me with a look and pointed out to the audience again.

Was there something I was supposed to notice? Something amiss? I shifted from one foot to the other, thinking about my crew downstairs. About Bucky running things. About Agda's professed ability to follow recipe directions in English. That made *me* squirm.

The camouflage guys and the black-clad snipers were busy organizing the displays on two of the long tables at the far side of the room. They'd peeled away the white coverings to reveal an odd assortment of gadgets. No doubt Gav here was supposed to be the warm-up act, and I the unfortunate audience volunteer.

I wanted to be back in my kitchen. Now.

When I bit my lip in impatience, I noticed Peter Everett Sargeant III grinning viciously up at me from the front row. Sargeant, the head of cultural and faith-based etiquette affairs, and I had never been able to see eye-to-eye about anything. I smiled back at him, as evenly as I could manage.

Finally, Gavin asked, "What do you see?"

I had an answer ready. "My colleagues."

"No." He shook his head somberly, as though I'd given a bad answer to a very easy question.

"No?"

"You see safety."

I could feel this little demonstration stretching out ahead of us. If he'd chosen someone else—anyone else—I might have been able to sneak out of this meeting after signing the attendance sheet. Here, out in front of everyone, I had no choice but to go along.

"You operate in a state of bliss," he continued. "You have no worries, no cares."

I wanted to ask him how often he'd plated a dinner for more than a hundred guests. From the looks of his down-turned mouth and icy-sharp gaze, I'd wager he didn't have enough friends to entertain often. Still, I didn't argue.

"One of these people here"—he pointed outward again—"could be a killer." He twisted to face me. "*You* could be a killer."

Was he joking? "I'm . . . not."

"We don't know that. None of us know that. Today you're a cook. . . ."

A *cook*? I bit the inside of my cheeks to keep from re-acting.

"Tomorrow, who knows? You could . . . snap!" He flicked his fingers in emphasis. Right in front of my rapidly heating face. "I will ask you again: What do you see?"

Obediently, I offered, "Safety?"

"Yes!" he said, smiling and raising two fists in the air like a TV evangelist wannabe. Even louder, he asked, "And *who* here could be a killer?"

I knew I should give him the answer he wanted. I knew I should resist temptation. But I couldn't stop myself. With a smile as wide as Gavin's, I pointed directly at his chest. "You!" I shouted.

The audience exploded with laughter. But old Gav was

not amused. "The cook has a sense of humor," he said without smiling.

Cook, again.

"How funny would it be if half the White House exploded on your watch?" he asked, pummeling the room's mood into the floor. "Then who would be laughing?"

I started moving toward the steps. "Are we done here?"

"We're only just beginning." His drill-sergeant demeanor grew stronger with every snarl. He tugged my elbow, forcing me back to center stage. "And when we're done with you—with all of you," he said, facing the crowd, "you will all know better than to just trust one another blindly. Do you understand?"

I held my breath, almost expecting everyone to yell, "Sir. Yes, sir!"

Instead, they fidgeted.

A camouflage guy smiled up at me sympathetically as he handed Gavin a weighty item. It looked like a dirty bottle one might find at the seashore, with a desperate message tucked inside its opaque shell. Gavin held it in both hands as he stared down at it, almost prayerfully, for half a minute.

Come on, I wanted to say. Let's get this show moving.

Keeping his head bent, Gavin's eyes flicked up, encompassing the shifting, murmuring crowd. "Do you all know what this is?" He waited. "Does anyone know?"

Silence.

"I didn't think you did." His grip tightened, as did his lips. I wondered how many times he'd practiced that meaningful stare in the mirror. "This, ladies and gentlemen, is an Improvised Explosive Device—an IED. A bomb."

With a collective gasp, and amid scraping chairs, staff members got to their feet. I jumped back.

"Sit down," Gavin ordered. "I wouldn't bring a hot IED into the White House."

When everyone resettled themselves, he continued, holding the bottlelike item high over his head. "This is the device we found in the West Wing this morning."

The West Wing. I'd been right.

"Although the exact location of the IED's placement is not being broadcast at this time, I can tell you that this is not now, nor has it ever been, a danger to the First Family—nor to any personnel. So, yes, you may all breathe a sigh of relief. Anyone can see that this was designed to mimic the workings of an IED." He hefted the bottle in front of himself now, frowning almost as though he were disappointed. "But it was never loaded with explosives. What that means, people, is that we have received a warning. Whoever placed it in the White House did so to test our diligence."

I started to back away, eyeing my seat at the far end of the room.

Sensing movement, Gavin half turned and directed his next question to me. "And what do you think this warning means?"

What else could it mean? "That we have to be more conscientious going forward."

The surprise in his eyes told me he hadn't expected my answer. He recovered quickly. "You are correct," he said, turning once again to face the audience and raising his voice. "What if this had been armed?"

No one answered.

"We don't even want to think about the devastation a weapon like this could cause, do we? But before today, how many of you had ever seen an IED before?"

No one raised a hand. Gavin cocked an eyebrow. "What would you have done had you encountered this? We are fortunate that one of our military-trained experts came across it. If any of you had found this where it had been secreted, you may have simply tossed it aside, thrown it away."

Watching him gesticulate as he paced the dais in front of me, I frowned. This guy didn't know our staff. We didn't take anything for granted. Perhaps none of us had ever seen something like this, but working in the White House taught us all not to take anything lightly. Finding a strange device in an unusual location would be enough to call for Secret Service support.

Gavin pointed to the camouflage-and-sniper contingent—the men were now standing at their tables, hands behind their backs, eyes staring straight ahead. Before them, they'd uncovered a display that resembled a collection of grammar school science projects.

"Today is the beginning of your training," Gavin said. "Over there, my men are waiting to demonstrate a variety of disarmed IEDs for you. We want you to acquaint yourselves with some of the known designs. But remember that terrorists are always improvising, dreaming up new models every single day. You must be on your guard, always. Take your time and learn all you can. We will keep the display available to you here for the remainder of the day. We will then move this exhibit across the building to the Family Dining Room, to continue your training tomorrow and throughout the week."

The crowd took their cue, getting up from their chairs. Some headed for the training tables. Others headed for the door.

I tapped Gavin's shoulder. "Thursday is Thanksgiving," I said.

Gavin twisted to stare at me. "So? Terrorists don't take days off."

"I realize that," I said equably. "But we're serving Thanksgiving dinner in the Family Dining Room this year." I pointed west. "You won't be able to set up there."

"This is the White House," Gavin said. "Don't tell me you have nowhere else to serve dinner."

"Mrs. Campbell requested—"

Before I could finish, Bradley stepped up to do what assistant ushers do best: He took control. "Let me handle this, Ollie," he said. When he faced Gavin, he shook his head. "Can't allow you to set up in the Family Dining Room. Sorry."

Grateful for the reprieve, I excused myself, hearing Gavin argue that safety was paramount, more important than a roast turkey's placement in a particular room. Although I knew old Gav would disapprove, I made only a cursory study of the bomb exhibit before heading back to the kitchen.

I'd just made my way to the ground floor, crossing the Center Hall, when I ran into Gene, muttering to himself. Wearing his tool belt and carrying a massive black drill, he looked like he'd just come in from a jog around the Ellipse. Streaming rivulets of sweat dripped down the sides of his face. His dark shirt was so wet that it could've used a good wringing out.

"You okay?" I asked.

He pointed to the Map Room. "Still no power. Manny says Vince bungled something up when he tried to fix it. Vince says it was Manny's fault. Damn idiots. Where did those two get their journeyman cards anyway? A cereal box?"

Since it was asked rhetorically, I let him vent.

Using the drill as a pointer, he indicated the rooms to my left. "Curly's out and the two screw-ups are nowhere to be found. So this repair, which should've been done already, is still waiting to be taken care of."

"So now you're stuck with the job?"

"You see anybody else stepping up to volunteer?" Shaking his head, he offered a wry smile. "Sorry, honey. I didn't mean to take it out on you."

"Don't worry about it," I said. "This time of year is always a little stressful."

"Yeah, and I shouldn't be standing here talking when there's work to be done." He pointed the drill skyward. "Wish me luck. I've got ten jobs that should've been done yesterday, and I'm working with this lousy equipment."

"What's wrong with it?"

He started toward the power closet behind the elevator, directly across the hall from the Map and Diplomatic Reception rooms. "This baby works just fine. But it's ancient. I keep these things around for emergencies"—his voice rose, almost as though he were hoping for the guilty parties to hear and respond—"like when people take my good equipment who knows where and don't bring it back when there's a job to be done. You know?"

"Same thing in the kitchen," I said. "My favorite mixer's a monster from way back. Maybe even Eisenhower's time." Laughing, I added, "It's huge and super noisy, but it handles heavy batter like nothing else. And I hate it when someone's using it when I need it."

Gene checked his watch. "I better get this done before Bradley calls me again."

"Stop by when you're finished. I have a couple of interesting dishes we're trying out. I think you deserve a treat after all this."

Gene swiped an arm across his sweaty brow. "Sounds great, Ollie. Count me in."

Back in the kitchen, Bucky and Cyan brought me up to speed. As she'd promised, Agda had indeed completed the soup without trouble. She was currently busy with the spiced pecans.

Cyan seemed impressed. "That girl is quick," she said. "Had everything put together in enough time to get started on the pecans for the appetizer tray. So I just handed her the next set of instructions and she was off."

"Wonderful," I said. "Things are finally going our way."

"How was the meeting?"

Before I could answer, the lights flashed off and on. A heartbeat later, like too-close lightning, a violent buzz seared the room.

Through it all, a scream so primal it froze all movement.

Except for the unmistakable *thud* of a body hitting the floor.

"What was that?" Cyan asked.

I was already running toward the sound. "Stay here," I ordered the wide-eyed staff. I had no idea what I would find, but if it were bomb-related, I didn't want all of us to be in danger.

With our kitchen so close to the Center Hall, I was the first on the scene. All the lights were out here; the passage was dim, but there was enough illumination to see the figure sprawled on his back, arms extended wide to his sides.

"Gene!" I cried, running to him.

Gene lay just outside the elevator power-closet door. His hands were empty, but one was blackened. A sudden stench of scorched flesh rose up, nearly causing me to retch. A metal stepstool had tumbled next to him, lying atop his right leg, while one of the stool's legs remained lodged against something inside the closet. I started looking around for a tool to free Gene's leg from beneath the metal trap. "Cyan!

Bucky!" I called, enunciating to make my panicked shouts understood. "Bring me the wooden rack. Now!"

The rack kept our most-often-used spices handy. About eighteen inches wide and just a few inches tall, it was the only thing I could think of at the moment that was safe to use in the presence of high voltage.

When neither of them answered, I cried out again. Finally, I heard Cyan yell back that she was coming.

One of the laundry ladies, Beatta, came running, as I had. "My God!" she said.

She reached down to touch Gene's face.

"Don't!" I shouted. "He might have been electrocuted."

Just then, Bucky arrived with the rack, Cyan running behind, carrying all the spices in a bowl. "Did you want these, too?" she asked.

I grabbed the empty rack, ignoring the question.

Cyan stepped out of my way as I pushed the rack beneath one of the stepladder's footholds. I tried levering the contraption away from its contact with Gene, but the rack twisted, slipping out of my fingers. "Damn," I said aloud.

"Be careful," Bucky said.

I took precious seconds to wipe perspiration from my hands and I inched forward to try again. A buzz emanating from within the room underscored the danger. Whatever electrical charge had hit Gene was still live. I scooted closer, my left foot less than four inches from his prone form, but I had to get close enough to get the leverage I needed.

"Get me a flashlight," I said. "And get the doctor."

Someone said they would, and hurried away.

More people came. Secret Service agents swarmed, then worked hard to manage the gathering crowd. One of the agents stepped in to take over for me, but I was so close I couldn't stop now. Although Gene was a big guy, it was only his foot that maintained contact with the metal ladder. I could do this. The agent must have sensed my concentration because he stepped back when I shook my head.

Amid shouts and questions and frantic babbling, I hooked the corner of the rack—the little lip at one end—under the rim of the stepladder's top foothold. Crouching, and using two hands, I forced the ladder upward, knocking it farther into the room.

All of this took less than a minute, but I felt as though hours had passed. "I think I'm clear. But I can't see. There's not enough light."

One of the agents came up with a flashlight. He shined it into the dark space.

"All clear," he said.

I dropped to my knees beside Gene, pushing my ear close to his mouth and nose. "Quiet, everyone!"

The hall rippled to silence.

The pounding I heard was my own heart beating—frenzied with fear for Gene. My CPR training rules rushed through my brain even as I pushed my head closer, hoping, waiting, trying to—

Warm air crossed my cheek. A baby-soft hiss followed.

"He's alive!"

I pulled my kitchen jacket off and covered Gene, hoping to stave off shock. A voice from behind the first circle of onlookers called out for everyone to make room.

The group parted. An emergency medical team raced in, the White House doctor heading the charge. Our on-staff nurse-practitioner followed two assistants, who carried a stretcher.

I was already scurrying out of their way when the team fell in around Gene, starting immediate care. The nurse-practitioner turned to me. "We've got him now."

Slowly we all backed away, giving the team a wide berth.
The sickening scent of cooked flesh hung in the air around
us; I wondered if I'd ever be able to forget that smell. The
Secret Service agents worked their crowd-dispersal magic,
and I sent Cyan and Bucky back to the kitchen.

As the corridor cleared, I caught sight of Manny. His
wide, lined face was pale gray, like the underbelly of a
dead fish. "What happened?" he asked. Nobody answered
him, so I made my way over.

"Where were you?"

He swallowed. "Me and Vince were outside." He pointed
south. "We had to get some wiring set up."

"It's raining."

"Not anymore. Stopped about an hour ago. That's why
we got out there. We were waiting all morning for the big
storm to clear up." Behind us the medical personnel spoke
in low tones as they ministered to Gene, preparing him for
transport. Manny asked again, "What happened?"

"Gene had an accident."

Manny shoved a hand through his thick hair, holding it
there for an extended period of time. The medical team
raised the stretcher, taking a moment to be sure they had
everything they needed. I thought Manny might be going
into shock.

"Where's Vince?" I asked, just to snap him out of it.

Staring at Gene's unmoving form, Manny could only
shake his head.

As though summoned, Vince came around the corner,
moving at his customary loping pace. About twenty-eight
years old, he had a chiseled look, from his solid muscular-
ity to his narrow face, so perfectly structured it looked to
be carved of pure ebony. His smile dropped the moment
he caught sight of the corridor's activity.

"Make way, folks," one of the technicians said. We moved out of the way, allowing them a clear path out the White House's south entrance.

"Was that Gene?" Vince asked.

I nodded. Manny remained speechless.

In his haste to get out of the stretcher's way, Vince nearly tripped. "Is he going to be okay?"

That was the one question I was wondering myself.

CHAPTER 5

JUST AFTER SEVEN O'CLOCK THAT EVENING,
the assistant usher showed up at the kitchen. I had already
sent Agda home, but Cyan, Bucky, and I were still hard at
work, trying our best to catch up.

The first thing out of my mouth was, "How's Gene?"

Bradley hesitated.

There's a sorrow people get in their eyes when news
is very, very bad. I've seen it often enough to recognize
the look even before I hear the words. Bradley's eyes held
that look now.

"Gene didn't . . ." He shook his head. "I'm sorry."

I dropped the knife I was holding, and steadied myself
against the stainless steel counter. Staring down, I was
vaguely aware of Cyan's gasp—and of Bucky backing up
to sit on a nearby stool.

Cyan snuffled, but I couldn't look at her just now.
I forced myself to focus on Bradley. "Electrocuted?" I
asked.

"The hospital said the damage was incredible. They were surprised he hadn't died on the scene . . . that he lasted as long as he did."

In unspeakable pain, no doubt. The little I knew about electrocution was enough to realize it was a ghastly way to go.

We were silent for a long moment, until I had to ask. "There's no connection between Gene's . . . death . . . and the bomb scare today, is there?"

Bradley grimaced, taking his time before answering. "We don't believe so. There will be a full investigation into the electrical system. In fact, that's going on right now. The Secret Service can't overlook any possibility of a correlation, of course, but preliminary findings suggest this is just a terrible coincidence."

I stared down at the diced mushrooms before me and as hard as I tried, I couldn't remember what I'd planned to do with them. I cleared my throat. "Thanks for letting us know, Bradley."

"We'll be sure to keep everyone informed about arrangements."

I nodded.

"Go home," I said to Bucky and Cyan as soon as Bradley was gone.

Cyan's eyes were red. "But . . ."

"We aren't going to get anything done tonight," I said. "Not after this. I'll clean up. It'll give me a chance to clear my head. You guys go home now. We'll just work harder tomorrow."

For once Bucky didn't fight me.

When they were gone, I stood in the silent kitchen, reliving Gene's final minutes in the White House. Could I have reached him sooner? Would it have mattered? Fragmented recollections raced through my brain, out of order and seemingly without purpose. Why had I noticed that the laundry lady's hairnet made her ears stick out? Why did it matter that the drill Gene had been holding cracked the marble floor when it fell? Why did I notice that salt was the top jar in the bowl that Cyan had erroneously carried out to us?

Instead of noticing these unrelated, irrelevant details, why hadn't I done more for Gene?

I closed my eyes, pressing fingers into my eye sockets, as though that could wipe the visions of his stricken body from my memory. Maybe, if I pressed hard enough, I could wake myself up and discover this terrible day had been a figment of my imagination. Maybe—

"Ollie?"

Startled, I jumped. Sparkles from the sudden release of eye pressure danced before me, but I recovered. "Mrs. Campbell," I said, ready to jump into action. "What can I do for you?"

Waving away my concerns, she made her way around the stainless steel worktable. "How are you doing?"

I opened my mouth, but no words came out. I bit my lip.

By then she'd reached my side and placed a warm hand over mine. "I wanted to see you because . . ."

Words didn't often fail the First Lady. She looked away.

When she faced me again, her eyes were shiny. She took several deep breaths before she spoke again. "I want to share something with you—something not a lot of people know." She took another deep breath and I got the impression she was steeling herself. "A very long time ago, when I was a teenager, a friend of mine drowned. We weren't twenty feet apart, Ollie, not twenty feet. We were in a public pool being watched over by lifeguards, and Donna was a good swimmer. But when I looked for her, she wasn't there."

When she took a breath this time, it was labored. "She was at the bottom of the pool and . . ." Mrs. Campbell stared up at the ceiling, wrinkling her nose as though to dispel the emotion. "By the time we got her out, there was nothing any of us could do for her."

I didn't know what to say.

She gave me a wry smile. "Everyone told me that I wasn't to blame. But I didn't believe them. I was seventeen, you understand, and I *knew*, I just knew, that she'd died because I hadn't been more careful. It was my fault."

Politeness urged me to contradict her, but good sense warned me not to.

"I lived with the guilt for a long time." She sighed. "A very long time. It wasn't until years later that I found out Donna had suffered a heart seizure that afternoon. It didn't matter that we were in a pool; she would've died at home in bed that day." Swallowing, Mrs. Campbell gave a resigned shrug. "Her parents never told me because they didn't know the guilt I was carrying. They were carrying their own. They believed they should have seen it coming, and that they could have prevented her death." She shook her head. "I'm telling you this because you were the first person to reach Gene. I know you feel responsible." She squeezed my hand. "Take it from someone who's been there. I'm here to tell you that when it's truly a person's time to go, there's nothing any of us can do about it."

My throat raw, I managed to say, "Thank you."

WHEN I FINALLY REACHED MY APARTMENT building that night, I'd taken to heart what Mrs. Campbell had said, yet I felt strongly that it hadn't really been Gene's time. With the new knee, his determination to be part of the

White House Christmas preparations, and the intensity with which I knew he approached safety issues, I couldn't shake the feeling that something was not right. With wonderment, I realized, too, that it had been just this morning that the First Lady and I had been sequestered with Sean in the bunker. It seemed like it had been weeks.

James sat in the front lobby. Although my building's owners hadn't hired James to sit at the front desk and screen visitors, they encouraged his continued cooperation by reducing his rent. A win-win situation. James, with his fixed income and empty apartment since Millie died, enjoyed the constant busyness. The building's owners liked the idea of the added, albeit limited, security James provided at the front door.

Though his build was slight, James had a deep voice. He greeted me with a gusty, "Hiya, Ollie! How's the president today?"

I answered as I usually did. "Great. He sends his best."

James laughed at our little joke. "You're home kinda late," he said. "I bet it's a lot of work to prepare for a White House Thanksgiving."

James loved any presidential tidbits I cared to share, and although I never gave him information that couldn't be found online or in the newspapers, he always felt as though he was getting the scoop from me. I started to answer, but a random thought stopped me. "Is Stanley around?"

"I saw him go up a little while ago. Why? You having power problems in your apartment?"

I shook my head. "I just want to ask him a couple questions." Realizing swiftly that Gene's death would make the early news tomorrow, I added, "We had an accident at the White House today and I just want to pick his brain a little."

"An electrical accident?"

"Yeah, but if Stanley's done for the night . . ." I let loose a sigh of frustration. Stanley was another of our building owner's priceless finds. He took care of building maintenance in return for a small stipend and free rent. I wondered if, when I retired, the mighty owners would consider putting in a restaurant on the main floor and give me free rent, too. "I'll try to catch up with him tomorrow."

But James was already dialing. "This may be a matter of national security," he said with mounting excitement.

"No, not at all—"

He waved me quiet when Stanley answered. "I've got Ollie down here at the desk," James said, his voice low, and heavy with importance. "She wants to talk with you about an electrical situation at . . ." He faltered a moment, looked at the receiver, then continued, very slowly, ". . . at the location where . . . she . . . works. You got that?"

He hung up. "Stanley will be right down."

"You didn't have to—"

His voice barely above a whisper, he asked, "So what happened? Are you allowed to talk about it?"

"You'll hear more tomorrow," I said. Before I could bring the words forward, my stomach dropped, silencing me. I didn't want to say it out loud. Gene was dead, but talking about it to someone who didn't even know the man made this afternoon's tragedy seem gossipy and trivial.

James's eyes were bright with anticipation. "Yeah?"

There was no question about it making the news tomorrow. Heck, I was sure it was racing across the Internet already.

"Our head electrician was . . . killed today."

James's mouth dropped. "Electrocuted?"

"Autopsy is scheduled for tomorrow, but that's what it looks like."

"Electrocution is a bad way to go."

I looked away. "I know."

"You didn't see him, did you?"

The elevator dinged its arrival, sparing me from having to tell James that I'd been the one to find Gene. I could already sense James's fatherly comfort welling up. In a minute he'd rise from his chair to pat me on the back. I didn't want that right now. All I wanted, really, were answers. Maybe I'd never get the ones I sought. But maybe Stanley . . .

He alighted from the first car on the right, his graying hair mussed on one side, his face creased, his pajama shirt tucked into blue jeans, and his feet in house slippers. "What happened?" he asked, bouncing alarmed glances between me and James. "What kind of emergency?" Stanley's words tumbled out fast, more slurred than usual. Probably owing to the fact that he'd been sound asleep up until a moment ago.

I reached him before he made it to the desk. "No emergency," I said, placing a restraining hand on his arm. "I just have a few things I wanted to ask you. But I didn't mean to wake you up. Really—this can wait till tomorrow."

James boosted himself from his seat, eager to join the discussion. "I told Ollie you'd want to help her right away."

Stanley blinked twice. "'Course. But I can't do much until you tell me what happened."

This was not going the way I'd planned. But there was no sense sending James back to the desk or Stanley back to bed at this point. Both were waiting for me to spill whatever revelation they thought I carried. Except for the three of us, the lobby was empty, the elevators quiet.

I wanted information. There seemed but one way to get it. I told them about Gene, about finding him outside the elevator closet, about the subsequent news of his death. The two men standing before me stood silent a long moment when I finished.

I got to the crux of my reason for being there. "I thought there were safeguards against electrocution," I said, addressing Stanley. "Gene wasn't working on power lines. He was inside the White House. A residence. Things like this shouldn't happen, right?"

We'd drifted back toward the entry desk and Stanley rested his hip against it. He scratched at his gray-stubbled chin. "Well," he said slowly, "the problem is, electrocutions do happen. Not too often these days, but still . . ." He ran his fingers across his chin again, staring just over my head. "What was he doing?"

"I'm not entirely sure," I said. "I know that one of the rooms was out of power, and I know he was drilling something."

"Go over it all again, real slow."

A phone call pulled James's attention away from our conversation. Still feeling guilty about waking Stanley up, I decided the best thing I could do was to make this interruption worth his time. I launched into a detailed play-by-play of the scene, starting when I found Gene on the floor.

"Back up," Stanley said. "How did you know he was restoring power to one of the rooms?"

"We'd talked about it earlier, and then right before he started the repairs. He had just complained that the power should've been fixed before and that he wasn't using his favorite tools. . . ."

"What was he using?"

I described the tool belt, the old-fashioned drill, the stepladder.

As Stanley pondered that, I continued, "Gene was always such a sweet guy, but he was in a bad mood today. With all the problems, though, I couldn't blame him."

This time, instead of rubbing his chin, Stanley ran his hand over his mouth. Talking between his fingers, he said, "Can you describe the drill?"

"It was old," I said. "Black, but shiny where the paint had worn off."

"Shiny?" he repeated. "He was using a drill that wasn't insulated?"

I had no answer for that.

"What was he drilling?" Stanley seemed agitated now. "Where was he standing when this happened? Describe it."

I desperately wished I had more details, but even scraping my brain to provide the best account of the incident I could wasn't working; I knew it came up short.

Stanley kept his hand over his mouth and his gaze on the floor. He was quiet so long I worried he'd fallen asleep. James finished his phone call and must have had the same impression because after a long, silent interval, he said, "Stanley? You got any ideas?"

His head came up and he pointed at me as he spoke. "A guy with that much experience knows not to take chances. If he was using a drill that wasn't insulated, he had to be pretty damn sure he wasn't puncturing anything hot. You with me?"

I nodded.

"Was he wet? Perspiring?"

I thought about it. "Yeah. A lot."

"I gotta tell you—he would have known better. Mind you, we all take risks, try for the shortcut. And I don't know this fellow, but if he was a master electrician—"

"He was."

"Then I have to think he knew exactly what he was doing. If he's been with the White House for all those years, then he knew that place inside and out. He wouldn't have taken that risk with the drill unless . . ."

Stanley's gaze dropped, and the hand came back to rub his chin.

"Unless?" I prompted.

He made a thoughtful sound. "We had a big storm today, didn't we?"

James and I nodded.

"Tell you what, Ollie. Let me think about this one. I'll get back to you."

CHAPTER 6

BY THE NEXT MORNING, A GREAT PALL HAD
settled on the White House. As I shredded sharp white
Cheddar for our baked farfalle, I tried without success
to fight the sadness. Today hardly felt like the day before
a holiday. Although Cyan, Bucky, and I went through the
motions of preparing this year's Thanksgiving meal, we did
so with little of the joy that usually accompanied our planning. There was no banter, no chitchat. Conversations were
brief, and even our more fun-loving assistants kept to
themselves when stopping in to pick up or drop off necessary items. Agda, of course, remained unaffected by the
situation's gravity, but as she kneaded dough that would
later become tiny rolls, she must have sensed our collective
sadness because she gave us sympathetic glances whenever she looked up from her work.

"We have another SBA chef coming in today," I told the
group.

Bucky had been adding chunks of pork roast to an

open pan on the stove. We always prepared the meat filling the day before assembling tamales. He turned. "Did you bother with an interview this time?" he asked with a pointed look at Agda.

"As a matter of fact, I didn't," I said. "We were able to get Rafe."

"Rafe!" Cyan said, exhibiting the first cheer this kitchen had seen all day. "That's perfect. He's a genius with sauces."

"Hmph," Bucky said, which I took as his version of support. Without an opening to badger me, he returned to his task, covering the pork with water and setting the flame below the pan to medium. Before long the kitchen would be filled with the succulent, roasty smell of the simmering meat. Keeping his back to me, Bucky asked, "Did you talk to Henry? About Gene, that is."

"I called him last night before I left here," I said. "Henry's planning to come to the wake."

"I figured he'd want to know." Despite Bucky's persistent crankiness and his singular ambition to prove himself right in all instances, he wasn't a bad fellow. His shoulders and arms moved around a lot as he worked—as though in an animated conversation with himself. The back of his bobbing head, freckled in the small patch where he'd begun to lose his hair, looked suddenly vulnerable and weak. He shrugged to no one, talking softly. "Hell of a way to go."

I was about to agree, when I thought about my conversation with Henry. He'd been shocked and saddened by the news of Gene's death, but then what he'd said next struck a chord with me. "I've had friends at the White House pass away before, but never like this. Never had to deal with an accident of that magnitude. I give you credit, Ollie. I don't know how I would cope."

I'd demurred, knowing full well that Henry always found ways to deal with new situations. He'd have certainly found a way to cope.

I stopped shredding the Cheddar to take a look around my kitchen. Agda kneaded her dough at one corner of the center workstation, humming softly. Cyan slumped before the computer, an open cookbook on her lap. Bucky moved as though by rote.

"Before Rafe gets here," I said, clearing my throat, "I think we all need to—"

"Talk?" Bucky asked. "Share our feelings? Should we stand around the countertop, hold hands, and sing 'Kumbaya'?" He blew out a breath, raspberry style. "This is a kitchen, not a grief support group."

Cyan looked taken aback. So did Agda, whether she understood or not.

But I'd caught the look in Bucky's eyes before he'd masked it with sarcasm. I realized our resident curmudgeon was afraid we'd see that he was hurting, too. If Henry had been here, male camaraderie might have allowed him to pat Bucky sympathetically on the back. Maybe that would've started the healing process. I didn't know. All I knew for certain was that I wasn't Henry. So I'd have to do what I felt was best, given the circumstances.

"I think we all need to recognize something." I wiped my hands and came around to his side of the kitchen. Cyan rounded in, too. Bucky took a step back, looking as though he expected bodily harm. I continued. "Gene was where he wanted to be when he died. He loved the White House more than he even loved his own home. Ever since his wife died, Gene's been more than a fixture here; he's been the embodiment of the White House itself." Cyan stared downward. Bucky's mouth twitched and he looked away. "If anyone else had just gone through knee surgery, they would've been slow coming back. But Gene wanted to be here for the Christmas preparations."

Cyan nodded. Bucky worked his jaw.

I lowered my voice. "And he *was* here. Doing what he loved most."

Arms folded, Bucky finally met my eyes. "I don't believe he was being careless."

For once he and I agreed. "Neither do I."

"That's what they're saying."

"Who?"

At that moment, Special Agent-in-Charge Gavin stepped into the kitchen, stopping just as he entered, holding his hands behind his back, surveying us. "Good morning," he said.

I started to make introductions, but he held up an index finger. His other hand swung around, holding a leather portfolio. "As you were," Gavin said. He eased over to where Agda was working, smiling as though engrossed in what she was doing. "Pretend I'm not here."

Oh, sure. Like that was possible. I focused my attention back on Bucky and spoke quietly. "Who's saying Gene was careless?"

Bucky lasered his gaze on Special Agent Gavin. "His guys."

Realizing our "Kumbaya" moment was over, I sent Cyan and Bucky back to their stations and returned to my shredding, my attention taken not by the hunk of cheese in my hand, but by the chunk of agent in my kitchen.

Agda offered Gavin a tentative smile. He smiled back. This happened several times while he stood next to her. She may not have known who he was, or what a man in a suit was doing in our kitchen, but she was clearly uncomfortable.

She inched away. The two were close in height, and every time she looked at him, he nodded encouragingly. Whether he was trying to ingratiate himself here because he was on a get-to-know-the-staff mission, or because he wanted to ask my new assistant chef out on a date, I didn't know.

I was about to break up this little meeting of the eyes when he spoke. "That smells delicious. What is it you're making?"

Agda nodded, smiled, and continued to knead the dough.

Gavin's grip tightened on his portfolio. He used his index finger to point. "What is it?" he asked again. "It looks good."

Agda kneaded harder, nodded harder. Her cheeks pinkened and her brows shot up.

Bucky exhaled loudly. "She's Swedish," he said. "She might not understand."

"Sweden?" Gavin asked. "I visited Göteborg last year."

"Göteborg!" Agda brightened. She exploded at once, chattering, speaking in lilting, excited, rapid Swedish, making me wonder if the famous Muppet might not have a human cousin counterpart after all.

"Sorry," Gavin said, backing away. Then to me: "She doesn't understand English?"

"Not much," Bucky and I said in unison.

Perplexed, Gavin asked, "Then how does she—"

I'd had enough of Gavin's kitchen inspection, and I was still more than a little annoyed with his belittling me on-stage yesterday. This was my territory and unless he was ready to start sniffing for bombs himself, I wanted him out of here. "Was there something you needed?"

Realizing she didn't have anyone to talk with after all, Agda's shoulders slumped and she moved back into her kneading rhythm.

Gavin licked his lips. "Your department was inadvertently left off the schedule for today's classes. I'm here to ensure you take the necessary steps to get all your employees to training." He shot a thumb toward Agda. "I don't know what to do about her. Don't you see her lack of communication as a security threat?"

"My job is to bring the best food to the table every time the president, his family, and his guests sit down to dine. Isn't it *your* job to ensure our safety?"

He waited a beat before answering. When he did, his words were clipped. "I'm glad you realize that. Makes things easier for me." His chin came up, surveying us once again. "We will call you out one at a time so as not to unduly burden your staff. Since there are four of you—"

"Seven."

Our man here didn't like being interrupted. Maybe that was why I enjoyed doing it. I explained: "Our pastry chef and his assistant are elsewhere at the moment. And we have another chef joining us later today. But the new chef and Agda"—I pointed—"are SBA chefs, which means they are not permanent employees of the White House. I don't know if they should be counted. Does that make a difference?"

"How long will they be in service here?"

"As long as we need them. Given that we have Thanksgiving tomorrow, the Mothers' Luncheon on Friday, and a couple of other events over the next week, I see them both staying until at least next Thursday. If the social calendar changes, I may keep them on longer."

Gavin shook his head. "Neither will be required to participate in our training sessions. Just send your permanent employees down. Here's the schedule." He pulled a copy from his portfolio and wiped the already sparkling countertop clean before he put it down. "All personnel are required to attend three sessions, designated A, B, and C. We will commence this afternoon and we expect to have everyone sufficiently trained by the weekend."

"This weekend?"

Gavin spread his hands and gave me a look that said, "Duh."

"Is there a problem?" he asked.

I bit back a retort. "No," I answered, deciding right then that I'd wait until Saturday to send any of us in for training. I'd consult with Marcel, of course, but I knew he'd agree. We faced an already hindered, overpacked schedule, and the next two days would be backbreakers. There was no way I could spare even one person. "How long are the classes?" I asked.

"Depends on class participation. Could be as short as an hour, could be as long as three. If people catch on quickly, we'll move quickly." Holding up a finger, he said, "But we can only move as fast as the slowest man. Er . . . woman." He smiled, like he expected me to laugh.

I picked up the schedule, glanced at it, and placed it with the rest of my important papers in the already overflowing computer area. "Got it," I said. "Thanks."

He tugged at his collar. He hadn't expected to be dismissed.

Recovering, he nodded. "As you were," he said, then left.

I WAS HEADING TOWARD THE FLORAL DEPARTment, just passing the basement bowling alley, when Curly Sheridan emerged from the long hall that led west to the carpenter shop. Manny shuffled behind him. They both wore workpants and chambray shirts with rolled-up sleeves. Manny was only a few years older than I was, but he seemed to have aged in the past couple of days. He grunted hello and turned away, but I stopped Curly. "How's your wife?" I asked.

He squinted at me. "How do you know about my wife?"

"Gene . . ." I started to say. My voice faltered. For the briefest moment I'd forgotten all of yesterday's horror. "Gene . . . He told me you'd been called to the hospital. Is she all right?" I'd met Mrs. Sheridan a couple times. Sweet woman. Tiny and dark-haired, she didn't talk much. I attributed that to her being foreign-born and the fact that she was married to truculent Curly.

He grimaced. "She's having a rough time."

I didn't know quite what to say to that. "I'm sorry."

"Yeah."

Not for the first time did I question Curly's nickname. The man was mostly bald, with a long scar like a *J* around his left ear, stretching up and across his shiny pate. It dawned on me suddenly that with Gene gone, Curly was next in command. Manny mumbled, letting Curly know that he'd be upstairs in the Blue Room. Curly started to leave, too, but I stopped him with a hand to his bare forearm. He reacted as if burned.

"What do you want?"

"What really happened yesterday?" I asked. "I mean, Gene was always so careful. . . ."

The squint came back. "Why you asking me?"

"You know these things. You understand them better than I do."

His perpetual scowl deepened and he shook his head, blowing out an angry breath. "Why does everybody think I know what happened there? I wasn't with him. I wasn't there. You were there."

I felt suddenly small, and the words came out before

I could stop myself from asking, "Could I have done something more? Could I have saved him if I'd done something differently?"

The scowl moved, fractionally. Enough for me to wonder if he harbored any sympathy at all, or if he was just trying to decide if I was a crackpot.

"Listen, I'll tell you what I've been telling everybody, including those explosives guys. What are they, anyway? Secret Service? Or military?"

I shook my head. "Not sure."

"Whatever." He took a plaid handkerchief out of his back pocket and wiped around the scar. "Gene hit something hot, that's for sure. I'm working on figuring out exactly what happened. That's my job today. That, and getting a million other things done." He grabbed at his empty shirt pocket, as though reaching for phantom cigarettes. Another grimace. "Gene was a big guy, and if you want to know what I think, I'm guessing he leaned up against something metal when he hit the power. He knew better, yeah, and there shouldn't've been enough juice to kill him, but he was using a bad drill. And Gene was always sweating. I think it just all added up to him being careless."

"You really think so?"

Taking offense to my skeptical tone, he said, "As a matter of fact I do, missy. You asked your question. You got my answer. Now go take care of the food handling and let me do the job they pay me for."

CHAPTER 7

WHEN I GOT BACK TO THE KITCHEN, RAFE
had arrived. But we had other company as well. I stopped
short. "Sean," I said in surprise. "I didn't expect to see you
today."

Sean Baxter was wearing a white apron over his char-
coal pants and pale gray shirt, standing at the center workstation, slicing red peppers. "Hey, I was wondering when
you'd show up. Look," he said, "they put me to work."

Cyan gave a one-shoulder shrug. "He wanted something
to do," she said with a grin. "I figured you wouldn't mind."

Just wait till security-crazed Gavin sees this, I thought.
But then again, Sean was cleared for much more classified
stuff than tomorrow's Thanksgiving dinner. If we couldn't
trust the president's own nephew, who could we trust?

Rafe called out, "Hey, Ollie, how's it going?"

I waved a hello. "Welcome to the team," I said to both
of them. Still trying to understand Sean's presence, I
turned to him. "What brings you down here?"

He fixed his attention on a pepper, giving it a good slice even as his cheeks rivaled the vegetable for redness. "Aunt Elaine and I were going over some of her decisions. You know, that financial stuff we talked about in the bunker yesterday."

He didn't elaborate, but behind him, Bucky raised his eyebrows and shot me a look that underscored his earlier comment about "cozying up to the First Lady."

I ignored him.

Sean continued. "She was called away and will probably be busy for about an hour. I had some time to kill, so . . ."

All I could think about was the time crunch we were under. "Are you sure you want to be down here?" I hoped to talk him out of helping. The last thing I needed was an unskilled amateur gumming up our plans for the day. It was one thing to have too many chefs spoiling the broth. It was another to have one who didn't speak the language. Add an assistant who didn't know his way around the kitchen and we'd be lucky if we managed to create any broth to spoil.

"Yeah," he said, concentrating on the peppers again. "I'm just about done here—so if you've got anything else . . ."

I thought about it. One of the surprises I'd discovered when I took over the position of executive chef was that I did less actual cooking than I had in the past. While I was certainly involved in the preparation of every meal, my duties were to create menus both for the family and for events. I also had a number of administrative issues to juggle, not unlike those of the director of a small company. In addition to managing each staff member's vacation time and sick days, I had to sign off on purchases, attend meetings, coordinate with other departments, and nurture my subordinates' growth as professional chefs. The administrative stuff took a lot more time than I'd expected, and I began to see why Henry had come in early and stayed late most days. That was what I'd been doing myself since he'd left.

Part of making this kitchen work was learning how to delegate. Why not put Sean to work? I didn't want to appear ungrateful. I reasoned that another pair of hands was another pair of hands. And we needed a lot of help if we were to get both big events plated on time with the panache to which Mrs. Campbell had become accustomed.

"Cyan," I said, "have you cleaned the shrimp?"

She gave me a mischievous look. "Not yet."

"Why don't you show Sean how that's done?"

"Sure," Cyan said, amused. I wanted to explain to her that I wasn't punishing him for helping out—shrimp cleaning was a job I abhorred—but rather it was a task that gave Sean a wide berth for error. No matter how hard he tried, he couldn't ruin things too badly. Once he got the hang of it, we'd have plenty of shrimp for our cocktail display. If any were messed up, we could chop those and use them for other purposes. This was a safe bet.

"Shrimp, huh?" Sean asked. "Is this for tomorrow?"

"Sure is. I hope you like it."

"One of my favorites." When he smiled at me, I felt my breath catch. There was that sparkle in his eyes that I usually saw only in Tom's. "Of course, I'm happy with anything you make, Ollie."

I didn't know what to say. Sean was a sweet guy. I liked him, even though I didn't know him particularly well. But he wasn't Tom. "Thanks," I said, moving in the opposite direction.

Bucky and Rafe were conversing near the stove as

I inched toward my computer station. Between the two men sat a large pan of cranberries, fresh from the oven. All the cranberries had popped and the tangy, sweet smell permeated the area, making me feel for the first time that Thanksgiving really was just one day away.

Agda had proven to be the quickest knife in the kitchen, and she was now chopping vegetables at the center island, full speed.

By the time Sean had followed Cyan around to the refrigerators, Agda had scooped up what was left of his peppers and had all of them chopped before Sean and Cyan returned with two huge bowls of raw shrimp. Sean caught my eye as he settled in to work. "I'm really glad to help out," he said.

"And we're glad to have you." Okay, so it wasn't exactly the truth, but Sean seemed so . . . sincere . . . that I couldn't have said anything else.

I sat on the stool at the computer station with my back to the bustling staff, Gavin's paperwork on my lap. Logging in, I immediately accessed the training schedule. He wasn't kidding when he said we'd been left out. There were enough training spots still open for all of us, but most of them were at times that conflicted with meal preparations. That figured. What was considered prime time for us was prime time for the rest of the staff, too.

The soft sounds of a busy kitchen—muted clatters, bumping, stirring—served to soothe my frazzled nerves. For as much as I'd tried to put the accident, the bomb scare, and the next two days' events in perspective, I realized how impossible a task that was. There was no perspective on situations like these.

A warm, yeasty scent rose up and I turned long enough to watch Agda pull a perfect tray of rolls from the nearby oven, her cheeks red from the heat. She caught my glance and smiled, her pride evident.

Back to the computer. Marcel would take care of his own training, I knew, and that of his assistant. I just had to worry about my own staff. When I'd finished placing Cyan and Bucky in A, B, and C classes that minimized impact on the kitchen, I set to the unenviable task of assigning myself.

Unfortunately, there weren't a whole lot of choices left.

As much as it pained me to do so, I took one of the open slots set up Thanksgiving night. I reasoned that dinner would be complete, Cyan and Bucky would have gone home to rest up for the next day's hoopla, and I would probably be staying late after dinner to clean up and prepare for the next day's luncheon. Tom had plans to go home for the holiday, so that left me free. We hadn't yet made the leap of meeting each other's family. I glanced toward Sean and wondered, idly, if by this time next year Tom and I would be willing to come forward with our relationship.

Regardless, I was destined to be by myself this year, so I might as well sign up for the security class. Let Cyan and Bucky enjoy the holiday with their families. And maybe, if I was lucky, old Gav would be sitting at the head of his own dinner table and I'd get someone else teaching the training this time.

Sean interrupted. "Ollie?"

I half turned. He'd made little progress on the shrimp-shelling, but he didn't seem overwhelmed. Yet.

"Hang on," I said. Returning to my task, I reserved two more open spots, one each on Friday and Saturday. There. Done.

With a flourish, I clicked the file closed.

"What's that?" Sean asked.

I told him.

He scratched the side of his face. "Would you mind me borrowing your computer for a minute? I didn't check my e-mail yet today."

"Sure," I said, thinking it an odd request. "Let me get you to the Internet."

Within seconds I had him set up and gave him some privacy. "Let me know when you're done."

Although we all shared the same computer in the kitchen, it felt strange to allow an outsider—even if that outsider was the president's nephew—access. But what harm could he do? Change the ingredients in one of our recipes? Unlikely.

I kept myself busy for about a quarter hour, until Sean raised his head. "Hey, Ollie," he said.

"What's up?" I asked, coming over to him.

"I just got an e-mail from Aunt Elaine. Treyton Blanchard is bringing his assistant instead of his wife to Thanksgiving."

"That's right."

He closed out of the Internet connection and headed back to his prior task. "You knew about that?"

"Sure. We're always informed about guest changes."

Sean pulled a shrimp from the pile and worked it. As he started up again, I could tell that he'd begun to develop a feel for the job—but the guy still had a long way to go. "Any idea why?"

Helping him, I grabbed a shrimp, removing the legs, shell, and tail with swift movements. I zipped the vein out and grabbed a second shrimp. "Mrs. Blanchard begged off," I said. "Something to do with keeping traditions at home."

He snorted.

I deveined the second shrimp and tossed it into a large bowl of ice. "You think there's another reason?"

He frowned down at the crustacean in his hand. "Maybe."

I tugged a new shrimp out of the bucket, disentangling its legs from the rest of them. "You think there's something between Blanchard and Bindy?" The words popped out before I could stop myself.

"No," he said with a headshake. "It's not that. It's just . . ." He glanced about the room. We were talking in low enough tones, and there was enough busy noise that the rest of the staff couldn't hear what we were saying. "You know about Nick Volkov's problems, don't you?"

I didn't.

"Well . . ." Another furtive glance around the room as he fought the little shrimp in his hand. "Do a Google search online. He's been having problems. He could use a windfall right about now to pay his legal bills. And I think he's convinced Senator Blanchard and Helen Hendrickson that it's in their best interests to sell Zendy Industries." Sean finally finished cleaning his shrimp and picked up another. I'd managed three in the interim.

"And you think tomorrow will be some sort of ambush?"

"That's what I was trying to tell Aunt Elaine," he said. "But she just sees the good in everyone."

I tossed another shrimp in the completed pile. "It's a nice quality to have."

"Unless people are out to screw you."

"You don't really believe that?"

Sean stopped working. "The problem is, I do. I'm just glad Uncle Harrison will be there. They can try to sway her, but if she holds her ground, I know he'll back her up."

"And you'll be there."

He smiled at me again in a way I wish he hadn't. "I will be. And so will you."

"My food will be there," I said, looking away. "The butlers will be there. I won't."

"Hmm," Sean said, beginning to work the shrimp again. "Maybe you could put a drug in the food that makes everybody tired. Then we'd all just have a great meal and go home and sleep. No business talk."

He laughed. I didn't think it was funny. Above all, the food that came out of my kitchen had to be safe. That wasn't something I ever joked about.

Sean must have sensed my displeasure because he sobered at once. "Listen, Ollie, I just have to tell you, I have a bad feeling about all this. The stakes are high. Aunt Elaine doesn't realize how desperate Volkov may be. I'd hate to see her get taken."

I put my hand on his, belatedly realizing that was probably a mistake. "Mrs. Campbell's a smart lady. She's strong. I'm sure she won't give in if she really doesn't want to."

Sean had just begun to answer when Peter Everett Sargeant III strode in, one eyebrow cocked at us. "Well, well," he said. "I see we've got a whole slew of new recruits."

Leave it to Sargeant to pop in at the exact wrong time. I sighed, reconsidering. Lately, with all the trouble and with two major events still behind schedule, was there ever a good time?

"Hello, Mr. Baxter," Sargeant said. Sean was the only person in the room he directly acknowledged. "It's a pleasure to see you again."

"Same here." Sean glanced from Sargeant to me. "Guess I ought to be going, huh?" He shot his last shrimp a distasteful look and gave me a sideways smile. "I think I'll stick to the turkey tomorrow," he said. "See you then, Ollie."

When he left I washed my hands and wiped them dry. "Peter," I said. Ever since taking on the role of executive chef, I had the privilege—if one could call it that—of addressing our sensitivity director by his first name. "What can I do for you?"

"What was Sean Baxter doing down here?"

I no longer had to answer to Sargeant. Gave me a good feeling, deep down. "Something you need, Peter?" I asked again.

He pulled out a notebook from his jacket pocket. "Friday's luncheon," he began. "I took the liberty of reviewing the guest list and I want to ensure you've provided for all the different religious and dietary issues we'll be facing."

I refrained from rolling my eyes. "We've got it covered."

"But I haven't had a chance to oversee the actual food preparation—"

"And you won't," I said, guiding him back toward the doorway. "I sent a copy of our complete menu to your office. If you chanced to read it, you'd see that everything has been handled with our usual aplomb."

I couldn't resist a tiny bit of bravado. We'd worked hard to come up with the perfect menu, with choices that would not only please a multitude of palates, but offer varieties to keep kosher, vegan, halaal, low-fat, low-carb, and non-dairy, among other things. To say this buffet had been one of my greatest challenges yet would be understatement. But everyone in the kitchen knew our guests would talk to the press afterward. We wanted—and expected—nothing short of a glowing account.

Sargeant was shaking his head. "I didn't read it yet. I would much prefer it if you walk me through—"

"And I much prefer to maximize the little time we have to get our meals together. So, Peter," I said, relishing the use of his first name again, "I have to ask you to allow us to do our jobs and to come back some other time. Preferably after the new year."

Blinking, he squared his shoulders and left without another word.

Bucky slapped his hands together in slow-motion applause. "Good job, kid. I didn't think you had it in you."

CHAPTER 8

ON THURSDAY, WITH LESS THAN AN HOUR TO go before Thanksgiving guests were due, food was flying. Not literally, of course. But we were all moving so fast that everything seemed a tiny bit blurred. Though there were only nine for dinner today, there were still dozens of last-minute details to attend to. We concentrated hard and talked very little.

I glanced at the clock. Just past noon. Mingled scents of roasting meat—the turkey breasts in the far oven, and the Virginia ham resting on the counter behind me—gave me enormous comfort. We were on time. Despite the fact that we left nothing to chance, I always panicked about the turkey; in my opinion, there was nothing worse than dried-out fowl. As I poured onion gravy from a pan into a tempo-rary tureenlike container, I shot a glance at the oven door. "Bucky," I called over my shoulder, "can you—"

"I just checked on them," he answered, reading my mind. "They're perfect. Nicely brown. Right on schedule."

"Thanks."

Agda was in charge of putting the finishing touches on each course. Every plate was arranged with exquisite precision just before it left our kitchen. At the White House, food did not simply sit on a dish—our meals required presentation. With her speed and accuracy, Agda was a natural to handle that job. Even though today's dinner would be served in a traditional, family-style manner, the trays and platters required her full attention before they were sent to the table.

Bent over the first tray of hors d'oeuvres, Agda was carefully placing fruits and cheeses in meticulous formation, interspersing crackers and spiced nuts to make for a beautifully appetizing display.

I glanced up when our head butler, Jackson, came in. He'd recently taken over the position, though he'd been on staff for many years. A tall black man with curly salt-and-pepper hair, he smiled often and could always be counted on for White House scoop. Right now, however, he wasn't smiling.

"The president is not returning to the White House until this evening," he said.

All activity stopped. "What?" I asked.

Jackson shook his head. "A change in plans."

Before inquiring as to what great world event prevented the president from attending his family's Thanksgiving dinner, I needed to know the truly crucial information. "Are we still serving?"

"We are," Jackson said, still not looking happy. "Sad day for the missus. She was counting on her husband's support with these guests." He met my gaze. "You have heard some stories?"

I had, and I remembered Sean Baxter's warnings. "This isn't going to be a friendly social dinner after all, is it?"

Jackson shook his head again. "I am concerned. But there is nothing we can do."

"Except feed them well and keep them happy," I said, "and hope that they're all so impressed with dinner that they forget about business."

The corner of Jackson's mouth curled up. "We can try. I will return when the guests arrive." Looking around the area, he asked, "Have you seen Yi-im?"

One of the newer butlers, a tiny gentleman of an Asian descent I couldn't deduce, Yi-im never seemed to be available when there was work to be done. It had taken me a while to get the hang of pronouncing his name: Yee-eem. I pointed downward. "He said something about heading to the cafeteria."

Anger sparked Jackson's eyes. "Lazy man."

"WE ARE READY," MARCEL SAID, AS HE CAME around the corner, wheeling a cart. The top shelf held a tall pumpkin trifle and a selection of four different varieties of minitartlets: pecan, orange chiffon, lemon cheese, and Boston cream. The cart's second shelf held Marcel's famous apple cobbler with oatmeal crumble.

"Do you need me to heat that up when the time comes?" I asked.

His dark face folded into worry lines—he hadn't even heard my question. "I hope I 'ave made enough."

I started to assure him that there was enough dessert to satisfy twenty hungry guests when he turned and beckoned someone behind. The missing Yi-im stepped into the kitchen carrying a large silver tray almost as big as he was. Just over forty, the junior butler was slim and so short that in his tuxedo he might have passed for a ring-bearer in a wedding. Except for his bald head, which he kept shaved and shiny enough to reflect lights.

"Just in case they are very hungry, I 'ave created another option," Marcel said, with a hint of superiority. "Chocolate truffles. Do you think they are a good choice?"

Again, as I was about to answer, Marcel's attention shifted. He ordered Yi-im to begin sending the desserts to the staging area: the Butler's Pantry just outside the first-floor Family Dining Room. I recognized in Marcel the same controlled panic I felt right before an important meal. He wasn't interested in my opinion—he simply wanted to bring me up to speed. And probably show off a little. The chocolate truffles would be a huge hit. Of that, I was certain.

When Yi-im left the area, I told Marcel that Jackson had been looking for the diminutive butler.

Marcel's hands came up in a gesture of supplication. "But he told me he had been assigned to help out here today."

I didn't have time to quibble. "At least we know he isn't shirking his duties," I said in a low voice. "And heaven knows we can use all the help we can get."

Marcel wiped his hands on his apron, looking thoughtful. "Yi-im has worked very hard today. As a butler, he is perhaps in the wrong department, no?"

I followed his logic. Marcel was always on the lookout for pastry assistants. With the number of dazzling and delicious desserts his department produced, he was usually understaffed. At the moment, however, I didn't have time to discuss personnel with him. "Let's talk about this next week," I said. "Monday morning staff meeting?"

"Excellent plan," he said. "Now I shall go upstairs to be certain my creations arrive safely."

Thirty seconds after his departure, Jackson returned,

making me think about one of those old movies where people chase one another and keep missing their quarry by moments. "Mr. and Mrs. Volkov have arrived, as has Senator Blanchard with Ms. Gerhardt. She has requested a few moments of your time."

I was surprised. "Bindy wants to talk to me?"

He nodded.

"Sure," I said. "You can let her come down after dinner."

"She would prefer to visit with you now."

Great. Another interruption. "Go ahead, Ollie," Bucky said. "We've got you covered."

He was right. One of the things Henry had told me before passing the potholders was that in order to succeed, I needed to be able to rely on the efforts of others. "You can't do everything yourself anymore," he'd said, chiding me. He knew how much I liked to feel in control. "You have to be able to let go. Let your staff show you how good they are." With a wink and a smile, he'd added, "That's how I recognized talent in you."

"Thanks, Bucky." I took a deep breath. "Okay," I said to Jackson. "Send her down."

Bindy Gerhardt had been a staffer in the West Wing during her tenure at the White House, and I liked her well enough. But she and I weren't the kind of girlfriends who sought one another out. Although she looked like central casting's answer to the nerdy girl with the heart of gold, she'd always struck me as a power groupie—doing her best only when people in authority were apt to notice. In fact, immediately after she'd accepted the position on Blanchard's staff, she'd stopped visiting the White House altogether. Probably to stave off any impression of impropriety. This was the nature of Washington, D.C.—rumor and innuendo ruled. We all knew that perception was often more important than reality. Especially where the news media was concerned.

Cyan sidled next to me. "That's weird," she said. "I hope she isn't looking for a special menu at this late date."

"I don't remember her having dietary restrictions." I was pretty good at remembering unusual requests. Plus, Bindy would have known to send her preferences early. I couldn't imagine why she'd asked to come down here, so I shrugged. I'd find out soon enough. "Maybe she wants to swap recipes."

Cyan laughed. I washed and dried my hands, taking a long look around my kitchen. It hummed. Without a doubt, this would be the best Thanksgiving dinner any of our guests had ever experienced. I savored the moment—the instance of absolute certainty that we'd achieved greatness. I couldn't wait for our guests' reactions.

Deciding it would be best to keep Bindy out of the kitchen proper—and hence out of the staff's way—I came into the Center Hall just as she made it to the bottom of the stairs. "Ollie!" she said when she saw me.

I almost didn't recognize her. Bindy had lost at least twenty pounds, and although I knew it was impossible, it seemed she'd grown taller, too. "Wow!" I couldn't stop my reaction. "You're . . . so . . ." I almost said, "slick," but caught myself before the word escaped. "So . . . chic. I mean . . . not that you weren't before, I just . . ." I'd fallen so far into the open-mouth-insert-foot trap that I couldn't escape without a massive recovery effort. "What I mean to say is that you look wonderful. The new job must be going great."

Sunny smile. "It is. And believe me, everyone has the same reaction. Quite the change, isn't it?"

Understatement, I thought.

She spun on a navy blue heel. Her dress was navy, too, a perfect contrast to her pearly skin. "What do you think?"

"You look fabulous." She did. Although she hadn't been exactly overweight before, the new, slimmer look suited her. The last time she'd been here, she preferred easy-comfort clothes and ballet flats. Back then she'd had loose, curly hair that she wore to her shoulders. No makeup. Now her hair was cropped short and slicked back, framing her carefully made-up face and exposing a pair of pert diamond earrings. The nose was still wide, the chin still weak, but she'd evidently been schooled in how to play up her better features because her eyes drew my attention first. Bindy would never be considered beautiful, but the change in her appearance certainly made her more attractive.

She tapped one of the earrings. "Fake," she said, "but aren't they great?"

At the moment, I would have much preferred to be discussing turkey dressing with Bucky than fake baubles with Bindy. "So, you're here in Mrs. Blanchard's place today?" I asked. I knew my voice held just enough curiosity to prompt her to get to the point.

"Yes, yes," she said. "There are some personal business items Senator Blanchard needs to discuss with the First Lady." Bindy wrinkled her nose, giving a little giggle. "Mrs. Blanchard didn't want to be in the way. I've done a lot of research for the senator. . . ." She waved both her hands at me. "That sounds so stilted. I do a lot for Treyton and his wife, and they both thought it would be smarter, strategically, for me to be here today when the partnership is discussed."

So Sean's fears had been warranted. Again, I was thankful he was due to arrive soon. "I thought this was supposed to be a Thanksgiving celebration."

"That, too. There's never any downtime in D.C., is

there?" She licked her lips. "But that's not what I wanted to talk with you about. I wanted to ask you about the gingerbread men."

"The ones Marcel is creating?"

"No, the ones being sent in from across the country." She giggled again. I'd forgotten that she had the tendency to do that when nervous. "Treyton knows that you're choosing the best ones from the thousands you've received to display in the Red Room next to the gingerbread house. Is that right?"

"It's not just me; Marcel has the final—"

"Yes, but you're in on it, right?"

"Sure."

"Treyton's kids are submitting gingerbread men they've been working on. It would mean a lot to them to have their work displayed in the Red Room during the holiday opening ceremonies."

I raised an eyebrow. "Where all the cameras will be?"

"Well, yes. . . ." She punctuated her words with another little laugh. "You know those pictures will be seen everywhere as soon as the celebration is complete. . . ."

She let the thought hang and I finally understood why she was uncomfortable talking with me. Treyton Blanchard wanted his kids' handiwork plastered all over every newspaper, White House–related Web site, and on TV. Rumor had it that the man was considering a run for the presidency. Getting his kids' artwork prominently displayed must feel a little like squatter's rights. A thought occurred to me. "Aren't his kids kind of young for this?" Blanchard had three little ones, and the oldest was eight or nine.

With a bouncy little so-so motion of her head, Bindy said, "They've had help with the project. The gingerbread men are really beautiful, Ollie. I wouldn't ask you to do this if they weren't worthy of presentation."

Sure, she wouldn't. Treyton Blanchard probably thought his kids' scribbles with a blue crayon were genius. And I knew that if the powerful senator asked Bindy to do something, she'd do it.

I shuddered inwardly at the thought of what these homemade gingerbread ornaments looked like until Bindy said, "If the kids had actually done all this on their own, they'd be snapped up as protégés." She laughed. "The family chef did some of the work. He's amazing." The spirit with which she added that last remark made me wonder if she and Blanchard's chef were the new hot item in D.C. I knew the guy. But I couldn't see them together.

"And the kids think they did it all themselves?"

She bit her lip, nodding.

"I'll look into it." I held up my hands, staving off further pressure. "But there's no guarantee the photographers will snap the right angle to get these in print, you know."

Tiny shrug. "I realize that. But I just wanted to ask you to do your best. The kids will be so thrilled. They've been invited to the ceremony, too. Their mom's bringing them. Can you imagine how excited they'll be to see their artwork in the Red Room of the White House?"

Realizing I wasn't going to get back into the kitchen until I gave her something to take back to Blanchard, I said, "I'll talk with Marcel and the decorating staff. That's the best I can do."

When Bindy smiled, relaxed now, I was taken aback again by the change in her. She'd morphed from ordinary to fabulous in just a few short months. And she seemed to have acquired a new confidence, too. "Thanks," she said. "It'll mean a lot to us."

She turned and headed for the stairs before I could ask

whether "us" meant her and the kids, or her and Treyton Blanchard.

I STEPPED OUT OF THE KITCHEN FOR THE dozenth time in the last hour. As Jackson passed me in the Center Hall, I grabbed his arm. "Any updates?"

Headshake. "No word. Nothing."

Five minutes before one o'clock and Sean Baxter hadn't arrived yet. We should have begun staging already.

"When do you think we'll be able to serve?" Visions of wilted lettuce, dried-out turkey, and soggy rolls raced through my mind.

"The First Lady suggested we wait until half past one. If Mr. Baxter still has not arrived, then we will begin without him."

A half-hour delay. Not great, but it could be worse. "Okay," I said, heading back in to deliver the news to my group. "Let me know if anything changes."

Over the next twenty minutes, I divided my time between overseeing progress in the kitchen and the Butler's Pantry upstairs. We staged our offerings in the pantry, waiting impatiently for the signal to serve our guests in the next room. The Family Dining Room occupies a space on the north side of the White House, with the pantry directly west. The State Dining Room—where most of our larger seated dining events are held—is a large area immediately adjacent to both rooms. In fact, we often used the Family Dining Room for staging when serving in the State Dining Room. The three-room setup is perfect whether we're serving a hundred guests, or fewer than a dozen.

I maintained a position in the empty State Dining Room, close enough to the gathering to listen and watch without being seen. Although I had every excuse to be there—to gauge how the hors d'oeuvres were going and to determine if I needed to make any last-minute changes to dinner—the real reason I parked myself at the door was pure nosiness. I knew Mrs. Campbell was a strong-minded and resilient woman, but I didn't know many of our guests. If they were planning on ambushing her, as Sean expected they might, I wanted to help him with information-gathering. I caught Jackson's eye. He stood nearby, facing the cross hall. I could tell he and I were on the same page.

I hadn't met Nick Volkov before, but I recognized him from the recent news items I'd checked online at Sean's suggestion. Volkov and his wife had had some trouble lately—involving allegedly bogus land deals, kickbacks, payoffs, and property liens. Volkov was a man—whether guilty or innocent—for whom a windfall would be salvation. No wonder he was pressuring Mrs. Campbell for a quick sale.

As they chatted and mingled with the other guests, the couple never seemed to lose physical contact with each other—his arm grazed hers his, fingers skimmed her back. Younger than the First Lady by about ten years, Nick was stout and fair, with youthful Eastern European features and a prominent brow. Mrs. Volkov, by contrast, wore her age like a road map. She looked considerably older than her husband and was a little bit hunched. Maybe all the jewelry she wore weighed her down. I hadn't seen this much sparkle since I passed Tiffany's in New York City.

"I don't understand your reluctance, Elaine," Nick Volkov said to the First Lady. His voice was even bigger than he was. "The sooner we put your uneasiness behind us, the sooner we can enjoy this blessed Thanksgiving day. Don't you agree?"

Mrs. Campbell held her hands together, clasped low.

She was the only diner in the room not carrying a glass of wine. "Oh, Nick," she said, with a touch of reproof, "I'm certainly not reluctant to talk, nor uneasy about my position with the company. I just don't want to discuss things twice. Why don't we wait for another opportunity, when both my husband and Sean can be here?"

I glanced at Jackson again. He shook his head. Sean still hadn't arrived.

Volkov lowered his voice. I almost didn't hear his next words. "If we wait too long, Elaine, we will miss our opportunity. Ten years from now the market may not be as good as it is now."

"And in ten years the market may be better," Mrs. Campbell said smoothly. "In fact, my father counted on that. He didn't want me to—"

"Your father didn't understand how things have changed."

"I believe he did." The First Lady's lips twitched. "And I certainly do."

Volkov's voice rose. "It comes down to this: We need to act and we need to do so right now."

"Nick," she said, and I caught the impatience in her tone, "once we sell, everything our fathers worked for will be gone. Zendy Industries will belong to others—to people who might take it in a direction we can't control."

"What difference does it make after we've been adequately compensated? Our fathers worked hard to provide us with security for our futures. Isn't this exactly what we're taking advantage of? Don't you think they would approve?"

"I don't think they would approve, no," Mrs. Campbell answered. She unclasped her hands and gestured around the room. "I don't think any of us is financially insecure right now. None of us needs the money—not for any legitimate reason."

Nick Volkov's face reddened.

He looked ready to say something unpleasant when his wife interrupted. "Where is Sean, anyway?" she asked. "I believe I've only met him once before. Such a nice young man."

Volkov sniffed. "Too young to understand the subtleties of business."

I backed away as Mrs. Campbell glanced toward the open door. "I don't know. I'm sure he said he was coming."

Nick Volkov cleared his throat. "He's irresponsible, if you ask me."

I slid around fast enough to catch Mrs. Campbell's tight smile. "Well, it's a good thing I didn't ask you, then, isn't it?" she said. With a pleasant nod to Mrs. Volkov, Mrs. Campbell excused herself to mingle with the other guests.

Call me Nosy Rosie, but I couldn't let it go. I continued to watch the interactions in the next room, listening closely to as many conversations as I could. The only people I knew who had the First Lady's interests at heart were the president and Sean. I hoped to overhear some tidbits of information that I could pass along to Sean later. Again, I wondered where he was. After our conversation yesterday in the kitchen, I couldn't imagine he would have forgotten the time. But things happen, and I decided that until he showed up, I was on spy duty.

Nick Volkov muttered under his breath. I didn't catch his words, but I couldn't miss the grimace he made behind the First Lady's back. Helen Hendrickson didn't miss it either. Practically sprinting away from Treyton Blanchard's side, she hurried over to join the Volkovs. Helen Hendrickson was not a small woman, nor a young one. The quick movement left her breathless. "Did she say she'll sign?" she asked.

"Hardly," Nick answered. "She's unwilling to even

entertain conversation until that damn Baxter arrives." Turning to his wife, he said something else I couldn't catch. She broke away from him to intercept Fitzgerald, who'd been heading toward them. Mrs. Volkov looped an arm through his and led him away toward the room's fireplace.

Helen Hendrickson chewed her thumbnail before addressing Volkov. "What can we do?"

Cyan came around the corner from the pantry. I walked over to meet her. "Still no news on Sean," I said, keeping my voice low. Looking at my watch, I added, "Not too much longer before we serve."

"I hate this tension," she said. "Can't do anything but wait and be nervous. Everything's ready now."

"I know, but we've been through worse," I said.

She glanced at the open door where I'd been standing. "Anything interesting?"

"So-so."

By the time Cyan returned to the pantry and I made it back to my unobtrusive position at the doorway, Treyton Blanchard had joined Nick Volkov and Helen Hendrickson. It was neat to be part of the wallpaper—seen but not noticed.

"What good gossip am I missing here?" Blanchard asked. The junior senator from Maryland had a pleasant face, but his natural charisma and wide smile made him seem even more handsome in person than he appeared on camera. "I hope you two haven't been talking about me."

Volkov made a noise. Frustration, it seemed. "We've been talking about our . . . partner." The way he said it made my skin crawl.

"Give it time," Blanchard said.

"Time?" Again, Volkov grew red-faced. "We don't have that luxury."

Blanchard took a small sip of his wine. "We have time

enough," he said. "Elaine can't be forced to make a decision without consulting her trusted advisers, can she?"

Volkov sputtered, "Some trusted adviser. That Baxter fellow can't even make it to dinner on time. How can we expect him to help her make the right decisions?"

"I'll talk with Elaine one-on-one when I get the chance," Blanchard said. "I think she's just overwhelmed right now. She's still grieving for her father. . . ."

"Her father's death is what precipitated this decision."

Blanchard held his wineglass to almost eye level, gesturing with it for emphasis. "Don't tell me things I already know, Nick. I understand what's at stake here. But today is Thanksgiving." He tempered his admonishment with a smile. "Or have you forgotten that?"

From the ping-pong movement of her head as the conversation went back and forth, Helen Hendrickson seemed unwilling—or too mousy—to join in. I was surprised when she focused her attention on Blanchard. "Easy for you," she said. "Nick and I don't have the benefit of political donations to help us make *our* dreams come true."

Blanchard replied, but I missed it because Jackson was on the move. As he passed me, he whispered, "Showtime."

I followed. "Sean Baxter?" I asked.

He spoke over his shoulder. "Not yet."

Within minutes, the guests were seated and we were ready to serve. I had Cyan in the narrow pantry with me and we scrutinized every dish to make certain it was absolutely perfect before one of our tuxedoed butlers carried it into the next room. I heard exclamations of delight as the platters reached the table, and I blew out a breath of relief.

When the door connecting the pantry to the Family Dining Room was open, I snuck a glance. With the president unavailable, the First Lady had taken her seat at the head of the table. Treyton Blanchard sat to her right, Bindy Gerhardt across from him. The Volkovs sat across from each other, too, with Nick next to Bindy. The male-female pattern continued with Helen Hendrickson next to Nick. Helen's guest, the elderly Mr. Fitzgerald, had settled himself across from her. Only the seat across from the First Lady was unoccupied.

As he passed me on his way back into the pantry, Jackson said, "We will seat Mr. Baxter when he arrives." A shrug. "If he arrives at all."

Cyan came close, whispering, "Do you think maybe Sean is with the president? I mean, that's his uncle. Maybe whatever's keeping President Campbell is—"

I shushed her. The other room had silenced. No conversation. No movement. Rather than push the connecting door open to peek, I hurried around into the State Dining Room where I could peer in unnoticed. I wondered if something was wrong with the meal. What could possibly have happened to stop everything so completely? I strained to hear, and was rewarded only by the flat-toned words from a voice I didn't recognize.

In a moment, I understood. Two Secret Service agents had positioned themselves inside the Family Dining Room. One of them had apparently requested Mrs. Campbell's presence away from her guests. I slowed to a stroll as I made my way across the expansive room, hoping I appeared nonchalant. Pretending I was heading into the hall.

Mrs. Campbell emerged just as I crossed her path. She'd been about to address the taller of the two agents, but stopped me with a hand to my arm. "Ollie," she said, "dinner is wonderful. I—"

"Mrs. Campbell," the agent said. He touched her elbow

in an effort to guide her toward the doorway to the Red Room. "Please."

She didn't move. "What happened?"

Both agents glared at me, making me want to shrink and run, but the First Lady gripped my arm, effectively freezing me in place.

She blinked rapidly, then took a steadying breath. "Is it my husband?"

"No," the shorter agent said quickly. "The president is safe."

"Thank God." Her grasp loosened, but she didn't completely let go. "Then what is it?" she asked the agents.

The taller one cleared his throat. "Ma'am, perhaps it would be better for you to come with us to the residence."

"No." Mrs. Campbell's jaw flexed. "Just . . . tell . . . me."

The agents exchanged glances.

She gripped me again. "Agent Teska, if you don't tell me what's going on—"

The thought hung there a long moment.

"With the president tied up in negotiations . . . we thought it best to talk to you first." The urgency in his face settled into the dispassionate expression that always heralds bad news. We waited. I barely breathed.

"There's been an incident," Teska finally said. "Please, ma'am. If you'll come with me . . ."

Her face was tight. Her voice even tighter. "Just tell me."

"It's Sean Baxter, ma'am. He's dead."

CHAPTER 9

THE FIRST LADY MANAGED TO FIND HER WAY
back to her chair in the dining room, waving away those of
us trying to help her. She sat for a long time, eyes covered,
head down.

There was no recovering from news like this—not surrounded by colleagues who had planned to enjoy Thanksgiving dinner and who all now sat, staring. Doing the best
they could, Secret Service agents quietly ushered the
guests out to waiting limousines. Helen Hendrickson broke
away from the group long enough to press Mrs. Campbell's hands between her own and hug the First Lady,
blinking back tears and murmuring condolences. All the
guests were gone in minutes. Their sudden departure left
us in suffocating silence.

Inexplicably, the First Lady asked me to stay with her
after the guests were gone. I had a tremendous desire to
beg off, but one look at the sadness in her eyes convinced

me otherwise. "Of course," I said. My staff would handle whatever cleanup and storage needed to be done, and though they'd wonder at my absence, they'd certainly manage without me.

Jackson brought Mrs. Campbell a glass of water, which she took but didn't sip. She held it in both hands, almost prayerfully, still staring downward. "Thank you," she said to the butler, and when he inquired what else he could get her, she said, "Nothing. Nothing now."

The two Secret Service agents remained: Teska and a female agent, Patricia Berland. They seemed perplexed by my presence. I couldn't blame them. I'd taken the seat vacated by Blanchard, my mind racing a hundred thoughts at once: how badly I felt about Sean, what I could do for Mrs. Campbell right at the moment, why she had asked me to stay, how soon I could get back to the kitchen, and why this had to happen today. Of all days.

Sean, who had been working in my kitchen just twenty-four hours ago—was dead. I couldn't get my mind around that. I couldn't grasp how he could have been here, so alive, so much fun, and now no longer exist. But I also knew I couldn't dwell on that right now. My first duty was to Mrs. Campbell.

She finally raised her head to face Teska. "You said, 'incident.' What do you mean?"

The two agents exchanged a glance. Teska squinted, as though he were fighting a hard internal argument. "His death is under investigation."

"What are you not telling me?"

Teska's face twitched. He spoke slowly. "Sean Baxter may have taken his own life."

"No!" Mrs. Campbell said, starting to stand. "I don't

believe that." Berland's gentle touch on the First Lady's shoulder was enough to keep her seated. "What happened? Where is he?"

At this point the two agents seemed to forget I was there. But the First Lady hadn't forgotten—she reached out and clasped my hand with hers. It was very cold.

Berland spoke. "Preliminary reports suggest that Mr. Baxter shot himself."

"No," Mrs. Campbell said again. This time, however, it was not an exclamation of disbelief, it was a flat refusal. "Sean didn't like guns. He never would have done that."

"Let me assure you, ma'am, the Metropolitan Police will fully investigate this as a homicide until the evidence proves otherwise. But . . ."

"But?"

"He left a note, ma'am."

Mrs. Campbell crumpled in on herself, her silent crying more poignant than if she'd wailed and screamed. I reacted instinctively, forgetting this was our nation's First Lady and seeing only a woman who'd suffered immeasurable loss. I stood next to her, putting my arm around her shaking shoulders, murmuring how sorry I was.

Berland's eyes met mine. "Let's get her upstairs," she mouthed.

I leaned in to whisper to Mrs. Campbell that it might be best to return to her own rooms. She nodded and stood, keeping her face covered with one hand, grabbing my arm with the other.

"We'll help you," Berland said, stepping between me and the First Lady.

She didn't release her hold. Instead, she tugged me close so that her whispered words were almost inaudible. "He cared about you, Ollie. He told me he saw a future with you."

Though tears raced down her face, she managed a wobbly smile. "He asked me to fix you two up."

I opened my mouth, but no words came out.

"He would have wanted you to know," she added, and she finally let go of my arm. Turning to face Berland, she gave a quick nod. "I'm ready now."

For the second time that week, I fought scalding pain in my throat, my eyes, and my heart.

CHAPTER 10

I WOKE UP CRAMPED AND ACHY FROM SPEND-ing the night on the small bed in my third-floor office. The mattress was comfortable enough, but I suffered from the dual distractions of not being in my own apartment and anxiety as I replayed the prior day's events.

Throwing on spare clothes I kept in my office for emergencies such as this, I made it downstairs to the kitchen while it was still dark. I usually loved the morning's solitary quiet—moving about at my own pace, transforming this cool stainless steel room into a warm, bustling nest of activity. I always felt as though I held the power to wake up the world.

Today, however, that simple pleasure eluded me. Despair weighed me down because again, one of our White House "family" had died—and again, under horrific circumstances.

I pulled biscuits out of the freezer, set them on the counter, and fired up one of the ovens. Sean hadn't struck me as despondent or suicidal. And yet the Secret Service had mentioned a note. That made no sense.

So acute was my concentration on Sean, and on preparing breakfast for what would be a long, grueling day for the First Family, that I didn't notice one of the butlers come in until he was almost next to me.

My head jerked up. "Red!"

His pale eyes widened in alarm. "I'm sorry," he said, taking a step back.

Red had been here forever, and though the man was spry, he'd crossed the line to elderly at least a decade ago. Along the way he'd lost the hair color that had given him his nickname. I hadn't meant to shake him. Waving off his apology, I pointed up, toward the residence. "How is she?"

"Bad times here," he said, with a sad shake of his head. "And no one is stopping long enough to grieve."

My puzzled expression encouraged him to explain.

"The president returned last night. He'll be taking breakfast early with his wife," he said. "Then he will depart for a meeting in New York."

I hoped that didn't mean the First Lady would be left alone at a time like this. "Is Mrs. Campbell going with him?"

Lines bracketing Red's eyes deepened. "The First Lady will remain in the residence to host the Mother's Luncheon this afternoon."

"What?"

"The luncheon will proceed as scheduled."

This couldn't be right. "But, after the news. After what happened to Sean . . ."

He stopped me with a sigh. "Yes," he said, "the family has much to deal with today. And on top of everything else, Gene Sculka's family is holding his wake tonight."

Dear God, I'd almost forgotten about that. I was about to ask if the president and First Lady were planning to attend, but Red anticipated my question.

"The president will not return to the White House until Saturday. The First Lady has called the Sculka family to pay respects."

I made a mental note to make an appearance myself this evening. But right now only one thing was on my mind. "I thought they would cancel the luncheon."

Red sighed. "Mrs. Campbell doesn't want to disappoint all the women and kids who have flown from all over the country—at their own expense—to be here today."

"But surely people would understand—"

"You know our First Lady."

I did. Selfless to a fault, she was notoriously stubborn but always looking out for the greater good. I admired her—and I hoped to achieve that serenity someday myself. "Well, then, I suppose I'd better move a bit faster here."

Cyan arrived moments later, followed by Bucky, Rafe, Agda, and a few more SBA chefs we'd hired for the day. I was glad I hadn't canceled the extra staff. Even if today's luncheon had been scrapped, we had a great deal of work ahead of us. The holiday season officially began Sunday afternoon—two days from now—when the president and First Lady would attend a presentation at the Kennedy Center. Extra hands in the kitchen were never a waste.

While managing breakfast and cleaning up, we got to work on the afternoon's event. Buffets were so much less stressful than plated dinners—for us, and for the waitstaff. We'd prepared as much as possible ahead of time, but there was still a lot to be done before the guests arrived.

More than two hundred moms and tots were expected, and we'd been careful to include plenty of kid-friendly fare in our offerings. One of the president's favorite sandwiches, peanut butter and banana, was on the menu today. We would offer a choice: served on plain white or on cinnamon bread. In fact, the staff had taken bets on which would be more popular with the kids.

Rafe expertly sliced away the crusts from a peanut-butter-on-white sandwich. "Kids will go for plain, every time."

"Cinnamon tastes better," Cyan said, sing-song.

Rafe raised his own voice up an octave, continuing the sing-song cadence. "Won't matter if they refuse to try it."

Shaking her head so her ponytail wagged, Cyan slathered peanut butter on yet another slice of cinnamon bread. "They'll try these."

I was happy to hear their chitchat. Although normalcy was not to be expected—not so soon after the two unexpected deaths—any little bit of happiness was worth grabbing.

Just as we started in on our next project, Special Agent Gavin strode into the kitchen. He stopped short a half breath before running into one of our SBA chefs who carried a massive bowl of salad on his shoulder.

"Watch where you're going," Gavin said, flattening himself against the wall just in time.

The assistant turned fully, in order to see the man who'd almost tossed our salad. "Sorry," he mumbled, then set off again for the refrigerator. Gavin's presence here just as time was getting tricky was enormously unwelcome. There was nothing this man could say or do to help today's event, and the sooner he got out of my kitchen the happier we would all be.

As he righted himself, he tugged at his suit coat and adjusted his tie. Before he could seek me out, I'd positioned myself in front of him. "What can I do for you?" My words were polite, my demeanor dismissive.

"You're scheduled for emergency response training."

So why was he in my kitchen now? I'd set the staff up myself; we were already on the hook for Gavin's classes. "We haven't forgotten," I said. "We'll be there. As scheduled."

"You're scheduled right now."

"No, we're not."

"Not them," he said, pointing. "You."

"No," I said, straining to process this. "Not possible."

He spoke solemnly. "It is my personal responsibility to see that department heads are fully trained. You missed your class last night."

"Do you have any idea what went on here last night?"

Gavin gave me one of those looks meant to make people wither. I didn't. "Ms. Paras," he said. "When someone's faced with a life-or-death situation, do you think it's more important that they've learned how to react swiftly, decisively, and accurately, thereby saving lives? Or do you believe it's more important that they've mastered the preparation of white roux?"

My eyebrows shot up.

Half of his mouth curled. "I am not so ignorant in matters of haute cuisine as you might imagine."

I didn't care if he was the next Paul Bocuse; I wasn't about to let him drag me away from the kitchen right before a major event. I tried again. "The reason I missed—"

He interrupted. "I know you believe your work here is important, but I'm sure you agree that the safety of the White House trumps all other concerns."

"I'm not saying—"

"Is your staff incapable of handling the situation on their own?"

"Of course not."

"Then come with me."

He turned, fully expecting me to follow. I stood my ground. "Special Agent Gavin," I said to his retreating form. "Just a minute."

He turned and his expression told me he wasn't entirely surprised that I hadn't complied.

"Today is a major event for the First Lady," I said. "She's depending on us. If you haven't already heard, and what I've been trying to tell you is, she suffered a devastating loss last night."

Gavin nodded. "Yes."

I continued. "If Mrs. Campbell is prepared to move forward with her luncheon today, then I'm damned certain going to stay here to make sure it's perfect."

I got the feeling I was amusing him. In a snarly sort of way.

"So you're telling me you refuse to attend training?"

"I refuse to attend *now*."

He made a show of looking at his watch. "And when, exactly, will you be finished here?"

I blew out a breath. "The luncheon is scheduled for one o'clock. . . ."

"One o'clock," he said, before I could finish my sentence. "I'll be back for you then."

When he left, I massaged my eyes. "There's always one, isn't there?" I said to nobody in particular.

Cyan patted me on the back. "Don't worry. We've got you covered."

CYAN WAS RIGHT. OUR LUNCHEON PREPARA-
tions moved with balletlike precision. We'd sent up trays of garlic–green bean bundles, blue-cheese straws, and

other savory side dishes to stock the buffet, with replacement trays on hand, ready for replenishing as the mothers helped themselves and attended to their children.

Jackson and Red made frequent trips to the kitchen, and I asked them how Mrs. Campbell was holding up. "She's a true lady," Red said cryptically. "Tough and soft at the same time."

My heart went out to her. I knew how terrible I felt, and I'd only just gotten to know Sean over the past few months. How hard it must be to lose someone you'd known since his birth.

The two men helped load the next batch of trays. Both rolled their eyes when I asked how the festivities were progressing. "Lotta whining going on up there," Jackson said.

Red shook his head. "In my day, children were seen and not heard."

For the first time since I'd come to work here, I was relieved not to be interacting with White House guests. "It can't be that bad," I said.

Jackson arched an eyebrow toward Red. "How many kids you figure are jamming themselves into that bathroom at one time?"

"Too many."

"What about the food?" I asked. "How do people like the cheese straws? What about the mint brownie bites?"

Red gave me a sad smile. "Those poor moms are having a devil of a time getting a chance to eat. The minute any of them tries to take a bite, their kid spills something."

"It really isn't that bad, is it?"

Jackson gave me a so-so. "They're well-behaved for the most part," he said. "They just take a lot more fussing than what we're used to."

"Not *more* fussing," Red corrected. "Just different fussing."

Jackson laughed. "Yeah. Different."

I was about to ask what he meant when Gavin returned. Without even a perfunctory greeting, he pointed at me. "It's after one o'clock," he said. "Let's go."

Realizing that it was not only useless to argue, but it was unnecessary because aside from cleanup, our work was done—I followed Gavin out of the kitchen and into the Palm Room.

"We're going into the West Wing?" I asked.

He didn't answer.

I rarely crossed into this section of the White House. The Palm Room connected the residence's ground floor—our floor—to the West Wing's first floor because of the lay of the land. The residence itself sat on a small slope. A casual area, with white latticed walls and a gardenlike feel, the Palm Room boasted two gorgeous pieces of art: *Union* and *Liberty*, both painted by the Italian American artist Constantino Brumidi.

Gavin walked with purpose, not looking back, and evidently not noticing how often I was required to scurry to catch up to his long-legged strides. He rushed me through the obstacle course of press corps offices, where eager reporters glanced up as we passed—each one startling into a hopeful, then disappointed expression when they realized it was only the chef coming through.

The air was different here. Too many bodies to avoid, too many wires to step over, too much electronic equipment to dodge, and the atmosphere of constant urgency gave the area a cramped, stuffy feel. I could hear the whir of a motor and I guessed air-conditioning ran in this section year-round. How else to cool off all the power equipment and panic?

"Where are we going?" I asked again.

Gavin didn't answer, but he stepped to the side to open the next door for me. And there we were: the Brady Press Briefing Room. I'd been in this room only a couple of times; it had been renovated a few years before I began working here.

Gavin took a few more strides to the center of the room, then stopped.

"What is here?" he asked. "What do you observe?"

I was sick and tired of Gavin's bizarre questioning methods. "I don't see a training class, if that's what you mean."

He graced my smart-aleck answer with a lips-only smile. "Due to your absence at last night's class, I have the dubious honor of bringing you up to speed by myself."

"It's not like I played hooky," I said. "Can't I just take one of the other classes?"

"When?" he asked. "All you've been talking about is how shorthanded you are. You have your staff scheduled tomorrow and Sunday. I highly doubt you'll find time to attend and shortchange your kitchen further."

He had me there.

"Listen," I said. "I'm a quick learner, and I don't want to waste your time. Can't you just give me some handouts and I'll catch up?"

"The next round of classes builds upon knowledge you glean from the first round. You can't expect to get anything out of further instruction without learning the basics first."

As he said this, he made his way up to the president's large, bullet-resistant lectern, also known as the "blue goose." When he positioned himself behind it and placed both hands on the lectern's sides, he seemed to forget I was there. His palpable craving for power washed over me like a wave. This was one intense guy.

Blinking himself back to awareness, he noticed me still near the door where we'd entered. "What do you observe?" he asked again.

The sooner I played along, the faster I'd get back to work. I took a deep breath. "Okay, give me a minute."

A picture of elegant efficiency, the bright room with the presidential motif boasted blue leather seats, state-of-the-art electronics, and a small raised dais at the far end of the room, where a door connected it to the heart and brains of the West Wing.

I didn't have a clue of what to look for. A quick glance at Gavin warned me not to ask.

Okay, fine. I was on my own here. Something out of place. Something that didn't belong.

Palladian windows adorned the north wall. I checked each one to ensure it was secure. I checked the doors, even the ones across the room that led south out onto the west colonnade. Everything clear.

But that would be too obvious. Special Agent-in-Charge Leonard Gavin was not the type to let me off easy. Whatever he'd set up in here would be designed to be difficult to find. I tried to think like old Gav. More precisely, I tried to think like an assassin.

Gav probably didn't realize I had a bit of experience in that arena. And I'd learned a few things.

What would an assassin do? He'd have to be better than clever. He'd have to be brilliant. Anything out of place would be noticed by our eagle-eyed Secret Service personnel. So if, say, a terrorist wanted to plant a bomb in the room, he'd have to ensure that it looked like something that belonged here. Up-front and obvious. Something so plain-as-day that every eye in the place would glaze over it without a second glance.

I stood in the fourth row of seats and I made a slow circle—a complete 360-degree turn—taking everything in at a pace that would make slugs weep.

"We're not here for the tourist show," he said. "You're supposed to be finding a security breach, not studying the symmetry."

I ignored him. Closed my eyes. Silently reasoned with myself.

Let's assume Gav planted one of those IEDs in here. He'd warned us that shapes and configurations of the deadly devices changed almost daily. So the one thing I knew I *wasn't* looking for was an opaque, bottlelike item.

Where would it do the most damage?

I opened my eyes. Right here, in the middle of the room, during a crowded press conference, a bomb would guarantee the greatest loss of life. But would that be an assassin's goal? Take out the innocent media folks, just like terrorists took out civilians on 9/11? Maybe, but if a fanatic killer was able to get this far—past White House security—then he'd be aiming for a bigger target.

I scooched out of the row and made my way up to the dais. "Excuse me," I said to Gavin.

With reluctance, he stepped away from the lectern, and I took a moment to stand behind it myself. The "blue goose" was tall, as speaking stands go, but I could still see over it with ease.

Running my hands along the sides, I felt the power, too. Twisting around, I cast a glance at the large medallion hanging on a curtained wall behind me. This wide blue oval, with an image of the White House at its center, was seen behind the president whenever he addressed the press from this room.

Gavin was watching me, his face expressionless.

I turned back toward the empty seats. Gav was setting me up to fail, I was sure of that. Maybe I should just give up and let him have his fun.

No. My personal pride rebelled. Not without a fight. Or at least, in this case, my best effort. But after the past few days, I didn't know how much effort I really had in me for Gavin's games.

I blew out a breath.

He sidled up. "Are you expecting the answer via ESP?" he asked. "When we held this exercise in the cafeteria yesterday, your colleagues at least searched the room before they gave up." He made a show of looking at his watch. "I'm giving you another minute. Then I'll explain what you should have been doing."

I could practically hear the clock tick as I gripped the lectern with both hands. Closing my eyes again, I thought about how *I* would wreak havoc on the White House if I had to do it in this room.

"Thirty seconds."

"Yeah, thanks," I said, wasting another two ticks to answer him.

This room was new. Why was that popping to the forefront of my thoughts just now? What was significant about its relative newness? Everything here had been changed. The place was practically sterile—and the housekeeping staff worked to keep it that way.

New. *Changed.*

A thought tickled my brain, just a breath out of reach.

"Fifteen seconds."

I opened my eyes. Turned to face the wall behind me. Stared at it.

"Ten."

The curtains were . . . wrong. This wasn't the right backdrop.

As I argued with myself—realizing that nothing prevented the president from switching backdrops from time to time—my hands searched the royal blue curtains. Last time I'd seen President Campbell speak, the background had been flat—as though made of drywall—and the medallion's suspension wires were visible.

This time, the medallion's method of suspension was *in*visible—a means of support I couldn't detect.

"What are you doing, Ms. Paras?"

I didn't bother answering. My fingers groped the medallion's edge—looking for what, I didn't know.

"Three . . . two . . ."

"Got it!" I shouted. I yanked at a fist-sized piece of plastic that had been duct-taped to the back of the medallion. Pulling it forward, I held it up for Gav to see.

"What exactly do you think you have?" he asked.

"This!" I said, feeling my face flush with pride.

He arched an eyebrow.

"This is what I was supposed to find, isn't it?"

Gav tilted his head, approaching me slowly. Taking the device from my hands, he said, "First of all, let me congratulate you, Ms. Paras. You're the first person to find one of our planted IEDs." He fingered two wires that reached out from the bottom of the plastic, playing with them so they bounced at his touch. "And guess what else you did that no one else did."

I shrugged.

"You just set off the bomb," he said.

"But—"

He stopped me with a withering gaze. How could anyone stay as cold and detached as this guy? He played with the two wires, pointing them at me.

"Know what this means, Ms. Paras?"

I shook my head.

"Kaboom!" he shouted into my face.

My shoulders dropped.

"It isn't enough that you're able to spot things out of place," he said, stepping back, again the picture of calm. "You need to learn what to do when faced with an emergency."

I opened my mouth to argue. I'd been in my fair share of emergency situations and I'd handled things nicely, thank you very much—but I realized he was right. When it came to explosive devices, I had no idea what to do. I closed my mouth without saying a word.

"Very good," he said with a tone that made me want to *kaboom* him myself. "Now that we've tested your powers of observation, let's work on reaction protocols."

Forty-five minutes later, he finally released me for the day. "Not a bad start," he said. From him, I supposed that rated as high praise.

"Thanks a lot," I said, pushing bangs off my damp forehead. He'd really kept me moving—in the hour we'd worked together, we hadn't had two minutes of downtime. Truth was, though, I'd learned more than I'd expected to and certainly more than I ever hoped to need to know. Throughout my tutorial, Gavin constantly prefaced his demonstrations with, "We didn't get a chance to do this with the big group . . ." so I got the definite impression that I'd received more in-depth instruction than had my colleagues. He really warmed to the subject matter when he taught one-on-one. Maybe I could even skip the next class.

We walked back toward the residence, through the Palm Room, in silence. When he and I were about to part company at the kitchen, I stopped him. "Special Agent Gavin?"

He turned. "Call me Gav."

Little did he know I'd already been doing that under my breath.

With a shrug, he added, "That is, use the nickname when we're working together. If we're out here, then use Special Agent Gavin."

"Sure," I said. But I sincerely hoped we wouldn't be working one-on-one again, ever.

"What were you going to say," he asked, "when you stopped me?"

Despite the fact that he was an arrogant jerk, and dismissive of my role as executive chef, I realized I was better prepared for emergencies even after today's short session. "Just wanted to say thanks," I said. "I learned a lot."

He frowned. "I'll be tougher on you next time." With a quick turn on his heel, he walked away.

Peculiar man.

I'd just about gotten into the kitchen when I ran into Bindy coming out. What was she doing here?

"Ollie!" she said, startling us both. "Where have you been?"

I didn't feel like explaining, so I pointed west. "Busy."

"The senator's wife, Maryann Blanchard, is upstairs," she said. "She wants to meet you."

"Me?" My hand instinctively brushed hair out of my eyes, and I was disappointed to discover I was still perspiring. "Why?"

Cheeks flushed, Bindy appeared a good deal more frazzled than she had yesterday. Although she was again super-snazzily dressed, she lacked the polish from the day before. "I was supposed to introduce you hours ago. Treyton insisted on it." Her eyes were restless—as though she were afraid that he would suddenly swoop down and scold her for taking too long. She giggled, which I recognized as Bindy's unusual expression of nervousness. We were all put in uncomfortable situations all too often. Her method of release didn't speak well of her professionalism. "Mrs. Blanchard wants you to meet the children."

"Now?" I glanced at my watch. The Mothers' Luncheon should be over. Guides should be taking groups of moms and tots on tours of the open rooms of the White House, and then everyone would gather in the East Room for a final discussion of the day's events. "Where's the First Lady?"

Bindy tilted her head, as though the question surprised her. "Upstairs with Mrs. Blanchard and a few others."

"How's she holding up?"

Finally, the light dawned. "Oh, of course. Yes. That's right. She lost her nephew yesterday."

My God, how could she have forgotten?

Bindy glanced away again. Maybe this job was too much for her. "I mean, we feel terrible about the First Family's loss," she said.

Too little, too late.

"But, Ollie, if you could just come upstairs for a little bit . . ."

"Does this have to do with the placement of her kids' gingerbread men in the Red Room?" I asked.

Bindy blushed more deeply. "Just five minutes, okay?"

I shook my head. "I can't. I haven't been back to the kitchen in over an hour and there are a million things to be done. Sorry." I started to move away, but she cut me off.

"Please," she said. "I promised her she'd get the chance to meet you."

"I told you I'd take a look at the gingerbread men the kids made. Isn't that enough? Tell her I'm busy. It's the truth."

"You have to do this, Ollie," Bindy said. Her voice had changed. "You don't understand what it's like."

I stared at her but she averted her eyes. "I don't understand what *what's* like?"

She bit her lip, wrinkling her nose. When she looked at me again, I thought she might cry. "Look at you. You've made it. You're at the top. You've gotten there."

I had an idea of where she was going, and though I didn't really want to travel down this track, I couldn't think of a way to stop the train.

"This is *my* chance," she said. "This is a dream job. This is what *I've* been working for all my life." She jabbed a finger into her own chest so hard it had to hurt. "But I'm still new. And I'm still trying to prove myself. What's it going to look like if I can't do something simple like make an introduction that Mrs. Blanchard requested?"

"You shouldn't have promised—"

"I know. You're right. I shouldn't have." Bindy looked as miserable as a person could, despite the trim suit and snazzy shoes, and she held out her hands, abdicating all power.

I had to ask. "Why are you so keen on keeping a job that makes you unhappy?"

For the first time since we started talking, Bindy smiled. "I love my job."

"I never would've guessed."

"It's just the pressure," she said. "I'm not used to it yet. But I'm getting better. And Treyton has plans. Big plans. If

I'm good at what I do, he'll keep me around. That's all I want."

Big plans. Like a run for the presidency? He was the same party as President Campbell. I doubted he'd make a primary bid against an incumbent, but I didn't doubt he fantasized about it.

I felt for Bindy, but I was sticky, tired, and not in the mood to meet anyone—especially one with a "choose my kids' artwork" agenda on her mind.

"Please," she said again.

I rubbed my eyesockets. "I'm a mess."

"Nobody will care."

And that was how I came to meet Mrs. Blanchard upstairs in the Entrance Hall. She was a dark-haired, petite beauty. Bindy introduced me. "Call me Maryann," Mrs. Blanchard said.

I knew I could never do that, but I smiled and said hello to the three young children hanging on her. "And what's your name?" I asked the oldest.

He squirmed and smiled. "Trey," he said. "Are you the cook?"

"I sure am," I said.

"The food was good," he said, ever so politely. "Except Leah didn't like the banana pudding. She smashed it on the floor."

His mother shushed him, and shrugged. "Sorry."

"It's okay," I said as I turned to the other two little ones. Leah was about three and John was five. They all looked like they couldn't wait to get home and out of their dressy clothes. Leah wrapped herself around her mother's leg and whimpered.

Behind us, small groups wandered in and out of the Green Room, Blue Room, Red Room, and State Dining

Room. Tour guides kept them moving. I was amazed at how well—relatively speaking—all the children behaved. I heard an occasional outburst and an accompanying reprimand, but the groups were more sedate than I'd expected, especially after Jackson's and Red's descriptions. I really wished Mrs. Blanchard had taken the tour.

Mrs. Campbell stood a few feet away, watching us. She maintained a serene smile, but from the look in her eyes, I knew she wanted to be away from all these people—to be alone to grieve for Sean. I marveled at the woman's strength in light of all that had happened.

"Are they touring the West Wing, too?" I asked at a lull in the conversation.

"They're almost everywhere," Bindy answered. "But we wanted a chance to talk with Mrs. Campbell alone. It's probably our only opportunity, isn't it?" she asked.

Mrs. Campbell nodded, without expression.

Couldn't they leave the poor woman alone?

Above the soft conversation and sounds of people moving around, we heard a speedy *click-clack* of two sets of high heels on the hard floor. A moment later, the social secretary, Marguerite, and her assistant joined us. Marguerite apologized for interrupting. "Mrs. Campbell," she said quietly, "you're needed upstairs."

The First Lady offered regrets for being called away. She thanked Mrs. Blanchard for attending the day's festivities and then procured a promise from the assistant secretary that everyone on the tours would be looked after properly.

Once the First Lady and Marguerite departed, I started to move away myself. "It was nice to meet you," I said. To the children, I added, "I hope you enjoyed your gingerbread man project."

Little Trey gave me a solemn look. "I didn't have fun making those," he said.

Bindy piped in. "This is the lady who will put your gingerbread men up for everybody to see. Right, Ollie?"

I didn't have any idea how to answer. "I'll do my best," I said.

Trey's mother gave his arm a tug. "Say thank you."

"Thank you."

Mrs. Blanchard smiled at me. An embarrassed smile. "We didn't turn them in with the rest. Bindy didn't want them to get lost in the confusion. She knows where they are."

"I'll make sure to get them into your hands directly," Bindy said.

"The tours are winding down now," the assistant secretary interjected, effectively ending this uncomfortable line of conversation. "Is there anything else you wanted to see before we return you to your car?"

What a nice way to shoo people out.

"No, we're done here," Maryann Blanchard said. She settled a high-wattage smile on Bindy, who winked at me.

"I'll call you tomorrow," she said.

I didn't answer. I couldn't wait for them to be gone.

CHAPTER 11

FROM THE FRYING PAN STRAIGHT INTO THE
fire.

That's how I felt at Gene's wake. I'd been here for about
fifteen minutes, but couldn't help but believe I'd inadvertently thrown myself into the flames just by showing up. I
hadn't anticipated the enormous impact my presence might
have. Standing next to the casket, I hadn't expected to be
surrounded by Gene's well-meaning relatives, all asking me
what really happened, what I'd seen, what I'd done, and did
I think Gene had suffered? With everyone asking at once, it
was difficult to know exactly what to say to give each of
them the most comfort. Above all, I wanted to be helpful.

Try as I might, I couldn't keep the family straight. A tall
woman rested her hand on my right shoulder, turning me to
meet yet another relative. An elderly, suited gentleman.
"This is the girl who found Gene," she said by way of introduction.

She was about to continue when a man to my right

tapped my arm. He, too, wore a suit—and the look of a successful businessman. "What was done for him?" he asked. "I mean, on the scene. Did you administer CPR?"

The woman to my right tugged me again, trying to pull my attention back to the elderly fellow, who I now learned was Gene's older brother. "I'm very sorry," I said, taking his hand in both of mine.

His eyes sagged under the weight of unshed tears. "Thank you."

"Excuse me," a familiar voice said. A big hand clamped my left shoulder with solid authority. "Ollie," he said, "I need to talk with you."

I turned to see a very welcome and familiar face. His hair had gone almost completely gray, but his customary cheer sparkled from those blue eyes. I started to smile, but remembered where I was and immediately tamped down my reaction. "Henry!" I reached to give him a big hug. Relieved to have an out, I turned back to the family. Again I offered my condolences—and then apologized for having to leave so soon.

"Thank you," I said as we moved to the lobby. "I didn't know how to answer them." I shot a look back into the room as the group clustered together again. Circling the wagons, as it were. "It's so difficult to know what to say. And what not to say."

"It's always hard," he said, his eyes scanning the large vestibule. "And a situation like this one makes it worse." He winked at me. "I've been waiting for you. I knew that unless there was some emergency, you'd be here tonight."

Henry had lost some of the weight he'd put on in his last few months as executive chef, and his face looked less flushed. Although his waistline would never be characterized as trim, it was certainly under control. In fact, the suit he wore gave the impression of being almost saggy. "You look good," I said.

He blushed. "How's your kitchen?"

"*Our* kitchen?" I asked.

That made him smile.

"I'll tell you all about it, if you want to go for coffee."

Henry's eyebrows lifted. "Such a beautiful young lady asking an old man like me out for coffee? I would be a fool to refuse."

I placed a hand on his arm. "With an attitude like yours, Henry, you will *never* be old."

There was a Starbucks half a block away, and though it was cold outside, we walked. I knew it wouldn't be long before Henry started peppering me with questions. He didn't disappoint. As soon as we'd settled at a small table, him with a cup of coffee, me with a caramel apple cider, he asked, "So, how are the holiday preparations progressing?"

I told him, then said, "You heard about Sean Baxter?"

His eyes, which had crinkled up at the corners when I'd talked about the menu, now drooped. "How could I not? It's been on every news station." He shook his big head. "I've often wondered why anyone would choose to be president. You lose all privacy." Waving a hand in the direction of the funeral home, he said, "Gene Sculka's family has had to deal with some reporters asking questions, but for the most part, they're allowed to grieve privately. They can be *family* to one another. They're able to hold one another up without worrying about the world staring in on them."

When he sighed, I picked up his train of thought. "I know. I've seen the papers. Any move the president or Mrs. Campbell makes is scrutinized and analyzed ten times over."

His eyes didn't hold the twinkle they usually did. "Sometimes the news needs to step back and let people just *be*."

We were silent for a long moment. I took a sip of my frothy concoction, and enjoyed the sweet, hot trickle down the back of my throat. "You've heard about the bomb scare, too?" I said, knowing he had. In this day and age, one would have to be as hermitlike as the Unabomber to avoid the deluge of news that constantly sluiced over us.

"Were you evacuated?"

I told him about being sequestered in the bunker with the First Lady and Sean. I watched emotion tighten Henry's eyes, and I shared with him my impression that Mrs. Campbell had intended to set me up with Sean.

Henry patted my hand. "This has been hard on you, too."

I swallowed, finding it a bit more difficult this time. "Yeah."

We talked about Bucky's constant temper tantrums, Cyan's burgeoning talents, and Marcel's quiet genius. When I told Henry about Agda, he laughed.

"Bucky was quick to remind me that you would never have hired her with such a language barrier."

Henry stared up toward the ceiling, as though imagining the kitchen. "He's wrong about that. We aren't there to talk. We're there to create superb food. To make the president of our United States forget his troubles long enough to enjoy a wonderful meal." He launched into one of his patriotic speeches. I smiled as he waxed poetic on the virtues of a good meal and how national leaders made better decisions when they were well cared for. I'd missed Henry's pontifications. "We're there to contribute to our country's success. We aren't there to make friends."

Now I rested my hand on his. "But sometimes we make lifelong friends anyway, don't we?"

He grabbed my fingers and held them. The twinkle was back in his eyes. "That we do."

Walking to my car after saying good night, I blew out a long breath, watching the wispy air curl in front of me on this cold night. Partly a reminder that I was alive, partly a sigh of frustration, I realized that, despite being able to visit with Henry, I was happy to be on my way home.

Back at my apartment building I wasn't terribly surprised to find James napping at the front desk. I tried sneaking past without disturbing him, but he woke up when the elevator dinged.

"Ollie," he said, getting up.

Politeness thrust my hand forward to hold the elevator doors open. "Hi, James," I said. "How are things?"

Making his way over, he waved his hand at the open car. "Let that one go. I've got some information for you."

Reluctantly, I let the doors slide shut. "Information?"

"Yeah, yeah," he said quickly. Still blinking himself awake, he amended, "Well, I guess I mean Stanley has information for you. He told me to let him know when you got in."

"Did he say—"

James raised his hand, and looked both ways up and down the elevator corridor. "It's about that incident the other day. You know, the one where you work?"

"The electrocution?"

James nodded, shooting me a look of mortified annoyance.

My curiosity piqued, I thanked him and pushed the "up" button again. "I'll stop by his place. He's on eight, right?"

The same elevator opened.

"Ah . . . you might try him at your neighbor's . . . Mrs. Wentworth's."

"Okay, thanks." I got into the car and wondered what electrical issues were plaguing my neighbor's apartment that required attention this late at night.

James blushed scarlet as the elevator door closed and it wasn't until Mrs. Wentworth opened her door, dressed in only a bathrobe—with Stanley behind her similarly attired—that I understood.

"Oh," I said. "I . . . I heard Stanley was here. Hi, Stanley."

"For crying out loud, Ollie, don't stand there gaping like a grouper," Mrs. Wentworth said. "Come in here. Stanley has lots to tell you."

They settled themselves together on Mrs. Wentworth's flowered couch and I suddenly realized I didn't know her first name. Stanley was always Stanley to me. She was always Mrs. Wentworth. Not knowing how to address them together added to the discomfort I was feeling right now, facing these two sleep-clad seniors, both wearing a contented sort of glow. . . .

"I had a thought, Ollie," Stanley said, breaking into my thoughts. Thank goodness. "Remember the day of the accident? It stormed that day, right?"

It had. I remembered Stanley commenting on it. "Yeah . . ."

"Well, I got to thinking that your electrician there— what was his name?"

"Gene." My voice caught as I relived the past few hours and Gene's wake.

"That's it." As Stanley talked, Mrs. Wentworth smiled up at him in the way lovestruck teenagers do. All of a sudden, my discomfort vanished. They weren't bothered by my interruption, so why should I be? These two were adorable. "Yeah, I wager he didn't get to be the top electrician at the White House by being stupid. If he knew he was going anywhere near high voltage, he would've taken precautions."

"Gene knew the layout of the electricity better than anyone."

"Exactly my point," Stanley said. "Which is why I'm betting Gene was killed by a floating neutral."

"A what?"

"A floating neutral," he repeated. "Dangerous, and unpredictable."

Mrs. Wentworth patted Stanley's knee. "Show her the thing you made."

Stanley blushed. "I put together a mock-up to explain it better." He padded out to the kitchen, with Mrs. Wentworth watching him until he was out of earshot.

"He's been at this all day making the mock-up to show you. And he's really proud of himself. Even I understand these neutral thingies now."

When Stanley returned, he carried a board, about eighteen by twenty-four inches. On it, he'd mounted five sockets. Two held forty-watt bulbs, three held fuses. In the center was an on/off switch. All of the parts were connected to one another with wires and the entire contraption was attached to a scary-looking triple-thick gray cord that sported a round plug as big as my palm. On it were three very long, odd-shaped metal prongs.

"This is a 240 plug," he said, holding it up. "You don't see too many of these around the house. But I bet you got one on your dryer." He waited for me to shrug—I had no idea. "No matter. Some appliances need 240 instead of the regular 120 volts. Like dryers. Check it out when you get back, you'll see."

"I will."

"I'm going to keep it short and simple, but you stop me if you got questions, okay?"

I promised I would.

"Storms can knock out your neutral—your ground. And that's a bad thing, because your ground is what keeps your house from catching on fire from too much voltage." He licked his lips. "You got a curling iron?"

"A couple of them," I said, even though lately I'd been foregoing using them in favor of a quick ponytail.

"Curling irons don't produce enough heat to catch your house on fire. So if you ever get worried you forgot to shut it off, don't sweat it."

"I have one of those auto-shut-off ones—"

"Even better." He waved that away. "But you most likely don't ever have to worry. Because your appliances are using 120 volts, and most of the time, if everything's working right, that ain't going to give you any headaches. But," he said, warming to his subject, "your house has to have 240 volts coming in so you can run your clothes dryer. It's too dangerous to send in 240 at once, so you got two wires coming in sending 120 each. Follow?"

"So far."

"The neutral acts like a buffer between them. I could get really technical here, but there's no need. All that's important to know is that if your neutral is broken, then the two 120s don't have anything keeping them apart. Your curling iron or your heating pad or your toaster can go crazy and heat up hot enough to catch fire."

He gestured to me to follow him. Mrs. Wentworth got up and came along, too. Stanley led us into the small closet that housed the furnace, washer, dryer, and slop sink. I was amazed at how pristinely clean the tiny room was. I sincerely hoped Mrs. Wentworth would never see the need to visit mine. She'd see delicates hung from cabinet handles, and to-be-washed items lying in piles on the floor.

The Lysol-smelling room was tight with the three of us, but Stanley urged me to lean over the back of the dryer. "See that?" He pulled the plug from a special outlet on the wall. The plug was a near duplicate of the one he'd attached to the board-contraption. "Now, I'm going to fire up my mock-up and I can show you what probably happened to your friend."

I stepped back, fearful of some explosion or something. Mrs. Wentworth hovered close, blocking the doorway.

When he plugged it in, the two lightbulbs went on. "Looks normal, right?" He flicked the switch, which I now noticed was labeled ON—NORMAL, OFF—OPEN. Nothing happened.

"These two lightbulbs take the same voltage," he said. "They keep things balanced. Even when the neutral is missing, you're not going to notice anything wrong." He unplugged the cord. "Now, watch what happens when we have an imbalance."

He replaced one of the forty-watt bulbs with a big spotlight version, turned the switch to "on"—meaning normal—and plugged it back in.

Both lights lit—the spotlight was, of course, brighter than the little forty-watt bulb in the accompanying socket, but I couldn't see anything amiss.

"Ready?" he asked.

Mrs. Wentworth stepped back. I said, "Ready."

"I'm now eliminating the neutral," he said, and flipped the switch.

"Whoa!" I said, raising my hand to protect my eyes.

Stanley pointed to the spotlight. "Big difference, huh?"

There was. The spotlight glowed so brightly I couldn't look at it. The light was so intense, the beam so strong, I felt as though the bulb was barely hanging on. At any moment I expected it to explode.

"Now, y'see, this here is an imbalance," Stanley continued in his unflappable manner. Mrs. Wentworth had backed out of the tiny room completely. I didn't want to be rude, but the bulb in the socket was unnervingly bright.

"Is it safe?" I asked.

Stanley made a so-so motion with his head. "You don't want to keep this on for long," he said. "Playing with neutrals is never a good idea. That's why this is all mounted on a wooden board. You see how I'm being careful not to touch anything metal? I'm sure it's not dangerous at the moment, but I like to take extra precautions just the same."

He must have noticed me squinting, because he reached into the center of the board and flipped the switch to "on." Immediately, the two bulbs resumed their normal brightness.

"Does that mean that all 240 volts were in this bulb?" I asked.

"Not quite. Can't say for sure how much was feeding into here. Maybe 220, maybe a little less. But that's the thing with neutrals. You gotta have 'em. Things are too unpredictable if you don't."

"So you think Gene was killed because of a floating neutral?"

Much to my relief, Stanley unplugged the contraption before answering. "Again, I can't say for sure. Something got him—and I'd be willing to bet it was something he didn't expect. If there were 240 volts flying through those lines, the man didn't stand a chance." He gave me a wistful look. "I'd know it if I got a look-see, but that isn't going to happen, is it?"

"Doubtful." I smiled. "The electricians on staff probably thought of this, right? I mean, this is something you'd look for in an electrocution."

Stanley cocked a white eyebrow. "Might be worth talking with them just to be sure. Floating neutrals aren't real common. People don't think to look for them. And I could be wrong about this—could be something else entirely that shot all that voltage into your friend. But storms are notorious for wreaking havoc with your wiring, including unpredictable damage—grounds, neutrals—you get the idea. I think it's worth a mention."

CHAPTER 12

MANNY JOGGED ACROSS THE CENTER HALL, his tool belt jangling to the beat of his pace. I called out to him, but he didn't hear me. Even though it was still before eight in the morning, the White House was bustling with activity. No matter how much time we allowed to get the residence ready for the official opening, it never seemed to be enough.

"Manny," I said again, this time loud enough to be carried across the hall.

He turned, his eyes narrowing when he realized it was me. I could practically read his mind. No matter what the executive chef was going to ask, he knew it wouldn't be good.

Without closing the distance between us, he said, "I'm working on the setup," jerking a thumb to the south. I knew he had a hundred tasks ahead of him, not the least of which was setting up the holiday lights for the massive tree that would be erected outside, but I needed only a couple minutes of his time.

I made my way toward him, wiping my hands on my apron. "I have a quick question."

His attention was at once caught by something behind me. I turned to see Vince loping toward us. "It's about time," Manny said. "Where have you been?"

"Curly's looking for you," Vince said, half turning as though he expected the acting chief electrician to materialize behind him.

"Again? That guy has been on my case all morning." Manny made a face, muttering in such a way that I knew if I hadn't been present, he would've let loose with a string of expletives. "What's with him anyway? He's been—"

I was about to interrupt, to ask Manny and Vince about the floating neutrals, when who should turn the corner but the man himself. "Hey, Curly," Vince said, hurrying away from our minigathering. "I'm heading out now." He pointed. "Found Manny for you."

Curly harrumphed. "What the hell are you doing still inside? I thought we were supposed to have the power up and running out there an hour ago."

Manny opened his mouth, but I interrupted. "I stopped him to ask a question."

"Go," he said to Manny, who took off like a shot. When Curly turned to stare at me with furious contempt, I nearly took a step back. He practically snarled. "What do you want?"

"It's about Gene."

"He's dead."

I bit the insides of my cheeks. "I have a question about how he died."

Curly's jaw worked. I jumped in before he could dismiss me.

"Listen," I said. "I just want to ask if you've considered the possibility that Gene was killed by a floating neutral?"

For the first time in my life, I could tell I caught Curly by surprise. He was dumbfounded. "What?"

"I said, I was wondering—"

"I heard that. How the hell do you know about floating neutrals?" His flabbergasted expression was replaced by the surly look I was used to. "Why are you pushing your nose into my business? Don't you have a kitchen to run?"

Though not entirely surprised by his reaction, I was still taken aback by his vehemence. I forced myself to hold my ground. "Have you considered the possibility?"

"I don't know what you've been reading, or think you know, missy, but floating neutrals don't just pop up out of thin air."

"But the storm—"

He snorted. "What, you think you're some sort of expert on our system now? Here, tell you what." With a flourish, he unfastened his tool belt. Removing it from his waist, he held it out to me. "Juncture number sixty-four is out. And we have a low-voltage issue at K-thirty-five. You take care of those while I go bake cookies, how's that sound?"

I fixed him with my most pointed, angry glare. "I'm just trying to help."

"Gene's dead," he said again. "Nothing you can do can change that."

"But I thought if we found out why—"

"Tell you what, missy," he said as he replaced his tool belt around his waist. "You get yourself a journeyman electrician's card—then I'll talk to you. But for now, I've got a White House to keep hot." He started down the same path Manny and Vince had taken. Two steps away, he turned and spoke to me over his shoulder, not breaking stride. "Don't bug me with this crap again."

RAFE TOOK UP A POSITION NEXT TO ME AT THE kitchen's center counter. "What did those chicken breasts ever do to you?"

I looked up, realizing I'd taken out my aggression by pounding the meat so thin, the breasts could've been served as high-protein pancakes. "Geez," I said, embarrassed, "I didn't realize."

"It's your first holiday season in the executive chef position," he said. "You're bound to be a little stressed."

If he only knew. I glanced at the clock. "I think there should be a law against aggravation before nine in the morning."

Rafe laughed. "Not going to happen. Not around here at least." He flicked a fleeting look across the kitchen, where Bucky was preparing a new salad dressing of his own concoction, and separately, stirring beef stock we would need later in the day. My second-in-command was murmuring, apparently having an argument with himself.

I took in the rest of the kitchen. Cyan was uncharacteristically silent, and even as Agda rolled dough out, I noticed veins in her arms standing out, and a crease on her forehead.

"How come you're so chipper?" I asked Rafe.

He shrugged. "Stress manifests itself differently in each of us."

I thought about Bindy's tendency to giggle. "Too true."

The phone rang. I was closest, so I wiped my hands with one of the antiseptic towels we kept just for that purpose, and answered it.

Jackson informed me that the First Lady would be out

all day, meeting with relatives to make arrangements for Sean's funeral. His parents lived nearby in Virginia, and Mrs. Campbell was not expected to return to the residence until after dinner.

"The president is returning this evening as well," he said.

"For dinner?"

"No. He'll be joining Mrs. Campbell at his sister's home first, and the president and his wife are expected back here after eight o'clock."

"Thanks," I said, and hung up. Not having to prepare lunch and dinner today made things easier on us, but I couldn't imagine how hard the day would be for the First Couple. It was a wonder that Mrs. Campbell had made it through yesterday at all, but having to prepare for the funeral of someone so close and so young had to be devastating.

I announced the change in plan to the rest of the kitchen staff, and I watched tension seep out of them—by the change in their stances, the position of their shoulders, their very breathing. "We still have a lot to get done," I added, unnecessarily. "Let's hope that . . ."

Before I could finish my wish that the rest of the day proceed uneventfully, Marcel stormed in, with Yi-im trotting faithfully behind him. Without greeting any of us, Marcel began ranting. "I 'ave no method to make use of these . . . these . . . childish efforts." He held out a tray displaying some of the gingerbread men that had been turned in yesterday. "These do not complement the gingerbread house I am slaving over. The house that is my crowning achievement this year. No. These are . . . *le pire*."

I stepped closer to look.

"Do you see?" he asked. "How can I use such a terrible mess as these? No one will look at the exquisite structure. No. Their eyes will all be drawn to this mishmash."

Although Marcel and I generally worked independently of each other, we had a friendly, symbiotic relationship. He needed to vent and I was happy to oblige him. But maybe there were options he hadn't considered. "Have you spoken with Kendra?" I asked.

"She is the one who presented these to me! She wants me to *fix* them. I have no time for such nonsense."

While I had to agree that the workmanship on the eight-inch cookies left a great deal to be desired, I thought they were kind of cute. "The idea is to showcase the country's kids," I said quietly.

"Are we raising a nation of imbeciles?" he asked, his big eyes bulging. "Look at this." He pointed to one of the corner pieces. The cookie man was missing one eye and half of one foot. The squiggled icing that decorated the cutout's perimeter had been squeezed off the edge repeatedly, but it was the smudgy unevenness of it all that made it look like it was put together by a bored kindergartner. Marcel practically sputtered as he spoke. "This was made by a boy of seven. By the time I was his age, I was creating three-layer cakes with handmade candies. Each one I produced was perfect."

I didn't doubt that. "Kendra is in charge of the overall design," I said soothingly. "And you know what a perfectionist she is. I'm sure she's hoping to use most of the submitted cookies." I took another pointed look. "Did you ever consider that these are the best she received?"

The horror on Marcel's face would have been laughable if I didn't know how much pressure we were under to get the residence together and ready for presentation in the next two days.

"I cannot work with this," he said. He dropped the tray in the center of the countertop and backed away from it, with an unconcealed look of contempt. "I will not use these. You may crumble them up and feed them to the dog."

Marcel left the kitchen. I blew out a breath as I stared after him. Although he occasionally had his prima donna moments, he didn't usually draw such a hard line. Bucky, Cyan, and Agda shared a glance of wariness before returning to their tasks. I locked eyes with Rafe, and it was as if we both shared the unspoken sentiment about stress manifesting itself differently in each of us.

"Ho, ho, ho!"

I turned at the exclamation to see chief usher Paul Vasquez come in, carrying a diplomatic parcel and wearing a wide grin.

"You're back," I said, stating the obvious.

"And the tree is beautiful," he said. "This year we have a magnificent Fraser fir. Breathtaking. I can't wait until we get it set up." His jovial expression dropped. "That's the good news. Unfortunately we've had our share of bad, haven't we?" He made eye contact with each of us in turn. Paul had a way of making every staff member feel important. "I've been in contact with the White House over the days I was gone," he said, "so I am aware of what has transpired. We will discuss everything at the next staff meeting. In the meantime," he handed me the diplomatic pouch, "this came for you."

"Me?" I said, surprised. Belatedly, I realized I knew exactly what this was. As I opened the parcel, Cyan edged up. I held my breath.

"More gingerbread men?" she asked.

I nodded. "These must be the ones created by the Blanchard children." And they were. A letter from Bindy accompanied them. I pulled the three men out, one at a time.

They'd been boxed separately, and wrapped in tissue paper surrounded by bubble wrap.

"Somebody isn't taking chances on these getting damaged," she said. Then, "Wow. His kids made these?"

We stared at the first cookie I'd removed from its container. "This is amazing."

Paul whistled. "Kendra must be thrilled. If this is the caliber of submissions she's receiving—"

"Eet ees not," Marcel interrupted, coming up behind us. *"Sacre bleu."* He held out both hands and I placed the little decorated man into them. "Where did this come from?"

Paul excused himself to return to his office and I took the opportunity to explain Bindy's request to Marcel.

"This is wonderful. *Marveilleux,*" he said, placing the cookie back into its box with great reverence. "Let me see the others."

The three cookies were whimsical and perfect. So perfect that not even Marcel could find fault with them. They were, of course, the right size, browned to perfection, and each of the three men sported a combination of patriotic red, white, and blue icing piped along their edges so perfect it looked fake. I commented on that.

"I don't care if it is plastic." Marcel said, beaming. "No one is to eat these. They are for display only."

The piped edge was the only requirement the White House had made for consistency's sake. I never would have thought to give them little sugar flags to hold, nor would I have come up with the idea of carving into the cookies themselves for a textured background. These were not cookie-gingerbread men; they were works of art.

"I promised Bindy we'd find a prominent place for these in the Red Room. I'm glad I did," I said, winking. "I had no idea the kids were so talented."

Missing my sarcasm, Marcel said, "Children did not make these." He pronounced the word, "shildren." He shook his head. "These are the work of a master."

"Bindy did hint that Treyton Blanchard's chef might have helped a bit."

Marcel barked a laugh. "I would say he created these single-handedly. And the project took several days, at least. I will have no problem including these with my own masterpiece."

I grinned, pleased to have one less thing to deal with, and handed him the three boxes. "All yours."

Marcel gave a little bow. "I accept with pleasure."

THE LAST THING I NEEDED WAS TO INCUR THE wrath of Curly again, but when I saw Manny later, still wearing the clanking tool belt, I couldn't help myself. In a repeat of the morning's move, I called out to him.

He turned, and this time when he saw me, he shook his head and backed away.

"I just have a question for you," I said.

"What did you do to get Curly all fired up?" he asked. "The guy's been on my case all day. Vince's, too. He said you ticked him off."

"I asked him about floating neutrals, and he—"

Manny looked just as surprised as Curly had this morning. "What?"

I explained about Stanley's mock-up.

"No wonder Curly's so pissed. He wouldn't tell us what was going on, just that you keep bullying him about Gene getting electrocuted."

"*I* keep picking on *him*? Since when does asking a question constitute bullying?"

"Hey, I'm just saying. Vince has gotten his head bitten off about five times today, and whenever we ask Curly why he's so ornery, he just gives us more work to do. He keeps checking on us, too. Like every fifteen minutes, he's there again. You shouldn't have started all this. You have no idea what you're doing. And now he's worse than usual. But at least now I know what's behind it."

"What's so bad about me asking?"

In even more of a hurry to get away now, Manny shrugged one shoulder and shifted toward the door. "I dunno. Maybe Curly thinks you're trying to show him up. Maybe he's worried you'll cost him the chief electrician position."

"Don't be silly." I could tell Manny was ready to bolt, so I pressed my point, explaining again what Stanley had explained to me. "Is there any way you can check to see if Gene's accident was due to a floating neutral?"

He shook his head even before I finished making my request. "Let it go."

"But I don't believe Gene would've made an electrical mistake."

"I wouldn't be so sure," he said.

"Just check, please?"

"No way. It's not a neutral. I guarantee it. And even if I could check on it, I wouldn't want to mess with this one. Not with Curly around. If it were up to me," Manny said, lowering his voice to a conspiratorial whisper, "I'd kick his sorry butt out of here. The guy's got too much on his mind with the sick wife and all. And now he's so worried I'm going to make a mistake, or that Vince is, that he's not letting us do our jobs. That guy should get canned before he does more damage. Seriously."

CHAPTER 13

WHEN THE KITCHEN PHONE RANG AT SEVEN-fifteen that evening, I was surprised to see the in-house ID indicate it was the First Lady calling.

"Hello, Ollie," she said. "I'm glad it's you who answered. Are you very busy?"

A visit from Gavin—who pilfered Bucky and Cyan for half the afternoon—had set us even further behind than we'd been. We had all hoped to leave by eight tonight, but from the looks of things now, we wouldn't get out until after ten.

"Not at all," I said. "What can I do for you?"

"My husband and I are expecting a guest this evening. I inquired and found that he hasn't eaten yet. In fact, neither have we."

That surprised me. I said so.

"Yes, I know," the First Lady continued, her voice just above a sigh. "We had planned to, but I don't find myself with much appetite today."

With everything that was swirling around in their lives—the president's high-level meetings, Sean's death, Gene's death—I couldn't imagine eating either. "I understand."

"I knew you would, Ollie. That's why I have a particular favor to ask. Would you be willing to prepare something for us and for our guest this evening?"

"Of course," I said. I was about to ask a question when she interrupted.

"There's one other thing. Could you take care of all this up here? In the family kitchen? I'd prefer to keep it informal. I don't want any other . . . anyone else . . . present. Would you be willing to do that?"

"I'd be glad to," I said. "Can you tell me who the guest is, so I can look up his dietary requirements?"

"Yes, of course. Senator Blanchard will be joining us this evening. He and I have much to discuss." She paused for a moment and I sensed it best to give her time to collect her thoughts rather than rush off the phone. "We have a lot to talk about that"—she hesitated before saying his name—"that matter Sean advised me on. You have been privy to information of which the rest of the staff is unaware. I would prefer to keep it that way. Just a limited contingent tonight. Dinner doesn't need to be elaborate. Do we have any leftovers you can use?"

In my mind, I'd already begun pulling together a menu. "How soon would you like to sit down?"

"Whatever works best for you. Just come up as soon as you can; the kitchen will be yours alone. After a day like today, I'd like to relax and not stand on ceremony for once."

WE KEPT SO MUCH ON HAND IN THE WHITE House kitchen that the First Lady's request made for no difficulty whatsoever. After assigning Bucky to take over holiday preparations—and it seemed there was no end to them in sight—I gathered ingredients, utensils, and assorted necessities onto one of our butler's carts and made my way up to the second floor.

The kitchen here was cozy—flowered wallpaper and warm-wood cabinets similar to those found in middle-class homes across the country. Although there would have been enough room for two of us to work comfortably together, I was content to handle this dinner for three myself. More important, that's what the First Lady had requested.

Dinner was to be served in the adjacent dining room. Occasionally referred to as the family's private dining room, it was often confused by non–White House personnel with the Family Dining Room on the first floor, or with the President's Dining Room in the West Wing. But we staffers knew the difference. This room, formerly known as the Prince of Wales Room, due to the fact that the Prince of Wales slept there during James Buchanan's presidency—before it was outfitted as a kitchen—became the First Family's private dining room under Jacqueline Kennedy's direction.

I'd just started breading the chicken breasts I'd pounded the heck out of earlier when Mrs. Campbell knocked at the doorjamb.

"I hope I'm not disturbing you," she said.

"Not at all. I'm hoping to be ready to serve at eight-thirty. Will that be all right?"

She nodded, and wandered into the kitchen. "I asked the butlers to set places for three, but now I understand that Treyton may bring Bindy along. Would it be too much inconvenience to prepare dinner for four, in the event she does show up?"

I'd brought extras up with me. One doesn't get to be a top chef without preparing for such exigencies. "Not a problem," I said.

Mrs. Campbell began opening cabinets. "Can you believe I haven't yet figured out where everything is in here?" She gave a sad laugh. "I'm getting too used to having people wait on me all the time. I don't think I like that."

"Enjoy it," I said. "We're happy to be here."

She had her back to me, two side-by-side cabinets open. "I'm glad you're here, Ollie. I trust you."

I didn't know what to say to that, but Mrs. Campbell wasn't finished.

"My husband and I don't believe Sean took his own life. His mother doesn't believe it either."

I hadn't expected her to talk about Sean, but I covered my surprise as best I could. She turned to me, tears swimming in her eyes. "You knew him, too. Maybe you saw something we didn't see? Do you think it's possible that . . . that he—"

"No," I said quickly. "I don't."

She graced me with a sad smile. "Thank you."

Although I was often sorry for speaking out of turn, this time I really couldn't help myself. "If I may say so . . ."

Mrs. Campbell inclined her head. "What's on your mind?"

"I just want to tell you how much I admire your composure." I groaned inwardly. Composure? There had to be a better word. That wasn't what I meant and it was coming out all wrong. "Dignity, I mean. I admire the way you handle everything. What I mean to say is, Sean's death has been so hard on you. On everyone . . ."

She flinched at Sean's name, but her eyes urged me to continue.

"I can't imagine how hard it must have been to entertain all those women yesterday. And yet you're still always . . ." I was trying hard to get my point across without babbling. Failing miserably. Summing up, I said, "You truly are the epitome of grace under pressure."

Another sad smile. "When my husband agreed to serve our country by taking on the presidency, we knew we would be held to a higher standard than we had been as civilians. As First Lady, my actions have a ripple effect across the country." She seemed to be speaking to herself. "It's frightening in some ways, empowering in others. I realize the effect my actions have, and try to comport myself in a way that deserves emulation, no matter how hard the circumstances." She squinted at me. "I see a lot of that trait in you, too, Ollie. We have a core"—she pulled both fists in, toward the center of her body—"that holds us steady even when the rest of the world is falling apart. You have the same strength you claim to admire in me. I just pray you never have reason to call upon it the same way I've found myself doing these past few days."

I felt my face grow hot. Worse, I was speechless.

Mrs. Campbell must have sensed my surprised amazement. Without waiting for me to reply, she turned her back to me again and grabbed a stack of white bowls in the cabinets. "You can use these," she said setting them on the table between us. "Like I said, I had dining places set out earlier. We can serve ourselves family style. After all, we are practically family. I've known Treyton since before he was born."

One of her assistants peeked around the door to let Mrs. Campbell know that Blanchard had arrived. I secretly hoped Bindy wasn't with him. If Mrs. Campbell was looking to share memories with an old friend, the last thing she needed at the table tonight was an ambitious political emissary who giggled whenever she got nervous.

IN FAIRLY SHORT ORDER I GOT ONE OF THE Campbell's favorite dinners started. Nothing fancy, a simple breaded lemon chicken served over angel hair pasta, with capers. The pre-course salad would be served with Bucky's newest dressing. I'd pre-tested it myself and pronounced it wonderful. Dessert would be simple, too. Fresh sorbet, in hollowed-out oranges, waited in the freezer for a whipped cream and peppermint leaf garnish. The preparation took some effort, but I wanted to bring a touch of cheer to what promised to be a difficult evening.

I was so immersed in preparation that I didn't notice Bindy until she called my name.

Startled, I glanced up, hoping as I reacted that my disappointment didn't show.

"This is nice," she said, walking into the kitchen. "I've never been in this room before." She carried a plate, silverware, napkin, and crystal water glass. In addition, she held a diplomatic pouch under her arm.

"What's going on?"

The disappointment on her face told the story before she could. "Treyton asked if I minded excusing myself." She flushed. "How embarrassing. We thought this was supposed to be a real dinner, downstairs, with a few other people. I guess I should've . . ." She shook her head. "Doesn't matter now, does it? I'm here. I'm stuck till it's time to leave. Do you mind if I sit in here with you?"

She arranged her place settings on the table, as though preparing to be served. With care, she placed the package on the chair next to hers. "That's for later," she said cryptically.

I'd planned to clean up as soon as dinner was served, and then beat a path back downstairs. My estimated ten o'clock departure was looking ever more unlikely. "Sure," I lied. "Have you eaten?"

She shook her head.

"Well, I've prepared plenty," I said. "Let me just take care of them first, okay?"

If I'd expected an offer of help, I was mistaken. But in truth, I was glad. Preparing a dinner for this small group wouldn't be difficult, and I'd rather do it myself than have to coach an amateur. Bindy sat at the table, watching me work, occasionally asking a question about preparation or presentation.

She had the good sense to speak in a whisper. Since we could hear most of the conversation going on in the next room, it stood to reason they would be able to hear us, too.

I wheeled out the salad, dressing, and bread, feeling more like I was serving my mother and nana at home than the president of the United States, his wife, and their guest. Meals in this home were usually served by tuxedoed butlers, amid much pomp and circumstance. Right now, in my tunic and apron, I felt positively slovenly.

"Good evening, Mr. President, Senator Blanchard," I said, nodding to each of them and to Mrs. Campbell. The president greeted me by name and Blanchard smiled. I saw in him what most voters must have seen. He exuded charm and confidence—so much so that it almost seemed as if he had the power to dispel the house's sad pall.

I set the food items on the table. "I'll be in the next room, if you need anything."

Having gone silent when I entered, they started conversation start right up again as I crossed the threshold into the adjacent kitchen.

"I know the timing is terrible," Senator Blanchard said, "but this is the situation we're faced with. This was brought on by our fathers. It's unfortunate that we're required to deal with their shortsightedness. Especially at a time like this."

Bindy made a face that let me know she was as uncomfortable as I. "Salad?" I whispered.

She nodded, so I set one in front of her and used the remaining time to finish preparing the entrée. As she ate, I couldn't help listening to the terse conversation in the next room.

"My wife has shown me the corporation's financials," President Campbell said. "Based on the company's projected growth, I don't understand why any of you want to sell right now."

"I beg your pardon, sir," Blanchard said, "but I believe my analysts have a better grip on the company's financials than either you or I could hope to have. We are, after all, in the business of serving our country rather than wizards in the financial world."

"Still," President Campbell said, "when Sean took a look at the books—"

"Your nephew would have advised you to sell, too."

"No," Mrs. Campbell said. "He advised me *against* selling."

I heard a chair scrape backward and I could picture Blanchard's reaction. As I poured sauce over the chicken breasts, I fought to tune out Bindy's mouth sounds and listen in to Blanchard's reply.

"You must be mistaken."

"I am not." A *clink* of silverware. I could imagine Mrs. Campbell sitting up straighter. "Don't you remember? I told you on Thursday." Her voice faltered. "Before we learned . . . before . . ."

"I truly am sorry to bring up such a difficult subject at a time like this," Blanchard said again. "But I can't imagine such a fine young man giving you bad advice."

Whispered: "Ollie?"

I turned. Bindy held up her glass. "Do you have anything stronger than water?"

I pulled open the refrigerator door, wondering why she didn't get it herself. Then again, she might not feel comfortable puttering around in someone else's kitchen, especially one in the White House. "Orange juice, milk, iced tea . . ."

"Iced tea, thanks."

As I served her, I listened again to the conversation in the other room. Bindy's body language suggested she was eager to keep me from hearing what was going on, so I strove for nonchalance, moving with care, trying to make as little noise as possible. Not that it mattered. The adjacent room's conversation came through loud and clear.

"No, I don't believe this is our fathers' fault," Mrs. Campbell was saying. "I believe they wanted to ensure their children's security. And my father would not have wanted me to sell out at the first opportunity after his death."

Blanchard spoke so quietly I almost couldn't make out his words. "But you must understand that my father, Nick's father, and Helen's all died years ago. We couldn't move on this business venture until . . . well, until you inherited your share. This can hardly be considered too quick of a decision."

"It is for me."

"But don't you see? That's the problem. Our fathers believed—erroneously, I might add—that the four of us needed to reach a decision unanimously. If they hadn't put that codicil in their agreement, I can guarantee Helen would have sold out within a year of her father's death. She's been waiting ten years for her portion of the proceeds."

The president chimed in. "What I don't understand is why the need to sell? None of you is destitute; you don't need the funds to survive. Why the rush?"

I carried a platter of succulent chicken breasts and steaming pasta into the dining room. As I set the dish down, I wanted to ask if there was anything else the diners required, but Blanchard was talking, so I held my tongue.

"It's Volkov," he said. Then, with a pointed look at me, he stopped talking and took a drink of water.

I grabbed my chance. "Will there be anything else for now?"

"No, thank you," Mrs. Campbell said. "Is Ms. Gerhardt faring well in the kitchen?"

"Just fine."

"Thank you, Ollie."

The moment I left, one of the president's aides, Ben, met me in the kitchen, coming in from the hallway. He gestured to me. "Where's everyone else?"

"Informal tonight," I said.

The assistant didn't hesitate. "He's needed downstairs."

"Now?"

Without answering, Ben strode into the private dining room and spoke quietly to the president. I watched from the doorway. Sighing deeply, President Campbell wiped his mouth with his napkin, then dropped it on the table. "If you'll excuse me," he said.

I ducked out of sight.

As soon as the president left, Blanchard spoke again, now more animatedly. "Volkov is going to bring us all down.

This scandal he's involved in is not going away anytime soon. In fact, I see it getting worse. Every day that we keep Zendy Industries alive with his name as one of our co-owners is a day that we risk losing everything."

I heard the sounds of passing plates, and then Mrs. Campbell said, "Surely, Treyton, you exaggerate."

"Not at all. In fact, he's the one spearheading this sell effort. At first I dismissed the idea, just as you're dismissing it now. But think about it. He may be desperate for funds to cover his legal bills, but he's right. We need to sell now, while Zendy's at the top of its game. Not later, when Volkov's troubles expand to include us all." Blanchard made a sound, like a *tsk*. "It's just a terrible shame that our fathers insisted on that unanimous vote."

There was silence for a long moment, with only scraping sounds of silverware on china and bodies shifting in seats.

"My father would not have wanted me to sell Zendy. Not this soon after his passing."

"Elaine," Blanchard said. "I know you're suffering still from the loss of your father. I offer you my sincere condolences on his passing and on Sean's, but we have very little time to make this decision."

"I disagree. We have ten years."

Blanchard took in a sharp breath. I assumed it was Blanchard, because he then said, "Perhaps you misunderstand. We have to wait ten years only if we decide *not* to sell at this time."

"And that's what Sean advised me to do."

The silence was so heavy I felt it in the kitchen. Bindy watched me with wide eyes. The chicken on her plate remained untouched.

"I hate to say this, Elaine, but if that's what Sean advised you, he was wrong. In fact, as distasteful as it sounds, I'm now beginning to wonder . . . if that's why he shot himself."

I heard Mrs. Campbell gasp. "No. No. Of course not."

"Can't you see it, Elaine? He might have believed he disappointed you by giving bad advice. He might not have seen any way out but to take his own life."

"Treyton, that's the most ridiculous thing I've ever heard. And I will thank you to not discuss Sean's death anymore. That subject is closed."

I heard him sigh. "I'm sorry."

"Yes, well, I would also like to table the Zendy discussion as well. We can talk about it another time."

A long moment of silence. "Just remember one thing, Elaine," Blanchard said. "Our window of opportunity won't stay open for long. And once it's closed, we won't have another chance to sell for ten years. There are buyers out there now. The time to sell is now."

"Actually, now is the time for two old friends to enjoy dinner together. No more business discussion tonight. Are we agreed?"

I couldn't see Blanchard's face, but I could imagine it as he said, "Whatever's best for you."

When they moved onto other topics, including the exploits of Blanchard's kids, I pulled the sorbet-filled oranges from the freezer and began to prepare them for serving. I liked to allow the sorbet to soften slightly for easier eating. Bindy broke the silence in the kitchen by asking, "How much do you know about this Zendy situation?"

I shrugged, shooting a look toward the other room. Even though she spoke quietly, I worried about being overheard. "Not much." I didn't want to tell her what Sean had shared with me. For some reason it seemed to be a betrayal of trust. I had no doubt that if Bindy perceived any value in my musings, she'd scurry to share them with Blanchard at her first opportunity.

The girl watched me work. Halfway between anxiety and expectation, the expression on her face told me she was hungry for any specifics I could give her. Little did she know that when it came to the First Family's business, I was as mute as a mime.

"Why all the fuss?" I asked, lowering myself into a chair opposite Bindy's so we could talk like girlfriends sharing a common concern. "I mean, really. Why can't the three other people sell and leave Mrs. Campbell to hold on to her share?"

"That's the thing," Bindy said. She seemed to fight back her natural reluctance to talk about her boss's business. Maybe she believed she'd glean some vital information from me. Bringing her head closer to mine, she whispered, "According to the company history, the four men who founded the company never wanted their children to sell. Zendy was set up as a research company with the mission of bettering the world. It's done that. In fact, the company has done it so well that it's made billions on research. Most of that money goes to philanthropic causes."

"Oh." I was beginning to understand. Although I trusted Sean's instincts, it had made no sense to me to put an investment on hold for ten years with no promise that the current successes would continue. I knew there had to be more to the story. "And Mrs. Campbell is reluctant to sell, because . . . ?"

Bindy glanced toward the doorway leading into the dining room. "They can't hear me, can they?"

I shook my head.

"The company looking to acquire Zendy intends to change its mission."

"How so?"

"Zendy is worth more in pieces than it is as a whole." She licked her lips. "If they sell now, Zendy will be split up into smaller units and sold off one at a time."

"What will happen to the philanthropic agenda?"

She shrugged, then gave a slight giggle. "That's one of the downsides. But that's a small price to pay for all the good the four partners can do with the proceeds."

"I understand now why Mrs. Campbell is opposed to the sale." I remembered her comment on Thursday, arguing that the new owners might not respect the same goals.

"That's it," she said.

"Sounds like Senator Blanchard is tired of giving away the money to the needy and wants to collect the proceeds of the sale for himself."

Put that way, my reflections made Bindy squirm. "It isn't Treyton," she said. "It's that Nick Volkov. You heard about all the trouble he's in."

"There's no way he's hurting for money to pay for legal counsel," I said. "I don't buy it."

"You have no idea how deep he's in debt."

"But you do."

She looked away. "I know stuff," she admitted.

I had a sudden thought. "Is Senator Blanchard planning to run for president?"

When her eyes met mine in that immediate, panicked way, I knew I'd struck a nerve.

"No," she said unconvincingly. "He's the same party as President Campbell. That would be silly."

"True."

I stood and finished setting up the serving trays, arranging the sorbet so it would look pretty as well as appetizing. I peered into the dining room and saw that both Mrs. Campbell and Senator Blanchard had pushed their empty plates just a little forward. They were done. Moments later, I had their places cleared and dessert served.

Back in the kitchen, I asked Bindy, "And so why are you here?"

"I told you. We thought that this dinner was involving more people."

For some reason I doubted her. But I couldn't think of any other plausible reason for her presence, so I let it go.

When the First Lady and the senator were finished eating, I cleared the table one final time, but since they were deep in conversation, I didn't interrupt. As I washed the remaining dishes and put everything away, Bindy and I discussed the gingerbread men. "They're incredible," I said.

"Thanks. We worked hard on them," she said.

"You and the Blanchards' chef?" I asked with a tilt to my head and a tone in my voice that asked if she and the chef were romantically involved. She turned away without answering and tried to listen in to the dining room conversation again. Mrs. Campbell and the senator had gone so quiet that there was no hearing them at this point.

"Oh, I almost forgot," she said, pulling her package onto the tabletop. She gave the top of the diplomatic pouch a little pat. "This is for you."

I was confused.

Bindy explained. "Treyton is so grateful you agreed to handle the gingerbread men that he asked me to give you this." She pushed it toward me. "Just to say thank you."

"I can't accept . . ."

"I know, but it really isn't for you exactly. It's for the kitchen. He figured that'd be okay."

As I opened it the weighty bundle, Bindy bit her lip. I wondered if she'd picked it out.

"Thank you," I said, as the object came free of its packaging. "It's lovely."

It was a clock. A bit large for a desk clock—about the size of a hardcover novel—it would have looked more at home in a French Provincial sitting room than in the White House kitchen. The clock face was small, but it was surrounded by a wide border of gold-colored heavy metal. Had it been real gold, I probably could have retired. As it was, the garish thing looked as though someone had picked it out as a joke, or for a white elephant gift exchange. "Thank you," I said.

Bindy breathed a sigh of relief. "You like it?"

"Sure!" I said. "I'll keep it in the kitchen right where we all can see it." To myself, I added that we'd keep it there long enough for Bindy to see it a couple of times. Then off to the warehouse with this clunker. "You really shouldn't have," I said, wishing she hadn't, "but thank you."

I offered coffee on my last foray into the dining room, but Blanchard declined. He stood. "Has Bindy been good company?" he asked me. "I'm so sorry we had a misunderstanding, but she said she hoped she might be of help back there."

She must have heard her name because before he finished asking, she was at my side. "I enjoyed reconnecting with Ollie," she said, with a little lilt to her voice that belied her words.

"That's great," Blanchard said. To Mrs. Campbell, he smiled and nodded. "It's been a pleasure, as always, Elaine. I hope you'll give some serious thought to the matters we discussed."

"Of course," she said.

"The clock's ticking," he said, tapping his watch. "I don't want you to forget."

With a smile that took the sting out of her words, Mrs. Campbell said, "How can I, when you're so eager to remind me?"

BY THE TIME I GOT BACK TO THE KITCHEN—my kitchen on the ground floor, that is—everyone had left for the day with the exception of Cyan and Bucky. They looked as exhausted as I felt. "Go home," I said.

Cyan tried to argue, but I shook my head.

"We'll start fresh in the morning," I said. "It's been a tough few days, but I think we made good headway. Tomorrow we'll turn the corner."

The relief in their eyes made me glad I'd insisted. "What time tomorrow?" Cyan asked.

With the president in residence, we'd be preparing full meals all day. As Cyan and Bucky traded information and agreed on plans for the next morning, I had a happy thought: The president back in town meant that Tom was back in town, too. Our schedules had kept us apart for too many days in a row. I needed to talk with him. Heck, I just needed to *be* with him.

Fifteen minutes after Cyan and Bucky left, I was headed to the McPherson Square Metro station for my ride home.

A train pulled into the station just as I made it to the platform. Perfect timing. I claimed a seat near the door and rested my head against the side window, allowing myself to relax just a little bit. I decided to wait to try calling Tom until I was walking to my apartment building. Less chance of losing our connection than if I tried to call while racing underground.

When I emerged outside again, it seemed the temperature had dropped ten degrees. We'd been in the mid-fifties lately, but tonight's raw air and sharp wind caused my eyes to tear. I shivered, pulling my jacket close, trying to fight the trembling chill.

I loved my jacket. Filled with down, I'd brought it with me from Chicago, where it very effectively blocked the wicked wind. January in Chicago always meant bundling up with a hat, a sweatshirt hood covering that, and big, insulated mittens. Today, here in D.C., I took no such precautions. It was just me and my jacket against this peculiarly icy wind.

With my head ducked deep into my turned-up collar and wisps of hair dancing around my face, I couldn't see much more than my feet beating a quick pace to my apartment building. I gave up the idea of calling Tom. My right hand pressed deep into my pocket, hiding from the cold, while my brave left hand pulled the collar close to my face so only my eyes and nose poked above it.

When the clouds above me opened and the rain came, I squinted against the sharp prickles of ice that stung my face. My quick walk became a hurried trot. It was then I noticed the accompanying trot behind me. Someone else was hurrying to get wherever he needed to go. Despite the fact that I was moving pretty fast, the person behind me was moving faster.

I glanced back. A man in a black Windbreaker was closing. With it being so dark, and with the icy rain blurring the street and my vision, I couldn't tell the guy's age, but he had to be fairly young—or in very good shape—to be moving at such a quick clip. Wearing blue jeans and shoes that made a unique double-clicking sound as he walked—almost as though he wore tap shoes—the man kept his head down. He wore a baseball cap with a dark hooded sweatshirt pulled tight around his face. Both hands were stuffed in his pockets.

Maintaining my own hurried pace, I eased to the right of the sidewalk to let the runner go by, peering over the edge of my collar as he got close enough to pass. He was tall—maybe six foot—and if the tight jacket was any indication, he weighed more than two hundred pounds.

There was a tree in my path. I could scoot left and possibly bump this guy, or go way off to the right, near the curb.

I veered right, hoping to reclaim my wide sidewalk berth once the guy passed me.

But he didn't.

Coming around the tree, I was forced to either speed up or slow down. He'd slowed his own pace and was now blocking my way. This was like a bad merge on an expressway.

I wrinkled my nose against the cold and eased in behind him. My apartment was just another couple of blocks away, and I rationalized that this big, bulky guy would block the wind for me.

But when I got behind him, he slowed down again. The trot lessened to a brisk walk, then lessened again to what could only generously be called a stroll.

Was this guy playing games with me? Did he not know I was behind him?

Whatever was going on, it was giving me the creeps. My building wasn't much farther, and I'd planned to cross the street at the light, but common sense told me to change my course right now.

I shot over to the curb and waited for a pair of shiny headlights to pass before racing across the street. My heart pounded as I skipped up the far curb. I chastised myself for my anxiety. Just my imagination working overtime again. I knew I had a paranoid streak, but the truth was, that paranoia had come in handy more times than I cared to count.

I pulled my collar close again, and tried to make out where the guy across the street had gone. The sleet was heavier and the cold seemed to worsen with every slash of rain against the dark cement. I couldn't wait to climb into my flannels and pull a cover over my chilled limbs. I couldn't see the opposite side of the street, but I took comfort in the fact that it meant he couldn't see me either.

Just the same, I resumed my trot. A moving target is harder to hit, as Tom always tells me. I smiled again at the thought of calling him. With any luck, he'd brave the elements and we could snuggle under those covers together.

My smile vanished when I heard the double-clicks again. Behind me. No way.

I was about to turn to see what I already knew—that the bulky guy was back—but by the time my head twisted over my shoulder, it was too late.

In a searingly hot second, he kicked me in the left knee. I shouted, both in pain and surprise. Unprepared for the attack, I flew facefirst to the sidewalk, my arms coming up just in time to break my fall. Even as I went down screaming, I prayed my hands and fingers wouldn't be hurt. They were my life, my livelihood.

The bulky guy didn't break stride, didn't turn.

Once I was down, he broke into a full-out run and was gone.

"Hey!" I yelled, noticing belatedly that my purse was gone. "Hey!" I said again, but by then I knew it was futile. I tried sitting up, but in the cold my knees felt as brittle as glass. At the same time, my palms burned from where I'd skimmed the sidewalk.

I shouted after him. "You big jerk!"

A soft voice next to me. "Are you okay?"

I felt a tug at my elbow. A small man hovered over me. Even from my seat on the wet sidewalk, I could tell he was shorter than I was. He pulled at my elbow again, trying to help me stand up. When I tried to get my footing, I slipped and sat down hard in wet dirt.

"Ick," I said, wincing as I struggled to my feet. "I'm okay."

"You are sure?" The man's voice held the touch of an accent and now that I stood up, I got a better look at my would-be rescuer. He was of Asian descent with hair so short as to be almost invisible. Although I couldn't peg his age, I guessed him to be on the far side of fifty. "What did that man do to you?" Using just his eyes, he gestured toward an idling car. "I was driving past and I saw him push you down."

I wiped my face with the back of my hand, trying to compose myself. The past several days had crushed the very energy out of everyone at the White House. But this was too much. After everything we'd been through, I shouldn't have to deal with this. Not today. I stared after the jerk who'd grabbed my purse, fighting overwhelming despair. All my ID was in there. Everything. I'd have to jump through a hundred hoops tomorrow just to get into work. I shook my head, then realized the little guy was waiting for me to say something. "I'm okay. He kicked me. Stole my purse."

"I am so sorry."

"Yeah," I said, blinking against the rain. "Me, too."

"I am Shan-Yu," he said, stepping forward.

"I'm Ollie," I said, responding automatically, thinking that I'd prefer to limp home in a hurry rather than stand in the sleet and chat. My mind was furiously trying to process everything that had just happened, but ingrained politeness kept me steady.

Shan-Yu gestured again with his eyes, keeping his hands together low at his waist. "May I offer you a ride?"

"No, thank you," I said, slapping my backside to release the dirt that crusted there. It hurt my hands, so I stopped immediately. "I live on the next block."

"As do I," he said, then mentioned his address.

"That's my building, too," I said.

He smiled. "Please, it would be my pleasure to help you after your encounter."

The biting rain had turned into a full-out downpour. I looked at the little guy standing next to me, his smile the only brightness in the dark enveloping rain.

"Thanks," I said. "That would be nice."

The Toyota Celica's windshield wipers were flapping as we made our way over. "Allow me," he said, and he glided ahead to open the passenger door.

We were directly under a streetlight, and as I started around him, I turned once more to take a look at my backside. "Oh," I said, "I can't get in your car like this. I'll get mud all over your seats."

"Not a problem," he said, just a little bit too quickly.

I turned, ready to explain again about the dirt on my backside, but the little guy's eyes suddenly shifted. Too close to me now, he said, "Get in."

"No, really, I—"

Before I could react, he hit me, hard, in the abdomen.

I doubled over and he shoved me into the open door, pushing me down onto the seat. Neither of us counted on the ground being wet, however, and to his dismay and my delight, I slipped and fell to the ground, out of his immediate reach. Scrambling toward the back of the car on all fours, I screamed, both in terror and from the pain. "Help me!"

Every ounce of me surged out in my screams. I tried to get my footing, but he kicked me in the side. The darkness impaired his aim and it hit me only as a glancing blow. Still, it was enough to throw off my balance. "Help!" My voice carried along the wet street and I thought I heard an answer. My voice strained with effort. "Please!"

The little guy had begun to pull at the back of my jacket, and though I already knew I was no match for him, I remembered what Tom had told me about the knees—a lesson recently reviewed with the passing tap-shoe guy. With Shan-Yu's hands gripping the fabric on my back, I wrenched sideways and lashed out at him with my foot. I connected with his knee, just as Mr. Tap Shoes had connected with mine. The little guy went down.

Fighting sparkles of pain that danced before my eyes, I made myself stand—just in time. Although he'd gone down, he didn't stay there. In one smooth roll, he'd bounced himself back to his feet and come at me again.

I dodged him, spinning around the back of the car and racing to the open driver's-side door. I'd thought to jump in and drive away, but Shan-Yu was too fast, too close. Just as I got near the door, I whirled to face him. He hadn't expected that. When I ducked, he toppled over me. Scratching, biting, and screaming, I fought my way out from under him, hearing footsteps—loud ones—and knowing I had almost nothing left with which to fight.

"Hey!" someone yelled.

Shan-Yu turned long enough for me to get another good look at his face. I scrambled out of the way of the back tires as he leaped into the car and tore off down the street.

A big guy wearing jogging pants and a do-rag leaned down to me, rain pouring down his bewildered face. "Are you okay?"

CHAPTER 14

I SPENT MOST OF THE NIGHT IN THE EMER-
gency room, giving the Metropolitan Police a statement, descriptions of both Mr. Tap Shoes and the man who identified
himself as Shan-Yu, and a description of the car. Two things
I learned from the cops—one: The bad guy hurts you, Good
Samaritan helps you game is one of the oldest in the book.
Two, the tap shoes were probably special steel-toed shoes
designed to inflict maximum damage on kicked opponents.

Once I'd been identified, the Secret Service was called
in to find out what sensitive items I might have lost in the
theft. Agents Kevin Martin and Patricia Berland showed up
while my knee was being examined. I was moved to a
room with a door so they could interrogate me in private.

"We need a comprehensive list of everything in your
purse," Agent Martin said. "I do mean everything. Even
personal items you believe may have no significance."

I came up with the best recollection I could. In addition to
my ID, I had keys: for my apartment, my car, and a number

of them for the White House. The two agents were not happy. "I have some notes, a few recipes. . . ." Oh, God, what a mess. "My Metro pass . . ." I named everything else I could think of, including personal female items that made me blush when I listed them.

They asked me if I thought I'd been targeted specifically. "No," I said, then stopped. "Wait. . . ."

"What?"

"The guy in the car," I said, thinking aloud. "He told me he lived in my building."

The two agents exchanged a look. "Was this before you told him where you lived?"

"Yes," I said, warming to the subject now. "He rattled off the address of my building, so that's why I believed him—but he came up with the address first. He must have known where I lived."

We talked a bit longer, both agents peppering me with questions designed to jog my memory.

"Keep all this information to yourself when you're back at the White House," Agent Martin said when the interview was over. "When do you plan to return?"

"Tomorrow," I said. Glancing at the clock on the wall over his head, I amended. "I mean, today."

Although they attempted to talk me out of returning in the morning, they didn't forbid me to do so. Their grudging acceptance might have been due to my spirited explanation of the difficulties of getting the residence together for the holiday opening. Or, it might have been my nonstop pleading. Mostly I think they just wanted to shut me up.

From the doorway, I heard a familiar voice asking for me.

"Tom!" I called.

Tall and muscular, Tom looked even more handsome tonight than he usually did. He wore his customary Secret

Service apparel—a business suit—but his hair was tousled as though he'd raced the whole way from the president's side to come see me. He edged around Agents Martin and Berland, acknowledging them with a nod. "I'll see Ms. Paras home," he said to them.

Kevin Martin's mouth twitched. "Yes, sir." He turned to me. "Are you comfortable with Agent MacKenzie escorting you home?"

At this point, despite my aches, I was all smiles. "I'm perfectly comfortable," I said.

Agent Berland was either in the dark about my relationship with Tom, or she pretended very well.

"Good night, then," Martin said. "We'll be in touch."

As soon as they were gone, Tom came close. He started to put his arms around me, stopped himself, and gently gripped my shoulders with both hands. "Are you okay?"

"Better now," I said. "God, you look so good." I started to reach around to hug him, but he held me at arm's length.

"I'm afraid I'll hurt you."

"I'm willing to risk it," I said, and pulled him close.

Yeah, it stung, but the hug was worth it.

I brought him up-to-date on the altercation that landed me in the emergency room, with him shaking his head the whole while. "Ollie," he said, "you've got to be more careful."

He was right, but I hated being told things I already knew. "I thought I was."

"Remember last time."

I shuddered when I thought about the terrifying incident right before I'd been promoted to executive chef. Tom took my reaction as an invitation to lecture me a bit more. Not that I blamed him.

"Those of us associated with the White House have to be extra vigilant."

"I know. I just can't imagine why anyone would target me."

"And that's why the criminals have the upper hand. Because no one expects to be attacked." With a pensive expression, he skimmed his fingers along the side of my face. "I wish I wasn't on duty tomorrow."

"I wish you weren't either."

Once all the hospital paperwork was complete, Tom helped me to his car. He had keys to my apartment, which allowed us to get in, and he'd arranged for a locksmith to meet us there. Amidst a lot of drilling and scraping—annoying my neighbor till two in the morning—my apartment was outfitted with spanking-new locks.

"Here you go, miss," Lou, the weary locksmith, said as he dangled the keys in front of me. "Good, solid brand I put in. You'll really enjoy these."

Enjoying locks was not something I anticipated, but I thanked Lou and tumbled into bed the minute he was gone. Tom insisted on staying with me, and I finally relaxed with him stroking my cheeks and forehead. Thank God for kindness in this world, I thought, and drifted safely off to dreamland.

"OH, MY GOD," CYAN SAID WHEN SHE SAW MY hands the next morning. "You can't work like that."

"I know," I said. "What horrible timing, huh?"

She cocked an eyebrow. "Like there's a good time?"

She had a point.

"One positive thing," she said, as we got started. "Turns out the president and Mrs. Campbell are out all day, after all. That'll take some pressure off."

I hated delegating every task, but I was faced with little

choice. Although I had no open cuts—that would have banished me from the kitchen completely for the duration of my healing—I wore an Ace bandage on my left hand and a splint on my right ring finger. The doctors told me I'd bruised my left ulna and jammed the finger on my right. Nothing debilitating, but bandages were hardly sterile when it came to working with food, so I found myself more the executive and less the chef for most of the morning.

Just as we started to hum, Gavin strode into the kitchen and came straight to me. "What happened last night?"

I'd taken to keeping my fingers clasped behind my back except when working at the computer. The move prevented me from inadvertently "helping" my colleagues.

"You mean this?" I asked, bringing my hands forward. "How did you find out?"

"It is my business to know about everything involving the security of the White House."

I figured as much.

Gavin fixed me with a piercing look. "I understand you fought off your attacker."

As much as I hated to admit it, I was still shaken by the experience, and I didn't appreciate the fact that Gav here wore an expression that told me he expected a blow-by-blow rehashing.

" 'Fought off' is a bit of an exaggeration," I said. "I screamed like an idiot. If that jogger hadn't come along . . ." I shivered, remembering. "The two guys who got me really knew what they were doing. They set me up perfectly. I'm embarrassed to have fallen for their scheme." Though it was hard for me to say so, I admitted my gullibility. "I trusted the little guy who pretended to help me."

"I was told he used martial arts moves against you."

My hand came up of its own volition, and I touched the

tender place under my ribs where he'd struck me. "Whatever it was, it hurt."

Gavin seemed about to say something else, but remained silent, staring at me. He finally said, "You aren't able to work?"

Bucky made eye contact from across the room. He arched an eyebrow and shook his head fractionally.

Message received. "I'm getting a lot done here, actually," I said, sounding more upbeat than I felt. "My predecessor, Henry, always told me I needed to learn to delegate more. Today I'm getting a perfect opportunity."

"I was hoping to continue your training."

Did this guy think I was planning to enlist in the military? How much more training did I need? My hands came up in response. I said, "I'm sorry," even though I wasn't.

I was, however, very glad when he left us again. "Tell you what," I said to the group. "Let me go get some of our holiday décor. While you guys work on the food, I'll start bringing a bunch of the fun stuff here."

They all looked up at me as though I was nuts. Rafe spoke. "With two damaged hands?"

I frowned. "I'll be careful. This really isn't that big of a deal."

Cyan shook her head. "You always get in such trouble, Ollie."

"How much trouble can I get into in the storage room?"

I MADE MY WAY THROUGH CONNECTING hallways, past the carpenter's, electrical, and flower shops. I fiddled with my replacement keys to unlock one of the storage rooms the kitchen controlled. My White House ID and other important items had been replaced much more quickly than I'd expected. Thank goodness.

The storage room was large, about ten feet by fifteen, and it was packed. There was limited floor space and the shelves overflowed with stuff I knew I should inventory. For about the hundredth time, I promised I'd get to it just as soon as things calmed down.

Large gray storage containers lined one wall. About four foot square and just over two feet tall, each wheeled container held presidential china. We kept the most popular patterns closer to the kitchen, and since this particular room was the farthest from our work center, it held the china patterns we used least. I pushed at the closest of the gray monsters—this one held Lyndon Johnson's pattern—to access the boxes I intended to scavenge.

Every year, grinning with holiday spirit, Henry made the trek down here to pull out fun things for the kitchen staff to use during the holiday season. He loved decorating the kitchen himself. Kendra and her staff didn't mind because none of what we used was ever seen by the public. Henry usually waited until the entire White House was completely finished before exercising his decorating muscle. He called the final kitchen embellishment his pièce de résistance.

I liked Henry's tradition, and I intended to continue it. With all that we'd gone through recently, however, I believed our festive mood needed a boost sooner rather than later.

I pushed another of the big bins out of the way, but realized, in doing so, I'd blocked my path out. There was only one solution: I pushed the two out into the hallway, and pulled out the boxes of tchotchkes I planned to make use of.

There was not, unfortunately, any type of cart I could use to transport my treasures to the kitchen. With my tender arm and splinted finger, I wasn't in the best position to carry the boxes myself.

Heading out again, I started for the electrical shop with two purposes in mind: getting a cart, and talking with Manny again, if I could pin him down. Based on our prior conversation, there was little reason to believe he would have checked out my floating neutral question. But I'm nothing if not tenacious.

Manny was nowhere to be found, but Vince sat on a stool at a small workbench, eating. "Do you have a minute?" I asked.

Startled, he just about fell off the seat. "You scared me," he said around one stuffed cheek. His gaze took in my bandaged arm and splinted finger.

"Sorry." I wandered in. "What do you have there?"

He held up half a sandwich. "Chicken."

Unsurprised, I nodded. Tradesmen generally didn't eat in the lower-level cafeteria. They went out, or brought their own food in. This was a throwback tradition from the White House's early days, when the household staff was mostly black, and the tradesmen white. Because nineteenth-century black employees couldn't find establishments to serve them in the nearby D.C. area, the White House provided meals. White tradesmen, having no such difficulty, went out for lunch or dinner each day. Over time the White House staff became infinitely more diverse. Of course, now blacks and whites occupied all staff levels, but the tradesman tradition—if you could call it that—continued. To this day, regardless of their race or ethnicity, tradesmen rarely ate in the White House cafeteria.

He stared at me as I moved closer. I got the distinct impression he didn't like the idea of the chef entering the electrician's lair. His constant jumpy glances toward the doorway behind me led me to believe he was expecting someone. Probably Curly. I'd have to make this quick. "Did Manny say anything to you about floating neutrals?"

Vince moved the wad of food from his cheek and chewed it before answering. I'd expected him to nod or shake his head, but he waited till he swallowed to say. "Uh . . . yeah."

"And?"

Vince glanced past me toward the doorway again. "And what?"

"Did you guys check? Was there something wrong with the ground when Gene got electrocuted?"

A voice boomed behind me. "What the hell are you doing here?"

I turned and there he was. Surly Curly, in the flesh. Knowing I could no longer press my question, I changed direction and offered him the friendliest smile I could. "I have to carry a few boxes to the kitchen, but . . ." I held up my injured hands. "No way to get them over there. I was wondering if you had a wheeled cart I could borrow?"

His mouth worked, as though pushing his angry grimace to one side. "Yeah, I got one." Shuffling to a nook just out of view, he came back with a gray dolly. "Boxes, you say?"

When I nodded, he switched the handle of the dolly, converting it from vertical to horizontal. "Here," he said, "easier to manage. You bring this back, you understand? I don't want to go hunting for it when I need it next."

"I'll bring it right back."

Vince hunched his shoulders as though to render himself invisible. I thanked Curly and headed back to the storage area, wondering if I'd ever get anyone to give me a straight answer to the floating neutral question.

FOUR HOURS LATER, AFTER HAVING DECORATED the kitchen to best of my holiday abilities given the collection of cute pot holders, trivets, and dish towels I'd pulled out, I headed back to the storage area to put the empty boxes away and to return Curly's precious dolly.

I wheeled it into the storeroom and had intended to replace the first box in its nook, when I realized that the china storage containers were not the way I'd left them. The Johnson china was pushed far to the right, completely out of place. That was odd. No one usually used this storage room except kitchen staff, and I couldn't recall anyone else mentioning a visit here in the past few hours.

Curious, I tugged the big gray bin, wondering what else might have been rearranged. Most of the time it wouldn't matter, but on the rare occasion we needed supplies from this area, I liked to be confident they were here. The idea that items had been shifted peeved me just a bit. Storage space was at a premium at the White House, and this area was designated for kitchen items only. Another department must have tried to encroach on our space, hoping no one would notice a stray item or two.

I pushed the wheeled bin of Johnson china out of the way and found an unfamiliar square brown box, crudely marked STORAGE on one side and along the sealed top. This did not belong to the kitchen. Worse, it hadn't been here this morning. Someone had snuck it in here, very recently.

I did a quick, cursory examination of the room to locate

any other stray boxes, but within a few minutes I realized this was the only unexpected addition to our stash.

There were no other markings on the box, and no way to tell which department had tucked it in here. I sighed with exasperation. I could just leave it here—it didn't take up an enormous amount of space—but doing so invited further incursions. Although this seemed like a trivial matter, and unworthy of the analysis I was affording it, I still suffered from the newness of my executive chef position. Sure, I'd earned the title, but I also needed to command respect. Were Henry here, I imagined he would nip this little nuisance in the bud.

I lifted the box onto the gray bin. I didn't have a knife to slice open the seal, but the dolly had metal clasps that Curly had used to readjust the handle. I pulled one of the silver clips from its anchoring hole, and pushed the metal end against the paper, ripping it. Within seconds I'd scored both ends and the center seam. I dropped the clip into my pocket and repositioned the box on the floor for leverage before attempting to open the flaps.

Whoever had sealed this thing had done a masterful job. I yanked three times before the first flap ripped free. The second flap snapped up with a quick pull and I pulled away excelsior to find out what was so important that had to be stored in my department's area.

More excelsior.

Finally, my fingers hit something hard. Metal or glass, I couldn't tell. I was on my knees, wrapping my fingers around the item's cylindrical shape, tugging upward. Stuck. Stray stuffing obscured my view of the article, but my fingers traced along its sides. Bottle-shaped, it seemed light enough, but as I pulled more shredded paper from around it with my left hand, my right discovered that both ends of the bottle were connected by wire to a flat board at the box's bottom.

I yanked my hand away. Heart racing, I felt my jaw go limp. I removed the remaining packaging material and stifled a scream of surprise when I saw the explosives.

This was an IED.

"Help," I said too softly, too weakly. I stood, calling out again, knowing no one would hear me. I ran out the door, intent on getting in touch with the Secret Service. But . . . I couldn't just run away. There were others in this area—in the carpenter's area, the florist's office, the laundry. I couldn't let innocent people there wait until something exploded.

I ran to the laundry room. "Get out," I screamed. "Hurry! A bomb. A bomb!"

I heard movement, and one of the laundry ladies came around the corner, looking confused.

"Get everybody out," I said, already running toward the florist's area. "Get out now, and get help!"

After warning as many people as I could, I ran into the nearest work area—the electrical shop. No one there.

Their phone was near the workbench. I picked it up and connected with the emergency operator. She told me to leave immediately and that help was on the way. I ran.

More than a dozen people were making their way quickly to the Center Hall, heading into the Diplomatic Reception Room, where they could evacuate via the south doors.

I skidded around the corner and rushed to the kitchen. My team stared up at me with wide eyes. "Everybody out," I said.

Bucky started to say something.

I waved them forward, toward me and the door. "Now."

They took one look at my face and filed out. Mentally,

I tallied them, making sure that everyone was accounted for.

Secret Service agents moved in fast. Before I could even think about what to do next, they'd covered every inch of the White House, urging people out the doors, barking orders, and taking firm control.

By the time I made it outside myself, I estimated we'd evacuated the residence in under three minutes. Not bad for a staff of more than ninety. I stared at the building, waiting. Wondering what would happen next.

I made my way over to my group. Bucky was talking with Rafe and Agda, and Cyan was listening in. They shifted their small circle to let me in.

"It's freezing out here," Cyan said, hugging herself. "I hope we don't get stuck outside for very long. What happened?"

I rubbed my own arms but as I tried to explain, the wind whipped my words away. I had to raise my voice as I repeated myself.

"You found a bomb?" Cyan said, with incredulity in her voice. "Are you sure?"

I opened my mouth to answer, realizing I wasn't sure at all. Maybe I'd overreacted. "It was . . ." My words faltered. I turned, taking a look at my colleagues—the rest of the White House staff—all of us huddled in small groups against the bitter chill. We were all out here, freezing, rather than inside doing our work. Just because I'd sounded an alarm.

"I think it was a bomb," I said finally.

"You *think*?" Bucky said. "You don't know?"

My stomach dropped. With the benefit of hindsight, I realized I didn't really know what a bomb looked like. Just because this one had some of the same features as the one

Gavin had shown us didn't mean that it posed any real threat.

Bucky wasn't happy. Breath-clouds poured out of his mouth as he asked, "Was it ticking?"

"No."

He exhaled sharply and walked over to join another group.

Maybe I should have simply called the Secret Service and let them handle it. Maybe if I'd done that, we'd all still be safely inside, and warm. The small groups of staffers snuck glances in my direction. I was sure they were discussing my "sky is falling" cries. The group around me chatted, keeping an eye on the activity just outside the south doors where a team of helmeted, black-cad individuals ran in.

"Bomb team," Rafe said.

We all nodded, silent now. Far enough away to feel safe, we could see the action but there was no way to make out faces from this distance. Secret Service personnel were maintaining a perimeter a distance away from the south doors, but I couldn't see who was on duty. I didn't expect any of them to be Tom, though; As part of the elite Presidential Protection Detail, he would be with President Campbell, wherever that may be.

Bucky wandered back with a swagger. "It's a fake."

"What?" we all asked at once.

Clearly pleased to be the source of insider information, Bucky took his time answering. "I was talking to Angela," he said. "She got a call from her brother, who has a friend on the bomb squad."

He continued. My stomach dropped.

"Nothing there. The thing Ollie found was probably just some junk. Not a bomb."

He kept talking about what a mess this was, and what a hassle we were all dealing with because of my too-quick-on-the-trigger response.

Feeling my face grow hot, I was about to argue that it's better to be safe than sorry, when Gavin stepped into our little group. Despite the bracing wind, he looked unruffled, though not pleased.

"Ms. Paras," he said. "Come with me."

Cyan gave me a pitying look.

"Is there some way we can get the staff inside?" I asked.

Gavin kept looking straight ahead. "It is being taken care of."

"What will they—"

"Ms. Paras, the comfort of your colleagues is not my immediate concern, but if it eases your mind, buses have been dispatched to pick everyone up and to keep them together."

I remembered how much time that took when I was sequestered with Mrs. Campbell and Sean in the bunker. I remembered Bucky's complaints. Had that been only a couple of days ago? So much had happened since then.

As we walked, I relived my adventure in the bunker and thought about Sean. My heart gave a little wobble. What had happened there? And how could I be missing someone I hadn't really known all that well?

A moment later it dawned on me that we weren't walking back to the White House. Gavin was leading me away, toward an idling black car. A Secret Service agent I didn't recognize opened the back door for me.

This was like something out of a spy movie.

"What—?"

"Just get in," Gavin said.

The car's warmth and smell of new leather helped lessen the goose bumps I bore from the cold. The ones from fear were still popping, mightily. "What's going on?" I asked when he sidled in beside me.

There was a driver and another man in the front seat. They both turned.

Gavin spoke, his enunciation so crisp, new goose bumps zoomed up the back of my arms and traipsed across my shoulders. "Tell me exactly what happened."

I did. They recorded my description of finding the box and opening it.

"Why didn't you call security the moment you saw the box?" Gavin asked.

I looked at him as though he was nuts. "It was a brown box in a storage room," I said with a little sharpness to my tone. "And it was marked for storage. Why would I ever be suspicious of something like that?"

The three men exchanged looks. I felt like the new kid at school, missing all the inside jokes because I wasn't considered "cool" yet.

"I already heard that I blew it," I said. "So why am I being questioned?"

Gavin gave me a puzzled look, but he answered. "In due course, Ms. Paras. Right now we need to go over your story again."

I sighed. "Okay." Again I recited the chain of events as best I could.

Gavin worked his lips as I spoke, his gaze never wavering from mine. I occasionally shifted my attention to the other two men, as though to include them in my narration, but Gavin grew more agitated by the moment. When noise outside the car drew the men's attention away from me, I had a moment of relief.

A man dressed all in black and wearing body armor rapped at the window. Gavin got out.

"You stay here," he said to me before slamming the door. I turned to the other two. "Did I do something wrong?"

They were both about thirty years old. The shorter one had dark hair and a pale complexion. The taller one was broad-shouldered, with sandy hair. Since he was in the passenger seat and I was directly behind him, I could only see his face in profile when he turned to me. The two men exchanged another look.

"You guys are making me nervous," I said. "Can't you tell me what's happening?"

The driver stared out his side window. The passenger said, "No, ma'am," and shifted his attention away.

I watched buses pull up and I could imagine Bucky complaining about the fact that I sat in a warm black sedan while he and the others were relegated to school bus—quality accommodations.

Silence in the car dragged me down. Gavin had gone off with the black-clad man and I attempted to put the time to good use. I began prioritizing tasks, working backward from our next target: the reception after the White House official ceremonies. Although I'd pressed Marguerite for an answer, she still didn't know whether the Campbells would participate this year or not. Sean's death had changed everything. The White House would still open on Tuesday to the public; but in the meantime, everything else was up for grabs.

"How much longer, do you think?" I asked my escorts.

The bigger guy replied. "Don't know, ma'am."

I watched minutes tick by on the dashboard clock. More than forty-five minutes later, Gavin finally returned. He opened the door and gestured me out. "Thank you, gentlemen," he said to the two men up front. "You may return."

He didn't say where they were returning to, and they

apparently didn't need to ask. As soon as I alighted and Gavin closed the door, they took off.

I felt like those little dogs who hustle their tiny paws to keep pace with their masters. Gavin didn't watch to make sure I was keeping up, he just made his way across the south lawn to the doors we'd exited from. "Special Agent Gavin," I called to his back.

He didn't stop moving, but his head tilted.

"What's going on?" I asked, a bit breathless from the wind and the running.

He didn't answer, but it looked as though he shook his head.

As we reentered the White House, I stole a look backward to see what was going on with the rest of the staff. The buses were filled, but stationary. I hoped everyone had warmed up. Reporters were everywhere. They surrounded the grounds like a pack of eager hyenas waiting to pounce. News vans, with high-perched satellite dishes and camera crews, were everywhere. Pointing their lenses at us.

Inside, I wiped away tears that had formed from the wind beating against my face. Gavin caught me and something in his expression softened. "Everything will be all right, Ollie. This is just procedure."

Ollie? That was the first time he called me by my given name.

I was about to explain that I wasn't crying, but he started off again, expecting me to follow. His shiny black shoes made snappy clicks against the floor and I followed him back into the corridor, past all the now-quiet shops, to the storage area where I'd found the box.

CHAPTER 15

GAVIN MADE ME GO OVER MY STEPS, AS PRE-
cisely as I could recall them. Very slowly. As I remembered
and recited—again—another black-clad man took notes.
Wearing body armor, a sniper rifle slung around his back
and, a heated expression, he neither spoke nor made eye
contact with me. I was sure everyone involved in this fracas was furious with me for having caused a major evacua-
tion over nothing. Agents, snipers, and other assorted
military folk were everywhere—the halls were filled with
people speaking to one another and into radios.

The press would have a field day with this one, I was
sure, and I only hoped I wouldn't be served up like a holiday turkey for them all to feast on.

After ten minutes of tracing my movements, we were
still only about five feet inside the storage room. Gavin was
insistent on stopping at each step so that the intense note-
taker could get down every detail. Problem was, there was
not much to tell. And I couldn't imagine why anyone cared

about any of this. Unless they had reason to doubt my story.

I caught a quiver in my voice. God, I hated that. "This is where I noticed that the Johnson china had been moved."

Gavin nodded.

I took that as encouragement to continue. "So I pushed the bin aside, and found the"—I hesitated—"the box." I described it, even though I knew they both must have seen it.

"What then?"

"Well," I said, trying to be as precise as possible, "I knew it didn't belong here, so I decided to see what was inside." Shrugging, I added, "I planned to return it to whatever department had left it here."

"You said it was sealed."

Nodding, I remembered the clip from the dolly, still in my pocket. I pulled it out. "I used this to slice through the tape."

Gavin grimaced.

"Better than using my teeth," I said, in an effort to lighten the mood. Neither man smiled.

"It opened easily?"

I considered that. "Not really. I had to pull hard a few times in order to rip past the tape."

This time Gavin winced. "Dear God, Ollie. You ripped it open?"

"Yeah," I said, a little defensively. "It's not like I suspected anything when I first saw it. And it was sealed pretty tightly." I glanced at the two of them. Even the note-taker had looked up, and they were staring at me as though I'd done the stupidest thing in the world. "Geez, I understand we're supposed to be careful when we see things out of place, but you have to admit it really did look like normal storage stuff. There was no way I knew it was a fake bomb."

Gavin's eyes snapped to mine. "Fake bomb?" he asked. "What are you telling me? You found something else?"

"No . . ." Again I hesitated. "I'm talking about the thing I believed was an IED. The reason I called for help." My hands spread as though to encompass the entire White House grounds. "The reason I started screaming for everyone to evacuate. It was a fake, right?"

Gavin licked his lips and I could tell it was taking every measure of patience he had to slow himself down. "Ollie," he began, surprising me again with familiarity, "the thing you found was live."

My knees trembled. "It was?"

"Yes," he said, with high-strung tolerance. "You found a bomb. A real one." He ran a hand over his face. "Let's get through the rest of this and I'll tell you what I can."

We finished the how-I-found-a-bomb-and-learned-to-start-worrying exercise and the tall man with the notepad finally left us. The minute he was gone, I sat on the floor. It was cold.

"You okay?" Gavin asked.

"I suppose it would be a stupid question to ask if the bomb has been safely removed."

He took a seat on the floor next to me. "It's been defused and it's gone. We've done a sweep of the area and it looks clean."

Looks?

I rested my forehead against my upturned knees. "Why me?" I asked. "Why am I always the one who gets involved in this stuff?"

Gavin took a deep breath and I lifted my head to watch him. For the first time since I'd met him, he didn't seem furious with me. He seemed to be contemplating.

Commotion in the hallways continued, but no one poked a head in. All things considered, it was pretty quiet.

"I've been around these sorts of situations a lot, Ollie," he said, staring away. "Been on the job for over twenty-five years."

I waited.

"There are people who things happen to. And whether you consider it a blessing or a curse, you appear to be one of them." He turned to face me. "I read your dossier."

I winced.

"Don't be embarrassed," he said. "It's not that you have a black cloud over your head—it's that you have the ability to see and to sense things better than most." He wagged his head from side to side. "I'm not talking about ESP or clairvoyance, although maybe describing it as a sixth sense is apt. You have a great deal of intelligence and an acute awareness—more than most people—which allows you to notice things out of place. And you have the curiosity to find out why."

"It's a curse, all right."

"I disagree. We hire people with your talents every day."

I realized he was giving me a compliment. Fear, adrenaline, and now self-consciousness combined to render me speechless. I cleared my throat. "Thanks."

Back to staring away, he said, "With that in mind, I'm going to tell you something that isn't for public knowledge. But I want you to know so that we have another set of eyes out there." Gavin worked his tongue around the inside of his mouth. "The bomb was on a timer."

"When was it supposed to go off?"

Squinting, he said, "Sunday, during the White House opening ceremony."

My stomach lurched as I tried to digest that. At the same time, I was thinking how odd it was to be sitting here on the floor with Special Agent-in-Charge Gavin discussing bombs.

"If there's any consolation," Gavin went on, "and it isn't much, the IED was small. Personal size, if you want to call it that." He was so calm, it gave me a measure of comfort. "We get the impression this was meant to target one person."

"Me?"

He shrugged. "I doubt it, but after your altercation on the street, we're not overlooking the possibility."

"If it wasn't intended for me," I said, glancing around the storeroom, and hoping to God it hadn't been meant for me, "why put it here? If the intention is to do damage, there are much better places. This area is usually empty."

Gavin smiled. "You're right. We suspect the would-be terrorist wanted to get the IED inside first. He probably intended to move it later, to somewhere closer to the action."

"Makes sense," I said, still thrown by the relaxed attitude of our conversation. "I take it you're looking at everyone, right? Staff included."

"Every single person who's been inside the White House over the past twenty-four hours, cross-checked against everyone who was here the day the original prank bomb was found."

"I can't imagine anyone on staff being guilty."

"Remember what I told you at the introductory safety meeting," he said, looking at me again. "Don't see safety around you. Don't trust anyone."

"Aren't you trusting me by telling me all this?"

"I told you, I've been on the job for a long time." He stood and offered me a hand up. "I can see and sense things, too. You're okay, Ollie. You did the right thing."

"HE'S GOT THE HOTS FOR YOU," TOM SAID that night, back at my apartment.

"Give me a break," I said, "Gav is probably fifteen years older than I am. . . ."

"Gav?"

Putting dinner leftovers away in the refrigerator while Tom rinsed the dishes, I gave a half shrug and turned away. "Yeah, he told me to call him that when we weren't around other staff members." All of a sudden I realized how that sounded. I spun. "It doesn't mean anything."

"He *definitely* has the hots for you."

Laughing now, I shut the fridge door. "Hardly. But I did catch something today that I didn't ever see before. I think he's actually beginning to respect me."

Tom wiped his hands on a dish towel. "He should. You single-handedly saved his backside."

"How so?"

"Gavin's the agent-in-charge, right?"

I nodded.

"You prevented a bombing. How would it look if it had gone off under his watch? If it weren't for you—"

"Just dumb luck," I said, waving away the accolades.

"Not just luck, Ollie. Gavin was right when he said you're one of those observant ones. Which is why I decided on the subject for tonight's lesson."

Over the past year and a half, Tom had taught me much—self-defense, gun handling, and target shooting, to name a few things. Many of these lessons had come in handy in the past and I was always eager for him to let me in on things that most people neither ever learn nor care about.

"Let me guess," I said. "Explosives?"

"Right."

I interrupted him before he could begin. "You do know that we've all had to take a class on this already, right?"

"Gavin taught it?"

"Yeah."

He made an unpleasant noise. "How is it that the executive chef can uncover an explosive device that the security forces missed?"

"Like I said, just dumb luck."

"No, Ollie. They should have found this one. And I hope to God they kept searching."

"They said they swept the place."

The look on Tom's face let me know what he thought of the team's competence. "*Now* they're pulling out all the stops. *Now* they're interviewing staff members. They should have done that when the prank bomb was found. They should have found the guy who planted that and found out why. The fact that they're taking so long to move on this is ludicrous."

"But how could anyone have known? Gav said—"

Tom silenced me with a look, and I realized I'd risen to Gavin's defense. "I'm not going to feel comfortable with the president—or you—in the White House until we get to the bottom of this bombing threat."

"Where is the president now?"

He frowned. "With family," he said. "I'll be headed to meet him in the morning. Then he's heading to Berlin. This is my only night off until Wednesday."

"Gotcha."

For the next hour, Tom walked me through Explosives

101. He was certainly more detailed than Gavin had been in class, but Tom suffered from not having examples on hand to share. He'd printed photos from declassified files and diagrams from Internet searches. By the time he finished, my head was chock-full of device strategies and configurations, all for methods of mass demolition. Fun stuff.

"The one thing you have to remember is this," he said, as he wound up. "There is almost always a secondary device."

"I'd heard that."

"It bears repeating. People in the business of destruction don't want to fall short. They set up fail-safes to ensure their plans move forward. To ensure their target is destroyed. Do you understand?"

A prickly feeling had come over me. "I do."

CHAPTER 16

SUNDAY MORNING, I RETURNED TO THE White House kitchen, knowing I wouldn't hear from Tom again until Wednesday at the earliest. My mind was still reeling from all the bomb stuff he'd tried to teach me last night. I worked hard to assimilate information I hoped to never actually need.

To say I was jittery was an understatement. We'd gotten word that today's decorator tour at the White House was still on. Although Mrs. Campbell would forgo the Kennedy celebration, she would be here to greet guests afterward. With President Campbell out of the residence until Wednesday, the First Lady would be required to handle the event solo.

I still wore the splint on my right hand, which kept me relegated to working at the computer rather than putting meals together. Angry at the two men who'd put me in this position, I knew I needed to push through my harsh disappointment. Working on food was so much more fun than tapping away on a keyboard. Still, I forced myself to focus.

While not as much fun as creating an entrée, updating files was a necessary chore, and I'd fallen way behind.

I took my seat in front of the monitor and glanced around the kitchen. My crew was preparing hors d'oeuvres for the afternoon's event—and they were doing so with terrific efficiency. Although I'd designed today's menu months ago—prepared samples and overseen the First Lady's tasting tests—today I felt utterly left out. My body still ached from the assault two nights ago, and my ego smarted from having to keep the bomb information secret. Not only could I not tell anyone else that yesterday's bomb had been real, I couldn't warn them that it had been scheduled to go off this very afternoon.

Bucky opened one of the cabinets. "Oh, my God!" We all turned to see him staring into the shelves with exaggerated, wide-eyed panic. He reached in and pulled out a bottle of cooking sherry. "Call security," he said, lifting the bottle over his head. "It might be a bomb."

I couldn't blame the kitchen crew for laughing. I pretended to, but I felt the heated rush of embarrassment fly from my chest to my face. Pointedly, I turned away to study the file open on my monitor. Nothing about it looked familiar, and yet it had been listed as one of my recent documents—which is why I'd opened it in the first place.

Bucky was now pretending the bottle of sherry was a machine gun. I ignored him for a long moment because we'd always bantered among ourselves and I didn't want to shut down our team's lighthearted teasing. But this time, mortification pounded in my ears. Suddenly too warm, I wiped the back of my hand across my brow. At least the rest of the kitchen staff was no longer laughing.

Changing tactics again, Bucky pranced around the center island, saying, "Get out before the cooking sherry explodes!"

I turned. "Enough."

"Can't take a little ribbing?" he asked.

If he only knew. "What I can't take is being behind schedule." I directed a look at the clock on the wall, then pointed to the eyesore Senator Blanchard had given us. "We've had plenty of interruptions this past week. Don't you think it's time we focused on our work instead of goofing around?"

Total silence in the kitchen while Cyan, Rafe, and Agda waited, wide-eyed, to see what would happen next.

Bucky strode over to the cabinet where he put the cooking sherry back and slammed the door.

I stifled an impatient response. Escalating the incident would only make things worse. I'd gotten what I wanted—what decorum demanded—but in doing so had I just quashed the easygoing cheer that characterized our kitchen? I bit my lip. Was it too much to ask that he comport himself like a professional rather than a troublesome fifth-grader? But that was Bucky, and such was the nature of temperamental geniuses. The man could nuance a dish in surprising and delightful ways, but put him in a social setting and all subtlety vanished like powdered sugar on hot pastry.

A voice behind me. "Ms. Paras. What are you doing here?"

I'd recognize Peter Everett Sargeant III's precise elocution anywhere. "Good morning," I said, turning. "What brings you to my kitchen today?"

He was perfectly pressed, as always. But today his characteristic etiquette was augmented by a nasty gleam in his eye. "I was under the impression you were scheduled for another emergency training session," he said. "After all, considering yesterday's . . . er . . . confusion it appears you're in need of remedial attention regarding proper protocols where security is concerned."

Did everyone intend to take a shot at me today? I wanted to scream the truth. But, to what end? To allow me to save face and possibly set up a panic situation? Yesterday, as we walked back to the kitchen, Gav had instructed me to keep quiet about what I knew. The Secret Service believed that the president's absence from the residence would prevent any future explosive attempts on the White House. At least until President Campbell returned. But by then, he assured me, they'd be ready.

"Thanks for checking with me, Peter," I said, minimizing the peculiar document I'd been studying. I slid off the seat. "But I think I'll be okay now. I was fortunate to be able to confer with Special Agent-in-Charge Gavin. He told me I did the right thing."

Sargeant had a squirrel-like way about him. He held his hands in front of his chest and tilted his head. "Wasn't that kind of him."

He looked ready to say more, but I interrupted. "Was there anything else?"

Nonplussed, he gave the kitchen a once-over. "Will everything be ready on time for today's reception?"

"Of course."

He sniffed. "I will return later."

As he left, I caught Cyan mouthing, "Much later."

I was beginning to think the entire place had turned negative. We were all stressed—this time of the year had that effect on us all—but Bucky and Sargeant were pushing it. If it hadn't been for Gav's pep talk and Tom's tutorial yesterday, I'd wonder if I were turning negative, too.

Back to the computer. I restored the minimized document

and reread the first line. "Shrimp processing for the uniniti-
ated."

What the heck?

Below that were crudely described directions for cleaning shrimp. I shook my head. I hadn't recorded this, and I
doubted anyone else on my team had.

"What's up, Ollie?" Cyan asked.

I pointed to the screen. "There's a document here I've
never seen before."

"That's weird," she said as she began to read.

"Yeah . . ." Then I remembered. I snapped my fingers.
"What?"

"Sean used this computer the other day," I said. "Remember?"

"To check his e-mail, right?"

I read the strangely worded preparations out loud:
"Shrimp in a big bowl. Take them out one at a time. They can
be slippery little buggers. Really hard to cut that vein thing
out. See below for important safety warnings." Mystified, I
turned to Cyan. "Sean must have recorded this, but why?"

"In case he ever came here to help again?" she said, but
I could tell she was as unconvinced as I. "So he didn't forget how to do it?"

"No," I said, scrolling down the page. "I think he
recorded this for us to find."

"For you to find, maybe." Cyan said. "I think he liked
you."

Heaviness dropped in my heart like a lump of cold
dough. Sean had indeed "liked" me, or so the First Lady
had led me to believe. As I tripped past his crazy notes, I
wondered why on earth he'd taken the time to write any of
this up when he said he was checking e-mail.

I stopped scrolling when I saw my name.
A letter. Directed to me.

Ollie,

  Hey. I don't know how soon you'll see this. Those shrimp
are a pain to work with—did you give me that job because
you think I'm a pain in your kitchen? Bucky seems annoyed
that I'm on your computer. I'd swear he's baring his teeth at
me. LOL. I hope you don't think I'm a pain. In fact I hope to
pop in here more often in the coming weeks.

My heart jolted again. I bit my lip and continued to read:

  Forget that for now. I've only got a second here before
Bucky the wonder dog gets suspicious. I wanted to talk with
you alone, but the more I spend time here, the more I realize
that isn't going to happen. Not today. And tomorrow's going
to be a tough one, too. I'll be here because Aunt Elaine
asked me to, and because you did. Aunt Elaine doesn't know
the people she's dealing with as well as she thinks she does.
They've been trying to muscle me out. But their threats are
meaningless. There's nothing to hold over my head.
  But that makes me a pretty good catch, don't you think?
LOL.
  Ah . . . I've said too much.
  Let me know when you get this. If I'm not already dead
of embarrassment, we'll talk.

  Yours,
  Sean

I felt my shoulders slump.
"What's wrong?" Cyan asked.

I scrolled back up the page, unwilling to share this with anyone else just yet. "I . . . I'm not sure," I said. Pressing my fingers into my eye sockets, I rooted in my brain for ideas. What this note meant, I had no idea, but I knew with certainty this could help prove that Sean hadn't committed suicide. I needed to get this to someone in authority— someone with the ability to prove that Sean hadn't taken his own life.

I clicked the print command and stood up. Easing the paper out of the machine as soon as it was done, I folded it and tucked it in my pocket, then closed out the file. My stomach jostled. If Sean hadn't taken his own life, who had taken it from him?

"You okay, Ollie?" Cyan asked. "You're awfully pale."

"I'm . . ." I swallowed. "I'm okay."

Marcel's arrival in the kitchen prevented me from having to explain further. In a tizzy, he stood in the doorway and begged for help.

"What's wrong?" I asked.

"The house. I cannot get it into the elevator," he said.

Bucky made a disparaging noise. "If we all run over to help him, who's going to get the hors d'oeuvres done on time?"

The clock was ticking. "Rafe," I said, "can you get Agda to help put the appetizers together?" He nodded. Agda, having heard her name, stood up straight, apparently ready for whatever task I would assign. "Bucky," I continued, "you're doing fine there. Cyan will stay here, too." I held up my splinted hand. "I'm off kitchen prep, so I'll work with Marcel."

More often than not, Marcel reacted first and thought things through later. I hoped that was the case now.

When I followed him into the hallway, I understood the

problem. The gingerbread house was enormous. "Marcel," I said, in awe, "this is incredible."

Larger than last year's gingerbread house by half, this year's version was a meticulously perfect model of the current White House. We'd had a hard time getting the house in the elevator last year. I couldn't imagine why Marcel had decided to up the scale. A quick glance at his distraught face convinced me not to ask.

The annual gingerbread house creation always fell under the purview of our executive pastry chef. The rest of us in the kitchen helped out where needed, of course, but Marcel enjoyed this project more than any other all year.

The house itself took more than two weeks to create. Last year's version had weighed more than three hundred pounds, and this one was most definitely bigger. Marcel had designed this tiny mansion with staggering accuracy, creating individual baked gingerbread pieces in varying shapes and sizes and bringing them together with architectural precision.

This was no half-baked endeavor. Marcel had, in fact, made several duplicates of each section in anticipation of breakage. Every single piece was hand-crafted in proportion to the whole. The gingerbread, though edible—and delicious—was never consumed. Marcel carefully shaped individual pieces, then baked and set them aside until needed for the final construction in the China Room. I'd walked in on Marcel and his team a few times over the past couple weeks. They worked with the quiet intensity of adults, but maintained the wide-eyed optimism of school-children. Every little detail, from side walls to windowsills, was identified, numbered, and set aside for placement at exactly the right time.

Marcel had five assistants for this project. Three were SBA chefs, and two were permanent. Marcel usually made do with only one assistant, but Yi-im had proven so adept at the pastry tasks, Marcel had seized him for his own. Cross-training happened now and again in the White House, but it wasn't the norm. Yi-im's change of status from butler to assistant chef had caused a few raised eyebrows—particularly from the waitstaff. They weren't happy at the prospect of having to fill another empty position.

When I finished my slow-circuit inspection of the house, I had to say it again. "This is incredible."

"Merci," he said, absentmindedly, his gaze flipping back and forth between the cookie house and the elevator doors. The giant structure sat on a massive piece of covered plywood, which itself sat atop one of our wheeled serving carts. The design took my breath away so completely that I nearly forgot the problem at hand—getting it up to the main floor.

Yi-im appeared from around the back of the gingerbread house. "I didn't see you," I said.

His cheekbones moved upward in a polite smile, but it came across more as an affectation than his being happy to see me. The dilemma of how to get this beautiful monstrosity to the Red Room was obviously weighing heavily on everyone.

"What are these?" I asked Marcel, pointing to the mansion's edges. Small postlike structures were attached to the miniature—and I use the term loosely—White House's corners. Like flagpoles, but without flying any banner, each inner and outer corner of the building had one of these, painted white with icing to make it less noticeable.

Marcel heaved a big sigh in front of the elevator. "I do not wish to disassemble my masterpiece," he said with a forlorn expression. "I have just now put it together. It is exactly right. If I were to take it apart once again, it will never be so perfect."

"Can't we just carry it up?"

"Are you insane?" he asked. "Do you know how much this must weigh?" He rolled his eyes and shook his head. "It would take the strength of six men to carry this up the stairs, and my assistants are not capable of such heavy lifting. Not only that, but if they were to tilt it to any extreme, the walls would crack and my masterpiece would be ruined." He looked ready to cry. "Do you hear me? Ruined!"

I blew out a breath. Marcel had been executive pastry chef for a long time. I couldn't imagine how he'd forgotten the limitations there were on transportation. Of course, when one is in the throes of creativity, sound reasoning often flies out the window. That's probably what happened in this case. Scope creep. A little flourish here, a little detail there, and pretty soon you've created a big monster.

I took another look at the grand cookie White House. I had to admit again it was gorgeous. Every window had icy corners, as though Jack Frost had decorated the panes himself. The Truman Balcony was not only perfectly represented, but it was dressed with snow, miniature evergreen roping, and wreaths decked with red bows. I couldn't see inside, but I knew Marcel had outfitted the piece with inner lights. I couldn't wait to see it lit.

Marcel paced as Yi-im fiddled with different sections of the structure. I asked him about the poles at each of the corners. He shrugged and did that nonsmile thing again but said nothing.

There was no way this creation would fit in any of the elevators. Not even close. I shook my head as I pondered our next move.

"You agree it is hopeless, no?"

"Nothing is hopeless," I said, walking slowly around it.

Six men, Marcel had said. Personally, I thought it could be handled by four. "Who's available to help us?"

Marcel gave me a wary look. "What do you have in mind?"

"If we can get four sturdy men to each take one corner of the plywood, and if they go up those stairs"—I pointed—"very, very carefully, I think there's a good chance of moving this in one piece."

Skeptical, Marcel pressed me for reasons why I believed a bunch of burly men wouldn't be clumsy with his masterpiece. After a ten-minute discussion, he agreed to give it a try. "But if the men cannot lift this easily—immediately—we will call off the experiment," he said, the corners of his mouth curling downward. "And I will return to my kitchen to take my beautiful building apart."

"Don't get defeated. We haven't even attempted this yet," I said.

Marcel nodded and spoke to Yi-im. "Can you find us several men to help?"

With a nod, he was off.

"What about the gingerbread men?" I asked, looking around the wheeled cart. "I don't see them here."

"They will come later," Marcel answered, still a bit more distracted than he usually was. "Yi-im will arrange those when the house itself is in place."

I glanced at my watch. Marcel noticed.

"I know. I know." He paced the corridor. "What was I thinking? Why did I not ensure the house was in place yesterday?" Turning to face me, he continued his one-sided conversation. "I will tell you why. Because I have had nothing but trouble with my assistants. Do they not know how important it is that we have our work of art in place when it is to be unveiled? Does that not follow? Do they have no sense?"

I glanced in the direction his assistant had gone and I gestured for Marcel to lower his voice. "I thought you said Yi-im was working out very well."

Marcel rolled bugged-out eyes. "He is, what you say . . . the harbor during the hurricane."

"Any port in a storm?"

He waved a hand dismissively. "Yes, yes. That. While he is willing to put in many hours, he is not trained in methods nor in kitchen procedure. He has much to learn."

Conversation from behind caused me to turn. Yi-im had drawn out the electrical staff. Curly, Manny, and Vince were following the small man; Curly looking ever unpleasant, and Manny and Vince sharing a joke.

Yi-im nodded, gesturing the other men forward. He'd snagged only three. We clearly needed four. Marcel, I knew, had no intention of helping carry the house, and Yi-im was just too small. I chewed the inside of my lip. I was strong for my size, but I had doubts about my ability to hold up my end of the structure. The last thing we needed was for the house to crash to the ground. And the very last thing I wanted was for it to be my fault.

Before I could step forward to lend assistance, however, Yi-im grabbed the corner nearest me. He grunted some imperative and the three other men took corresponding positions at each end. Marcel covered his eyes. "I cannot bear to watch."

The four men, with set expressions, wrapped their fingers around the curved ends of the platform, and as one, lifted the board into the air.

Marcel moaned, turning his back now. "Ollie, you must oversee this. Tell me when I may look." Hands covering his eyes like horse blinders, he started back to the kitchen.

"Marcel," I called.

He turned, but only enough to face me. "Take the cart in the elevator," I said. "We'll need this as soon as we get up there."

With pain twisting his aristocratic features into a horrified frown, Marcel quickly stepped forward, grabbed both handles, and maneuvered the cart out from beneath the men's pole positions.

Within moments, Manny and Vince were four steps up the staircase, Curly and Yi-im still on the floor, raising their end high to keep the house level. Marcel chanced a look back, let loose another groan of total despair, and practically ran the cart to the nearest elevator.

I hated accompanying the four men on their painstaking crawl up the stairs, but I sensed they hated my presence even more. They had all obviously carried cumbersome, heavy items up staircases before, because they used minimal conversation to guide the collective group effort. Although I had faith in the strength of these men, I sweated out my position, low on the steps as they climbed up. If, heaven forbid, the house did topple, I could just see myself now, crushed below it, my feet sticking out like those of the Wicked Witch of the East.

I scampered up past them and breathed a little easier.

Curly, Manny, and Vince labored against the project's weight, grunting as they inched up each individual step. Yi-im's face showed no such strain. All four were careful to keep the board level. Too late, I thought about borrowing an actual level from the carpenter's department; I could have monitored the progress up the stairs.

One look at the contorted expressions on these guys' faces, however, and I realized my coaching and calling out levelness might have tempted them to dump the house smack on top of my head.

Marcel met me at the top of the stairs, cart ready.

Several long, sweaty minutes later, Manny and Vince cleared the top landing, holding their ends low until Curly and Yi-im were able to join them. Relief washed over every one of their faces when the board was settled softly atop the cart. We wheeled the house into the center of the Entrance Hall.

"*Merci*, er, thank you," Marcel said to the men, but he clearly didn't care whether anyone heard him. Walking around the giant confection, Marcel slowly examined his masterpiece, inspecting every inch. If I would have had a magnifying glass on me, I would have offered it to him.

Curly was just starting back toward the steps when Paul Vasquez called out to him to wait. Our chief usher hurried across the hall, his shiny black shoes clipping in sharp measure. "I just left a message for you. I didn't realize you'd be up here."

Curly scowled, looking at me with contempt. The fact that he was helping us out instead of doing his own work needled him and I could tell he blamed me. I smiled innocently.

"We're having problems in the Red Room again," Paul continued. "Did you cut the power there?"

Manny and Vince were about to head downstairs, but Curly stopped them with an unintelligible command. "What did you two do to the Red Room's power?" he asked.

Manny looked at Vince, who shrugged. "Don't know what you're talking about," Vince said.

Manny lifted his hands. "No idea. But we've got a lot to do, so . . ."

They were almost to the steps. "Hang on, there," Curly said, his voice raised. He swore under his breath. The scar that stretched across his head reddened and a vein throbbed at his temple. "Listen," he said to Paul, "I've been at this all day. I checked the Red Room, everything's hot. You tell me something's wrong. I check it again, and there's still nothing wrong. You think maybe your staff don't know the difference between the on and off switch?"

Ever unflappable, Paul shook his head. "I checked it myself, Curly. In fact, I just came from there. We have no power in the Red Room."

Curly raised a hand to his two assistants, then pointed down. "You go see what's what. And I want a complete report."

"Hold off on that a minute," Paul said, preventing the two men from leaving yet again. "I'm also here to inform you about a change in plan. I've just gotten word that the First Lady will *not* be entertaining here this afternoon. We will not have the traditional decorator tour after all."

I breathed a sigh of relief. Not just for my team's sake, but for that of the First Lady. She needed a break, and it seemed that finally she'd be able to get one. "We aren't serving, then?" I asked.

Paul shook his head. "Today is off. Completely."

Pulled from his mesmerizing study, Marcel straightened. "The house is not needed for today?" he asked. With an indignant tug of his tunic, he shot blazing eyes at Paul. "Why was I not told sooner?"

Paul raised his hand in a placating gesture. "I just found out. There have been . . . developments . . . in Mr. Baxter's funeral arrangements."

My hand immediately flew to my pocket, where I'd stowed the letter from Sean. "Developments?"

I knew Paul was reluctant to share any information he didn't deem necessary. "Mrs. Campbell has opted to spend more time with the president's family. She's needed there."

"Did they say anything more about whether they're investigating this as a homicide?"

Paul looked away. "We'll let you know more when we can, Ollie."

Curly had lowered his chin and now sent us piercing looks as he rolled his head back and forth between us, his eyes wide with boredom. "And this affects the electricity how?"

Marcel muttered to himself about being left out of important decisions, but he'd gone back to studying the gingerbread house and was mostly quiet. Yi-im stood away from us, his hands clasped at his waist.

Tiredness settled around Paul's expressive eyes as he addressed Curly's concerns. "I'm bringing you all up to date right now. A memo will go out shortly. Please plan to have everything ready for display on Tuesday."

I piped up, "The day we reopen to the public?"

Marcel muttered. Paul nodded. "We plan to tie the opening ceremony for the holiday season with the decorator tour. The only difference between the two events is size. And once we put both together, don't be surprised if Tuesday turns out to be a wild media event." He relaxed his features. "Curly, you'll see to the Red Room?"

"These two will see to it right now. And I guarantee I'm going to check it myself when they're done."

Only too happy to get the heck out of there, Manny said, "Okay, thanks." He looked to Curly. "We good to go?"

Curly jerked a thumb. "Get."

Vince started toward the Red Room, but Manny tugged his arm. "We got to check it from downstairs, first."

"Oh, yeah."

Paul clapped his hands together, thanked us all, and left.
Curly looked like he was ready to depart, but I stopped

him. "I think Marcel needs help getting this into the Red Room. Don't you, Marcel?"

Our pastry chef seemed to become suddenly aware of the recent departures. "I cannot do this alone. Where are the other two?" he asked.

If laser-eyed stares could kill, I would have been dead on the floor. Curly worked his jaw. "Let's get this over with," he said, taking a position at one end of the house. He ordered Yi-im to the opposite side and told Marcel to push the cart.

"But there are so few of us," Marcel said. "How can we—"

"Just push the damn thing," Curly said.

Marcel closed his mouth, fixing the other man with a glare of condescension. "But of course, you have no appreciation for art."

Curly ignored him.

We all quickly realized that Marcel had neither the upper body strength nor the inclination to push the heavy load across the massive hall. I was about to suggest that we ask a couple of other staffers to help when Yi-im took over for Marcel, and I took Yi-im's position. As though the huge structure weighed nothing, he pushed it smoothly and quickly into the Red Room, where we left it in the room's center. Kendra had given us strict instructions not to place it on its display table yet. That would come later, after she'd ensured that everything was exactly where she wanted it.

As we left Marcel to coo over his creation a bit longer, and Yi-im to continue to assist in his quiet, capable way, I tried one of the room's lights. It went on, nice and bright. "Looks like your guys got the power going in here again."

"Couple of idiots," Curly said.

We were in the cross hall now. "Hey," I said, turning. "The Red Room is right above the Map Room."

Curly didn't stop walking.

"Curly."

Impatiently, he turned.

I took that as an invitation to continue. "The Map Room is the room Gene was working on when he got that power surge."

"So?"

"Remember? The day of the electrocution, the Map Room had gone powerless."

"I don't remember," he said.

"That's right," I said, recollection dawning on me. That was the day Curly's wife had been taken to the hospital. "You weren't here. The Map Room didn't have power. Gene thought it had been taken care of, but when it wasn't, he set out to fix it himself."

Curly's calloused fingers skimmed his scar. "I don't know what this has to do with anything."

"Don't you see? Whatever killed Gene may be happening again. Remember those floating neutrals I asked you about?"

Curly scowled, throwing his hands violently sideways— as though swatting a giant fly. "You don't know what you're talking about. You learn one little thing, you think you're an expert. I told you once: You show me your electrician's card, and only then I'll start listening to what you have to say."

"But—"

"Just . . ." He shook his head, and held up his hands, swatting the air again. This time when he turned and left, I didn't call after him.

CHAPTER 17

BACK IN THE KITCHEN, I GAVE MY TEAM THE news. "Slow down, everyone. Today's reception has been canceled."

Relief brightened their faces as they all stood back from their tasks and took a breath. Agda stared a long moment. "I stop now?" she asked.

"We all stop now," I said.

"What are we supposed to do with all the extra?" Bucky asked. "Look at how much we've already done."

He had a point. There were hundreds of appetizers lined up on enormous baking sheets, waiting to be served. "Let's freeze what we can," I said, letting them know that the event had been rescheduled for Tuesday. "And we'll take the rest down to the cafeteria to share."

"Tuesday?" Bucky said. "Won't that be a madhouse?"

The general public—those who had the foresight to pre-arrange a visit—and congressional leaders and their fami-lies were all due here to vie for photo-ops at the opening ceremony. The event today was supposed to have been for the local press and other highfalutin magazines. Dubbed the Decorator Tour, the Sunday event traditionally gave the world a sneak peek at the year's White House extravaganza.

"I can't even begin to worry about it," I said. "Since the decorators are coming Tuesday now, too, we'll just have to add what we can from today's menu to what we have planned. We'll be fine."

I kept my tone light, but I was concerned nonetheless. Today had been the day I agonized over because of food preparations, but I was also preoccupied with safety concerns. Last night Tom and I had discussed how today, Sunday, had been the bomb's target day. We agreed that if the Secret Service believed a threat still remained, they would have canceled today's event.

Now suddenly it *was* canceled.

I swallowed before continuing, rationalizing that if there were any real threat, we would have been evacuated by now. With the president out of town and the White House closed to outsiders, the likelihood of an attempt was cheerfully slim. The same held for Tuesday, when the First Lady would open the White House to the public—the president was scheduled for a trip to Berlin. No president meant no bomb.

That gave me comfort. And to be honest, I was happy for the recent change of plan. In fact, I was feeling better than I had in a very long time. President Campbell was safe for now. And the next possible chaotic situation—Tuesday's opening—would happen without him in town. That should buy us some safety.

Fingering the note in my pocket, I realized that things were not completely perfect. The note from Sean convinced me that those in authority needed to look more closely into the manner of his death. But who could I talk to? Tom would have been my first choice, but he was away and wholly incommunicado until Wednesday.

As if reading my mind, Cyan wandered over and spoke in a low voice. "That document Sean left you," she said. "Are you going to do anything about it?"

"Did you read it?"

When she flushed, I had my answer. "It doesn't sound like it was written by someone about to commit suicide," she said.

"I didn't think so either."

Inching closer, she whispered. "You always seem to get in the middle of things, Ollie." When I reacted, she was quick to add, "That is, things seem to happen to you— around you. All the time."

She was starting to sound a lot like Gav.

"I can't help that," I said.

Keeping her voice low, she said, "I don't mean to hurt your feelings. It's just that I know you well enough to know that you're probably trying to figure out what happened to Sean all by yourself."

I shook my head, but Cyan wasn't finished.

"All I'm saying is to be careful."

"I am being careful."

She gave me a wry frown. "I know you don't believe Sean killed himself, but if he didn't . . . well, that means somebody else killed him. If you're trying to investigate this, and you've got a note like that"—she nodded toward my pocket—"you could be asking for trouble."

"I'm not trying to investigate."

Her look said she didn't believe me. "You're always poking around, Ollie. We both know that." Her wide-swept glance took in the rest of the kitchen. "We all know that."

Bucky, Rafe, and Agda were beginning to shoot curious looks our way. It wasn't often two people held a private, whispered conversation in front of the giant mixer. I grabbed Cyan's elbow. "I swear, I'm not touching this one." I gave a helpless shrug. "I don't even know where Sean lived. And so far, there hasn't been anything I can do to help anyone in this investigation, even if I wanted to." My hand curled around the note in my pocket and I pulled it up high enough for Cyan to see a corner of it. "Well, at least not until now, that is."

She gave a resigned nod. "Just be careful, okay?"

I WOULD HAVE PREFERRED TO TALK TO AGENTS Teska or Berland, who'd been with Mrs. Campbell when she first received news of Sean's death, but they were again with the First Lady—wherever she was right now. I could have talked with any of the other agents assigned to the White House, but that would have involved explaining the whole story to them. No, I needed to talk with a person in the know, with the authority to get things done.

I found him downstairs in the cafeteria, alone, reading papers out of a manila folder, arms resting on the tabletop, fingers wrapped around the handle of a steaming mug. He wore gold half-moon reading glasses perched at the very end of his nose. The place was quiet, but at this time of day, and at this time of year, it wasn't surprising. No one had time for coffee breaks. Well, hardly anyone.

"Do you have a minute, Gav?"

His gaze and eyebrows arched over the tops of his glasses, and his mouth tugged down. Dressed as always in a suit and tie, he looked totally at ease, which is more than I was at the moment.

"What can I do for you, Ollie?" he asked, holding a palm out toward the chair next to his.

I sat. Then pushed a hard breath out.

"Feeling the effects of yesterday's scare?" he asked.

"Yes," I said, rubbing my upper arms. "But that's not what's bothering me this time."

He sat back, removed the glasses, and placed them on the table next to the mug. "Talk to me."

I dragged the note out and spread it before him on the small table. He was fully versed in the Sean situation, so there wasn't much to explain before he read it. "I found this on my kitchen computer," I said. "Sean Baxter left it for me."

Gav leaned both arms on the table and held the paper far from his face. One second later, he pulled the glasses back on and started skimming.

I added, "He wrote this the day before he died."

Gav looked up. For the first time, I noticed his eyes. Pale gray. "And you're bringing this to me because . . . ?"

"Isn't it obvious?"

Gav continued to read. I waited.

"You believe this is proof he didn't commit suicide?"

I nodded.

"I'd have to agree the wording doesn't sound like it came from someone depressed enough to take his own life."

"Can you show that to someone? Would you be able to get that into the proper hands?"

Gav sucked on his lower lip for a moment before answering. He stared at the page, rereading. "This is on your computer in the kitchen?"

I nodded again. "I almost didn't notice it. He'd opened it under an obscure heading."

"Obscure," Gav repeated. "But you found it."

"It seemed out of place."

One corner of his mouth turned up. "Just like I told you. You have an eye for things."

That was all nice and complimentary, but I wanted to be sure this paper did some good. "Can you get it into the proper hands?" I repeated.

He folded it into fourths and placed it into his shirt pocket. "Can anyone else access this letter?"

"Sure," I said. "But no one else will." I thought about Cyan and amended, "Hardly anyone. The kitchen staff only accesses recipes and other necessary documents. I handle the administrative issues. This is under my set of documents."

"Is it password-protected?"

"No, but there's no reason—"

"Ollie, what did I tell you about trusting people?"

"No one in the kitchen—"

He held a hand up. "Even if you're right and no one in the kitchen means anyone any harm, how do you know that individuals from other departments aren't accessing your files?"

I opened my mouth to argue, but realized I had nothing to say. Although I was savvy enough to manipulate recipes, files, and spreadsheets, I knew nothing about firewalls or security stuff like that. That wasn't my area of expertise. Now that I thought about it, however, I supposed it could be possible for others to access my files when I wasn't looking—either in person, or through the quirks of cyberspace.

He jumped into my awkward silence. "Has anyone else seen this?"

"Cyan."

"She's the little redhead?"

"Yeah."

"Anyone else?"

"No."

Gav seemed to weigh that information. "Probably best if you keep this to yourself. Can you trust Cyan?"

"Absolutely."

"Then tell her to keep mum, too."

"What will you do with the note?" I asked.

"Make copies. Show them to the officers in charge. I'll get one to the First Lady as well."

Any uneasiness I'd felt about sharing the letter with Gav had dissipated. My mood lightened. "Thanks," I said.

"When I say to keep this to yourself, I really mean that."

"I know."

He stole a look to the right and then to the left. The only other humans in the room were two maintenance men, who were wiping down the far countertop. "Ollie," he said, leaning forward, "if Sean was murdered—and I'm not saying he was . . ."

"I know."

"Then whoever killed him won't want this information out there."

I thought about how similar Gav's warnings were to Cyan's. "I understand."

He tapped his breast pocket. "But this gives us a place to start looking for suspects."

CHAPTER 18

I MADE MY WAY TO THE FIRST FLOOR TO TAKE a look at the decorating in progress. Most days of the year we had crowds wandering through the White House to tour the public rooms. But today and tomorrow would be quiet now that the Decorator Tour had been canceled. I wanted to steal a selfish minute to breathe in the beauty of the holiday before things got crazy again tomorrow. I wandered through the Entrance Hall and, as always, appreciated its grandeur. While the White House was permanently a showplace and forever gorgeous, this time of year the mansion sparkled with holiday spirit.

I crossed the plaque in the floor that commemorated the White House's original construction and all the renovations that had taken place since—1792, 1817, 1902, 1952—and found it curious that most of the construction occurred in years ending in two. The building's most recent renovation, during Truman's tenure, had been so comprehensive that I couldn't imagine another one occurring in my lifetime.

Just ahead, Mrs. Campbell stood in the Blue Room, her back to me. She watched as one of Kendra's teams put the finishing touches on the tree. Hundreds of gingerbread men decorated the branches, peeking out from behind the white poinsettia blooms that sharpened the Fraser fir's intense green.

All the president's gingerbread men, I thought.

I wondered what the First Lady was thinking about right this minute. With all the beauty and cheer going on around her, it had to be difficult to face this happy time of year knowing Sean would not be here to celebrate. Not wishing to disturb her, I walked very softly to the adjacent Red Room.

One of the White House state reception rooms, the Red Room was always impressive, but decorated as it was today, with lighted garland surrounding the fireplace, handmade gingerbread men in every possible corner, and wreaths hanging in the tall windows, it was breathtaking. In prior years, the gingerbread house was showcased in the State Dining Room, but Mrs. Campbell had requested the change. This year, we had originally intended to use the State Dining Room for the very large, very busy reception following the Decorator Tour this afternoon. Now those plans had changed, too.

I scratched my forehead, assessing this last-minute rearrangement. The reception, rescheduled for Tuesday, including both days' invitees, would be larger in scale than anyone had anticipated. Maybe it was a good thing the house was set up in the Red Room after all. But I did find myself curious about all the power outages. Could it be that the Red Room wasn't electrically equipped to handle everything? Was that why we were having so much trouble?

The gingerbread house sat between the room's windows.

Their swooping gold draperies, topped with fringed red swags, framed Marcel's creation to perfection. I sighed. Despite all the crazed goings-on these past few days, the comfort of this room filled me with a warm sense of contentment.

Opposite the wall with the fireplace, the waitstaff had set up a champagne fountain. Dry now, it would be primed and ready to go before the reception on Tuesday. Two of our butlers would flank it, serving directly from the cascading fountain, so that none of our guests would get his or her fingers sticky.

Everything sparkled, looking warm and wonderful. Standing by the fireplace, I ran a finger along the edges of some of the gingerbread men turned in by our nation's kids. These simple, homemade decorations added just the right touch.

I wandered into the State Dining Room. Decorated trees in the room's corners were heavy with dazzling white and silver decorations. Matching ribboned arrangements hung from the wall sconces and draped the fireplace. A long table ran down the middle of the room, topped with complementary centerpieces. And everywhere I looked—on the trees, the walls, hanging from sconces—were more gingerbread men. Kendra was on her knees in the room's far corner, strategically arranging two more little men on the lowest branches of a tree.

"This is gorgeous," I said.

She turned, her flushed face breaking out into a huge smile. "It does look good, doesn't it?"

"That's an understatement." Standing near her, I turned, slowly, in order to take in the whole display. To just appreciate the beauty of it all.

"I'm relieved to have the extra time," Kendra said, wiping her forehead with the back of her hand. "We would have had everything done by noon if we needed to." She glanced at her watch, then grimaced. "But I'm happy for the breather. Gives me the chance to do a little extra."

"This theme is fabulous," I said, stepping close to the east wall and touching one of the gingerbread men's arms. "It gives the White House such a cozy feeling."

"This is a first for me. I didn't know how hard it would be to sort through submissions from all over the country." Her eyes widened and her voice lowered. "It was a nightmare," she said. "Which is why we're running later this year than I expected. There's so much more involved with accepting decorations for the White House from people. Everybody has to be checked out thoroughly before we even think about using their pieces." She took a slow look around the room, a satisfied smile on her face. "But it was sure worth it."

"Did you turn anyone down?"

She wrinkled her nose. "A few. Some arrived broken, some didn't follow directions and sent gingerbread men that were the wrong size, or the wrong shape. Part of what makes an overall design work is consistency in the right places." She shot me a conspiratorial grin. "Of course, we don't tell people that their kids' artwork has been relegated to the basement cafeteria. We just send them the official thank-you letter and let them know their efforts are appreciated. They'll never know."

"Speaking of gingerbread men," I said, "I gave Marcel some from the Blanchard kids. I didn't see them in the Red Room like Senator Blanchard requested."

Kendra's eyebrows raised. "Preferential treatment?"

"You know it." I ticked my fingers. "One, he's a senator. Two, he's a special friend of the First Lady's, and three . . . the decorations are really well-done."

A skeptical look. "From Blanchard's kids?"

I winked as I started back to the Red Room. "Rumor has it the Blanchard chef put them together."

She shook her head. "Why am I not surprised?"

Back in the Red Room, I happened upon Yi-im, who was touching up the house with a cup of powdered sugar and a tiny paintbrush. "Did the house survive the move all right?" I asked.

He canted his head, nodded, then went back to work.

After a few minutes of checking the room, I approached him again. "Where are the gingerbread men from Senator Blanchard?"

Yi-im's jaw moved sideways, as though he were considering my question. Finally, he shook his head and shrugged. Did this man never talk?

Just as I was about to ask him again where they might be, Marcel came in, his face shiny from exertion, but his demeanor high and cheerful. "She looks marvelous, no?" he asked us.

Yi-im straightened and I told Marcel how fabulously things were coming together.

He beamed. "It is time to ensure that my masterpiece is fully functional," he said, moving to the rear of the platform upon which the house sat. He plugged it into the wall. "We must see." Turning to Yi-im, he waved his hand, one finger aloft, encompassing the room's illumination. "Please lower the lights."

Yi-im obliged. The moment the room was darkened—not terribly dark since daylight still brightened the windows—

Marcel stepped back and rested his hand on the switch located behind the gingerbread building. "We are ready, yes?"

I nodded.

When Marcel flicked the switch, the gingerbread White House lit up from the inside. A warm, golden glow emanated from each frosty window and suffused the creation with a curious joy.

"Oh," I said, unable to conjure up anything else.

"But wait," Marcel said. "As they say on the television—there is more." He fiddled behind the structure for a moment. "Yi-im is seeing to it that the First Lady will be able to light this with a single control, aren't you, Yi-im?"

The smaller man nodded.

Marcel flicked a second switch and the corner poles I'd asked about before came alive with sudden brightness. "Sparklers?" I asked.

He shook his head. "No, but they mimic the illusion, do they not?" He drew me closer. "They are able to continue sparkling for hours by using a method of constant feed." He pointed to the bottom of one of the corner poles. "I have added these—they are spring-loaded to provide . . . what is the best word? Fuel? To each little flame."

"Aren't these a fire hazard?"

Marcel fixed me with a frown. "Do you not think that I have made certain to clear this with our Secret Service?" He shook a finger at me. "This is very low-grade. And not hot. Try touching it."

I waved my finger over the top of the bouncing brightness. "It's cool," I said, surprised.

"But of course."

"I'm impressed, Marcel. As always."

He smiled, the feathers I'd unintentionally ruffled back

in place. Clicking the house "off" again, he asked Yi-im to restore the lights. When he did, Marcel explained, "I have more of this fuel in my kitchen to replace as necessary."

"Sounds like you have everything covered."

"Again I say: But of course." Big grin this time.

"By the way," I said, when Yi-im resumed his sugar painting, and Marcel started his own personal inspection, "have you seen the gingerbread men the Blanchard children made?"

"The children?" he said, with a snort. "Certainly not. But I do have the gingerbread men sent to us from the Blanchard household, if that is what you are asking."

I smiled at his clarification. "It is."

"We will incorporate those with the house." He pointed to a position on the wall just above the gingerbread building. "They will be placed there," he said. "I wanted to fully test my house first and then we shall add in finishes as necessary."

A soft voice from behind us. "Oh, Marcel."

We turned. The First Lady had come in from the Blue Room, her hands clasped high to her chest. "How exquisite."

Marcel's dark face blushed and I noticed a drip of perspiration wend its way down near his ear. For all his bravado and bluster, Marcel was just as nervous as the rest of us to make sure everything went perfectly well. "Thank you, madame."

Yi-im scampered out of the way as Mrs. Campbell made a slow show of inspecting the gingerbread house. "I am in awe," she said.

Not wanting to disturb her while she talked with our pastry chef, I began to back out of the room.

"Just a moment, Ollie," she said, holding up a finger. "If you don't mind."

What could I do? I mumbled acknowledgment and stood near the door to the cross hall, watching.

Mrs. Campbell took a few long moments to study the frivolous yet inspiring details worked into the piece. She smiled, but I thought it a sad smile. "At a time like this, it is good to be reminded of beauty. I am humbled by your talent, Marcel."

Marcel gave a little bow. "You honor me, madame."

"Thank you," she said, in a near-breathless voice. Nodding to Yi-im, she made her way to me and guided us both into the cross hall. She didn't stop there, however, instead waiting until we were in the center of the Entrance Hall to talk.

"Would it be too much trouble to arrange for a dinner tomorrow evening?" she asked.

"Of course not," I said quickly. When the First Lady asks for anything, the answer is always an enthusiastic yes. "For how many?"

"Four," she said. "My colleagues Nick Volkov, Senator Blanchard, and Helen Hendrickson will be joining me here."

I opened my mouth to say something, thought better of it, and clammed up again.

Mrs. Campbell blinked moist eyes. "You have been privy to a great deal of information lately," she said. "I apologize for that. I sense your apprehension."

"It's not my place. . . ."

"Perhaps not, Ollie, but I plan to get this matter settled once and for all."

I couldn't stop myself this time. "Have you decided to sell?" Horrified that the question popped out, I raised my hand to my mouth. "Sorry."

She didn't appear to get angry. Rather she smiled,

then sighed, deeply, looking away, as though speaking to herself—convincing herself of what she planned to say to her three friends. "No matter what they tell me, I can't believe Sean took his own life. I also cannot believe that he gave me bad advice. I trusted Sean." She met my eyes again. "I can't make such a monumental decision with so much that hasn't been explained."

I hesitated, but knew that if I didn't speak up now, I'd be sorry later. "I have a letter," I said, "from Sean."

My words puzzled her. "What are you talking about?" she asked. "He sent you something? When?"

"He left it for me, on my computer," I said, explaining how I'd found it, and what the letter had said. I finished by adding that I was also convinced that the letter's tone was such that I couldn't imagine Sean taking his life either.

"Where is it?" she asked.

"I still have it on my computer," I said, pointing down toward the kitchen. "But I gave a copy of it to Special Agent-In-Charge Gavin."

She considered that. "Would you please make a copy for me?"

"Of course," I said, starting for the stairs. "I'll do that right now."

"I'll come with you."

Everyone in the kitchen stopped what they were doing to welcome the First Lady. Her visit wasn't completely without precedent, but it wasn't the norm. "Thank you," she said, with her characteristic grace. "I won't be in your way for very long. Ollie has something of importance to share with me, and then I'll be out of your hair."

When her back was turned, Bucky's eyes rolled so far up into his head I thought he might be on the verge of collapse. I warned him with a glare.

Mrs. Campbell took time to speak with Cyan, Rafe, and Agda while I pulled up my files. Bucky whispered close: "Always nice to cozy up to the First Family, isn't it? Lots of perks can come your way when you're buddy-buddy with the boss."

"Back off," I said.

He did, but took a long moment to stare at me. I couldn't tell what crazy thoughts danced behind those murky eyes. I could tell he'd been surprised by my sharp retort, but I wasn't sure if the added emotion was amusement or fury. And I didn't have time to bother.

As I clicked at my keyboard, my stomach jittered. What if it had been deleted? Or what if someone else had come across Sean's letter and modified it? I eyed Bucky, who I discovered was eyeing me back. It would be just like him to think he was funny by messing with my stuff—and I remembered Sean's concerns about Bucky being annoyed with him for accessing my computer.

My head pounded with worry and potential embarrassment as I pulled up a list of recent documents. Even as I rationalized that a true copy still existed—with Gav—I worried that this one would be gone and I'd be the laughingstock once again. After the bomb incident—the bomb that everyone believed was fake, but I knew to be real—even *I* thought I was starting to sound like Chicken Little.

"Come on," I whispered, urging the computer to move faster. I double-clicked on the file, exasperated when I was rewarded by the little hourglass that warned me to wait.

The computer made that unwelcome and not-very-nice sound when it can't find what it's looking for.

"No," I said, softly.

Cyan broke away from the First Lady. "Are you looking for what I think you're looking for?"

Her eyes today were amber brown. I stared into them. "It's not here."

"Hang on." She leaned in to where I was working and commandeered the mouse. She double-clicked on a file titled "YEO" and then typed in a password when prompted. Winking at me, she whispered, "Buckminster." Bucky's full name. Good choice, I thought.

A split second later, Sean's document was on the screen. "There," she said.

Amazed by her foresight, I thanked her. "YEO?" I asked.

"Stands for 'Your Eyes Only.' In my culinary school, students were always trying to steal one another's ideas. I learned to password-protect early." With a shrug, she started back toward the counter, but leaned forward to add, "I thought this one was worth protecting."

"You're good," I said, clicking the command to print.

"Just watching your back."

Mrs. Campbell continued talking with the other chefs as I pulled Sean's letter from the printer. When I had it in hand, she turned to me. "A moment, Ollie?"

We walked out across the Center Hall into the Map Room, where Mrs. Campbell read the letter. I would have preferred to allow her to read it by herself, but she asked me to stay when I offered to give her privacy.

When she looked up, her eyes were shining. "Thank you," she said. "I know just what to do with this."

"You know that Gav has a copy, too?"

She smiled. "I'm certain he's doing the best he can. But one of the benefits of my position is that it allows me to cut through red tape when I need to. You have done me a great favor, Ollie. And you've done the president a great favor as well."

I felt myself blush.

"I know you have a lot to do, so I won't keep you longer, but I want you to know that my husband and I appreciate all you do for us." She looked down at the letter, then up at me. "Today . . . and every day."

ON MY RIDE HOME, I STAYED HYPER-ALERT FOR any sign that I was being followed—any hint that people were out to get me. Today's stand-down on the reception, however, meant that our work load lessened and my commute home was at a more busy time than when I'd been attacked. It was getting dark, but it wasn't terribly late. There were people everywhere—and so many on the Metro that I had to stand for part of the trip. I didn't mind. Oblivious humanity provided a degree of comfort.

I reached into my replacement purse and smiled. How appropriate, I thought—the chef carrying pepper spray to defend herself. After my last altercation, I realized I needed to take a more proactive approach to guarding my safety.

I had to admit that I didn't expect to be attacked again, but what I really didn't expect was a reporter outside my apartment building. I didn't realize at first that the woman sitting alone in an idling Honda Civic was waiting for me.

"Olivia Paras?" the woman asked too eagerly as she alighted.

My stomach squeezed. What now? There were so many things going on—the two recent deaths, the fake bomb, the real bomb, the cancelation of today's event at the White House—that I couldn't begin to guess what this lady wanted to talk with me about.

I tried getting past her but she stepped in front of me. She spoke into a handheld microphone that appeared to be connected to a recorder on the hip of her fur coat. "Olivia Paras, you're the White House executive chef. . . ."

Tell me something I don't know.

"What can you tell us about tomorrow's dinner?"

She shoved the microphone at me. I blanked. "Dinner?"

"We understand that the First Lady is meeting with Nicholas Volkov."

As she said Volkov's name, she widened her eyes and slowed her speech, giving the name additional weight.

The microphone popped in front of me again. "I'm sorry. I'm going in now." I pointed up toward my floor. "And I'm cold."

"But don't you think the American public deserves to know if the First Lady is planning to meet with an accused murderer?"

My jaw dropped. I started to say, "What?" then thought better of it. Although I wanted to ask a million questions, I said, "I have nothing to say."

The reporter's shoulders drooped. "Ms. Paras, please," she said, her voice quietly entreating. "My name is Kirsten Zarzycki. I'm with Channel Seven News. May I call you Livvie?"

Livvie? My reaction must have shown, because she started to apologize. "Channel Seven?" I said, my eyes raking the Honda behind her. "I—"

"You've never seen me. I'm new," she said. "But I've been looking into all this for a while now and I think I'm onto something." She lifted one shoulder. "I can't get clearance to talk to any of the big shots involved, but I thought that maybe, since you're planning the dinner, you might have some insight into what's going on there."

I rubbed my forehead and stared at this girl. Kirsten Zarzycki was younger than I was, by at least five years, and taller than me by at least five inches. Blonde, eager, and looking as though the high-rise pumps she wore were squeezing her feet, she pleaded, with both her eyes and her words.

"Listen, I'm trying to make a name for myself here," she said. "You've got to be able to share something with me." Now both shoulders shrugged and I wondered how many innocent foxes gave their lives for her protection against the night's chill.

"I don't have anything, and even if I did . . ." My mind raced. Volkov accused of murder? Could he have been the one who—

"That's it," she said, the excitement in her voice pushing it up an octave. "I see it in your face. You do know something. I know you do. You just might not realize how much you know. Come on," she said, blinking rapidly. "You're where you want to be in this world. Can't you give a hand up?"

Plying me with almost the same argument Bindy had, she blinked again. I wondered if this tactic worked to better effect on men. I hoped not.

"Sorry," I said, starting for my front door. My woolen coat was no match for the cold air, although little Miss High Heels seemed toasty in her fur.

"What about Zendy Industries?" she asked, desperation shooting her voice even higher. "I hear that Mrs. Campbell refuses to sell out. But does she realize how much Volkov's involvement will hurt her investment?"

"Mrs. Campbell's investments are none of my business." I smiled. "Nor are they yours."

She called after me. "Don't you think this makes Mrs. Campbell a target now?"

I turned to face her. Anticipation sparked Kirsten's eyes.

"What do you mean?" I asked.

"I've been doing some research into Zendy," she said. "I'm trying hard to make this into a story. But nobody seems to care."

I shivered and wanted her to get on with it. "What did you mean when you said that the First Lady was a target?"

"It all revolves around Zendy." She bit the insides of her cheeks and I could tell she was weighing how much to share. "Volkov needs the money from the sale of the company, right?"

I shrugged.

"It's in the news. No secret there. His legal troubles are no secret either. The other thing that's only slightly more confidential is that the company can't be sold unless all four of the heirs vote unanimously to sell it."

I knew that much. This girl wasn't going to make it big in the media unless she could come up with something hotter than that.

"Who did Nick Volkov supposedly kill?" I asked.

"You don't know?"

I saw my capital dropping fast in her estimation. I shook my head.

"Mrs. Campbell's father."

That took me aback.

She frowned. "You really don't have any information, do you?"

"And you think Mrs. Campbell is a target because . . ."

"With her father dead, she's the only person standing in the way of the sale of Zendy Industries," Kirsten said with exasperation. "I'm connecting the dots here. I think when Volkov killed Mrs. Campbell's father, he assumed she'd be ready to just sign everything away."

I decided not to remind her that in America people are

innocent till proven guilty. That wouldn't have stopped this girl's cascade of information. By the way her breaths spun out into the night in short, agitated spurts, I could tell she was so tightly wound up with this story that the truth wouldn't stop her now. "But if you're right," I said, "and Volkov is arrested, then the danger's gone, isn't it?"

"Maybe," she said. "But I have to convince someone he's guilty."

"What else do you know?" I asked.

She twisted her mouth. "You're getting more out of me than I'm getting out of you."

"Maybe that's because there's no story here." I started for my front door again, not acknowledging any of the questions she shouted to my back. I waved without turning, and called, "Good night!"

CHAPTER 19

"WHAT'S GOING ON OUT THERE, OLLIE?" JAMES asked when I made it through the building's front doors. Tonight Stanley was with him. The two of them wore nearly identical looks of concern.

I waved away James's inquiry. "Just more of the same. Everyone wants secrets spilled, but why they think I have them is beyond me."

Stanley had been resting his hip against the desk. Now he shifted his weight. "You ask anybody about those neutrals?" he asked.

James perked up immediately. "What are you talking about?"

Again I tried to dismiss his concerns. "Just a theory we discussed. About the . . . you know . . . electrocution." I addressed Stanley. "I asked three people already. The acting chief electrician and two of his assistants. None of them is interested in what I have to say."

Stanley fisted the desk, making James jump. "Damn it,

they should. The more I think about it, the more I believe that's what got your friend. And if I'm right, it could still cause trouble. You got to get somebody to listen before another person gets fried."

His words shook me more than I cared to admit. What if something else did happen . . . if Curly, Vince, or Manny were electrocuted and I could have prevented it? How would I feel then?

I knew the answer. I couldn't live with myself. Despite the fact that I'd done my best to warn them, I realized I needed to push harder. And pushing was something I was good at.

"I'll tell you what," I said. "The guys I talked to think I'm just butting my nose in where it doesn't belong. I'll be sure to let the fellow in charge know that I talked with you." I smiled at Stanley. "I'll let him know that a real electrician is behind my questions."

Mollified, Stanley eased back to leaning. "I don't need no credit, y'understand, but if you think it'll make them listen, you do that, Ollie."

IN MY APARTMENT, AND COMFORTABLY READY to relax, I turned on the television, hoping for some mention of Volkov, especially after Kirsten Zarzycki's claims. My first choice was, naturally, her station, WJLA. Nothing. Nothing at all. I switched to CNN, then switched away again when no mention of Volkov, nor of Mrs. Campbell, hit the airwaves. If indeed this Kirsten was right, then news of this nature would have been splattered everywhere. Hers was an explosive allegation, and definitely too hot to let simmer.

After a half hour of channel surfing, I realized the

rookie reporter had apparently gotten her signals crossed somewhere along the line. I tried searching the Internet, but found nothing there either.

As I got myself together for the next day and prioritized my tasks, I removed my splint and flexed my fingers. Felt good to have the freedom of movement. Better yet, I'd be able to really dive into food tasks in the kitchen tomorrow. I sorely missed the hands-on work I was used to.

Tomorrow was Monday, the last day the White House would be closed to the public before the big holiday unveiling on Tuesday. I set my alarm for a little earlier than usual, snuggled under my covers, and wished I could talk to Tom.

MOST MORNINGS, I WOKE TO MUSIC, BUT THE fifteen-minute lead time I'd built in the night before set my wake-up to smack in the middle of a news report. A voice like dark chocolate roused me from deep slumber. I missed the first few words, but twisted my head toward the voice when I heard him intone: "It is not known whether Ms. Zarzycki knew her attacker. Police are canvassing the area, looking for clues to this shocking murder. They have no suspects in custody but are asking witnesses in the area to step forward if they have any information to help find her killer." The announcer continued with a hotline number to call.

I shook my head. This couldn't be right. I must have misunderstood the name.

Staring at my clock radio, I waited for the story to repeat. But all I got was weather and traffic.

Heading into the living room, I tried to convince myself

that this was all a dream. That all the events from recent days were conspiring to play with my mind. But my bedroom floor was cold to my bare feet. The apartment was chilly, and I could see the dawn of a new day outside my balcony window. Dreams were not usually so rich with such sensory stimuli. As my TV came alive I searched the room, hoping for some out-of-place vision, some signal that this was not real.

Instead, the two on-air personalities at WJLA were speaking disconsolately into the camera. One male, one female. I didn't know these commentators well enough to know their names, but the elegant black woman spoke for both. "Our hopes and prayers go out to Kirsten's family tonight. Although she'd just joined us here at WJLA, she was part of our family, and she will be missed." The woman's lips tight, she glanced to her co-anchor.

He took the cue. "Anyone with any information should call the number you see on your screen."

I dropped back into my sofa, curling my knees up, wrapping my arms around them. I continued to stare at the TV, even after they shifted away and cut to commercial. What the hell was going on?

With a beseeching glance at my clock, I willed the hours to speed by so that I could talk with Tom. But he wouldn't be here till Wednesday. Two long days away.

I changed the channel repeatedly until I caught the story again elsewhere. I got a few more details each time. I kept trying, looking for more, but soon I realized I had as much as I could get. There just wasn't much information out there. Not yet.

Dropping my knees, I held my head in my hands and tried to make sense of it all.

Kirsten was dead. Attacked at home, in her apartment, she'd been shot in the head. This could be a random act of violence, I told myself. But I didn't believe that for a minute. She'd talked about Nick Volkov being responsible for Mrs. Campbell's father's death. Kirsten was dead, and yet the information she claimed to have was nowhere to be found on the news.

Murder has a way of adding deadly credence to unproven conspiracies. Could Kirsten have been onto something after all?

LATER THAT AFTERNOON, RAFE JOSTLED MY shoulder. "What's wrong, Ollie?" he asked. "You're usually in your element when your hands are deep in dough."

Cyan didn't wait for me to answer. "Maybe you forgot what it was like to do the real work around here," she said, winking.

"That's it. You found me out." I forced a grin. As much as I wanted to be able to join in their cheer, I couldn't shake the news report on Kirsten's murder.

Rafe had been working with Agda a lot over the past week and now she joined in the good-natured teasing. While she divvied up parsley, she eyed the ball of dough before me. "I do that with eyes closed," she said, blinking hard. I expect she'd meant to wink at me. "And I do in half of the time."

"You're right," I said, soberly, then smiled to take the despondency out of my words. Agda had proven herself to be a huge asset to our kitchen. In recent days, with all our setbacks, and with me being sidelined with the splint, she'd more than taken up the slack. And she'd started to join in on conversation as well. She'd even impressed Bucky. Now that he was coming around, I knew the girl was starting to be considered part of the team. It did my heart good to see how well everyone was working together. And I needed that boost right now.

I eyed the forlorn ball of dough before me. I should have had these icebox rolls done fifteen minutes ago. I was falling behind. Too much weight on my brain seemed to cause a drag on everything else. Twice today I'd tried calling the Kirsten hotline number to let them know I'd talked with her last night, but I'd gotten a busy signal each time. Maybe that was for the best. I slammed the dough onto the countertop and kneaded it hard. I'd talk with our Secret Service personnel, or with Gav. They'd know what to do.

"How soon before the guests arrive?" I asked.

Bucky shot me a weird look.

"What?" I asked.

"That's the third time you've asked."

Was it? Geez, I really needed to get my head back in the game. "Well, you know how fast things change around here," I said to soothe my own ruffles. "And so far, we're still serving just four people tonight, right?"

"Last I heard, no change."

Agda perked up. "Change. Yes."

"A change in the guest list?" My heart raced. I'd been playing one of those if/then games with myself all day: If Volkov shows up tonight, then he's *not* guilty of killing Mrs. Campbell's father, and also not involved in Kirsten Zarzycki's murder. I could breathe easier if that were the case. But if we found out he wasn't coming . . . it could mean . . . "What is it?" I asked. "What's the change?"

Cyan put a hand on my arm. "Ollie, what's wrong? You're the one who just said we're always dealing with changes here. What are you worried about? You're pale again."

Waving a floured hand, I worked up a cheery demeanor. "Nothing, nothing at all," I said, keeping my voice light. I turned to Agda again. "What change did you hear about?"

Her hands came up to either side of her head, fingers spread, and she shook them—excited, it seemed, to be able to contribute her piece of knowledge. She spoke slowly but clearly. "Not dinner in residence. Now serving in Family Dining Room."

That *was* a change. We'd been instructed to send everything upstairs, where the First Lady intended to meet privately with her colleagues. "Who told you?" I asked.

Agda smiled and nodded. Then, belatedly understanding my question, her eyebrows lifted and she nodded again. "Paul."

I rubbed the back of my wrist against my forehead. "Why the change?" I asked, rhetorically. "I didn't think the First Lady wanted to have anyone see the first floor until the official opening ceremony tomorrow."

Cyan shrugged. "No idea. But with all she's been through lately, maybe she just wants to keep her private rooms private again."

"You're probably right," I said. Addressing Agda, I asked her if there were any other changes.

She shook her head. "No."

"What are you expecting, Ollie?" Cyan asked again.

"Just wondering if the guests are still the same."

"Why wouldn't they be?"

Now I shrugged. "Just a hunch."

Rafe had been right about one thing: Keeping my hands busy in the kitchen had been the perfect panacea for my uneasy mind. We were serving chicken-fried beef tenderloin tonight. Topped with more of the white onion gravy we'd made earlier and served with my late-to-the-party icebox rolls, we rounded out dinner with a basic salad, some in-season vegetables, and homemade peppermint ice cream for dessert. About an hour before dinner was to be prepared, I had my first chance to steal out of the kitchen and find Gav.

I'd seen him earlier when I passed the China Room. Now that the gingerbread house was complete, Marcel had given up squatter's rights and Gav had been using it as a lecture hall. When I walked past, he'd been in the midst of talking to some of the staff, so I hadn't interrupted. But I definitely needed a few minutes of his time.

He was still there.

"Got a minute?" I asked.

They'd brought a folding table into the room, and he sat at it, staring down, elbow propped, holding his head. The rest of the room was empty.

When he looked up, he didn't seem very happy to see me. "What is it?"

I'd intended to ask his opinion of the Kirsten Zarzycki situation, but I faltered. "Is something wrong?"

When people's eyes crinkle, it's usually because they're smiling. In this case, Gavin looked as though he'd suffered a quick pain. He took a long moment to speak. "Why did you give a copy of Sean's letter to the First Lady?"

I started to answer, but he cut me off.

"She's involved a lot of . . . others." He shook his head, and it looked as though his phantom pain intensified.

"We were talking," I said. "She and I . . ." I stopped myself from the apology that nearly tumbled off my tongue. "Why shouldn't I tell her? The situation involves a family member."

I watched Gavin force himself to be patient. He came close to losing the battle.

Another hard pain-squint. "When you first presented the information to me, I had a unique opportunity to make discreet inquiries. Now," he said, bitterness creeping into his voice, "I have been shut out of the investigation by the agencies involved."

I didn't know what to say to that. All I could think of was that if other agencies were investigating, then at least some good was coming of my bringing it to Mrs. Campbell's attention. "Who's handling it now?"

His mouth set into a thin line. "What is it you needed from me?"

I felt stupid bringing up the Kirsten Zarzycki issue after being scolded. "Forget it," I said. "It's nothing."

He rubbed his temples and spoke with clipped consonants. "You came in here intending to tell me something. What was it?"

I really didn't want to get into it, but I also didn't want to bear the burden of this information myself. "Did you hear about that reporter who was murdered late last night?"

"Shot in the head?"

"That's her," I said, dejectedly. "She came to visit me yesterday evening."

"Here?"

I shook my head, then gave him a quick rundown of our discussion.

When I was finished talking, Gav's anger had all but dissipated. "Where did she get the idea that Nick Volkov was responsible for Mrs. Campbell's father's death?"

"She didn't tell me."

He stared upward, toward the ceiling, before meeting my eyes again. "Mrs. Campbell's father died in a car accident."

"I know."

He stood. "Who did you talk to about this?" he asked. "Besides me?"

I shook my head. "No one."

"This time, keep it that way," he said. Without another word, he bundled up his papers and left the room.

CHAPTER 20

IT WASN'T LONG BEFORE MRS. CAMPBELL'S dinner guests began to arrive. With a sad sense of déjà vu, we staged dinner in the Family Dining Room's adjacent pantry, just as we had on Thanksgiving—when these same guests were present and we received the terrible news that Sean was dead. I couldn't help but question Mrs. Campbell's decision to choose this particular venue for tonight's meal. In addition to the recent sadness associated with the room, it wouldn't be very private. Staffers in adjacent rooms were working around the clock tonight to complete everything before tomorrow's opening.

Cyan and I intended to handle tonight's dinner ourselves. With three guests—possibly only two if Volkov didn't show—there was no need to clutter up the pantry with extra bodies.

I warmed the onion gravy on the stove, about to ask Cyan a question, when I heard Treyton Blanchard's voice in the next room. "Elaine, thank you for having us. A shame about Volkov, isn't it?"

Turning down the heat, I inched toward the wall, hoping to hear more. A shame? That hardly seemed an appropriate reaction to Volkov being responsible for her father's death.

"I hope Nick is all right," Mrs. Campbell answered. "And I hope we hear more soon."

"Let's hope we hear from him directly."

I pressed my fingers to my forehead. This conversation made no sense.

Jackson came in, letting us know that dinner would be served a half hour later than we'd planned. When I asked why, he shook his head. He didn't know, he just wanted to relay Mrs. Campbell's request. I thanked him and kept listening in.

Mrs. Campbell and Senator Blanchard moved into discussion about other things, family and such. I heard him murmur his repeated condolences about Sean, and Mrs. Campbell said something in return I couldn't catch.

"Hey, Nancy Drew," Cyan whispered. "What's so important in there?"

I moved away from my eavesdropping perch. "They're talking about Volkov."

"So?"

"He's still coming, right?"

Cyan twisted her mouth. "What's with you today? I think they're all coming." She glanced at her watch. "And no one is officially late, yet. But Helen Hendrickson hasn't arrived either. . . ."

"Helen," Mrs. Campbell exclaimed in the other room. "I'm so glad you could make it."

I lifted my eyebrows. "She's here now."

Cyan and I arranged stuffed cherry tomatoes on one plate and set out another platter for the bacon-and-cornbread muffins while I waited for some word as to whether Volkov was coming or not. At the same time, I kept my ears open for any further mention of his name.

The silly bet I'd played with myself now rose up to mock me. I tried reasoning with myself. Even if the man didn't show up, it wasn't as though I could take that fact to the nearest police station and claim that he was guilty. But as the minutes ticked by and Volkov became officially late, I became ever more convinced that Kirsten Zarzycki's allegations had more going for them than just ravings of an eager-to-be-promoted reporter. The fact that she was dead sealed it for me. I wondered who else she may have talked to.

Then a thought hit me so hard it made me stagger.

"Ollie? What's wrong?" Cyan asked.

I held on to the edge of countertop, forcing my brain to slow down instead of making the terrible conclusions it preferred to leap into.

If Kirsten indeed had access to information that incriminated Volkov—and she had been killed to maintain silence—then I had to worry about who else she might have talked to. Because whoever was responsible for her death might have known she talked to me.

My fingers formed a vise around the counter edge.

"Ollie?"

"I'm okay," I whispered to Cyan, though I was anything but. The horrible thought bounced around in my brain— what if Kirsten had mentioned me? What if whoever killed her was looking to tie up other loose ends?

I'd had an assassin after me before—and although I'd survived, it had been close. Too close. The recent incident on the street took on new meaning. What if these were the same people who'd killed Kirsten? What if they'd planned to get me first? Would they stop now, or had I made myself an even bigger target by talking with the reporter?

"I think you ought to sit down," Cyan insisted.

"No." I wiped the back of my hand against my eyes. "I just had a moment there. I don't know what's wrong."

"Maybe you're coming down with something."

"I'll be okay."

Her look told me she didn't believe me. I wouldn't have believed me either.

I made my way to a stool near the door to the Family Dining Room. "You know what? Maybe I'll just sit for a minute." I gathered some of the baby greens we intended to use for the salad, and four plates. "I'll get the salad started here."

While Cyan worked at the far end of the room, she cast occasional glances my way. For my part, I listened for mention of Volkov, for mention of Mrs. Campbell's father. Instead, the three old friends seemed intent on keeping the conversation light.

"There he is," Treyton Blanchard boomed.

I nearly stood up to see, but didn't need to. Within moments I heard the greetings indicating Nick Volkov had arrived—and in apparent high spirits.

"He came?" I asked aloud.

"Why shouldn't he?" Cyan asked. "We set a place for him."

As much as I knew my little he's-guilty-if-he-doesn't-show reasoning meant nothing, I felt relief begin to seep into my consciousness. Last night, Kirsten had made it sound as though an arrest were imminent. Volkov showing up here today suggested that the late reporter's musings could have been just that—musings. Solid logic was rapidly extinguishing the irrational fear that had gripped me. Perhaps Kirsten met her untimely end in a strictly coincidental fashion.

That didn't feel quite right to me, but the fact that Nick Volkov had shown up gave me enough release to let go and enjoy the rest of the dinner preparation.

Jackson came into the pantry, all smiles. "We are ready to serve at any time."

"Any idea why the delay?"

"Mr. Volkov was apparently in a fender-bender on his way over. His driver is still at the scene, and Mr. Volkov needed to remain until the police arrived."

"Is he okay?"

Jackson nodded and began mixing a drink using sweet vermouth, Tennessee whiskey, and bitters. "Both Mr. Volkov and the driver were uninjured."

"What about the other guy?"

He shrugged. "Hit-and-run."

"Poor Volkov. Is he shaken up?"

Jackson strained his mixture into a lowball glass and added a maraschino cherry. "First thing he asked for was a perfect Manhattan," he said, holding up the concoction. "And told me to keep them coming."

"Yikes," I said. "Think he'll be in any mood to discuss business with that much in his system?"

Jackson backed into the doorway, lifting his shoulders in silent response. He mouthed, "We'll see."

Plating and serving dinner took my full concentration. The little snatches of conversation I caught between tasks weren't much. It seemed as though, by tacit agreement, all four diners had agreed to table contentious discussion until after the meal.

Before the empty dishes were brought back to the kitchen, Cyan and I began to prepare for dessert. She had her back to me, one hand on the coffeepot, when she turned to ask me a question.

Instead of Cyan's voice, however, Volkov's rang out. "Why can't you see reason, woman?"

We both froze.

Mrs. Campbell's voice came next. "Nicholas—"

"Goddamn this stupid arrangement. Where the hell did our fathers come up with this ridiculous idea?" Then, a *whump*, sounding a lot like a fist, slammed onto a tabletop.

"How many did he have?" I asked Jackson in a whisper.

He held up four fingers.

Another one for our "Do not serve" list.

Helen Hendrickson attempted to say something, but Senator Blanchard interrupted. "Nick, this isn't helping. Elaine, you know as well as I do that if we don't move forward now—quickly and decisively—we won't be able to sell for another ten years."

Mrs. Campbell spoke up. "We have until December fifteenth."

"You think that's a lot of time?" Volkov shouted.

"I think it's plenty of time to wait to discuss this."

Volkov kept at it. "That's why this arrangement is such idiocy. You may very well have inherited your share of the company, but you have certainly not inherited any business sense."

A chair scraped. I imagined Mrs. Campbell standing up. "Excuse me?"

Volkov's words slurred. "We have a buyer interested, which means this is the time to strike. You may have all the time in the world to make up your mind on other matters, but for now, this is the most important item on my agenda.

If you don't agree to sell, then I can't be responsible for my actions." Another *whump*. Louder this time.

I peeked around the corner. Secret Service agents had moved into the room, close enough to act, should the need arise. Mrs. Campbell, however, held them off with a raised hand. "I thought it would be a good idea to talk tonight," she said. "I see I was wrong."

From my vantage point, I watched her make eye contact with each of her colleagues, one at a time. She spoke softly. "Despite the range of our ages, we practically grew up together. Have you forgotten? Our fathers were friends, close friends. As I believed we were." She clasped her hands in front of her. "Time and distance and circumstances have caused the four of us to lose the closeness we once had, but I'd hoped we'd be able to reach an agreement." She sighed.

Helen Hendrickson remained seated, and Volkov, his energy spent, dropped back into his chair. Blanchard, standing to Mrs. Campbell's left, leaned forward, fisted hands on the table. "We can still reach an agreement, Elaine."

She shook her head. "I no longer believe that."

"If you'd only listen to reason."

She held up a hand. Blanchard stopped talking. "Our fathers were wealthy men." Again she stopped long enough to make eye contact with her guests. "They envisioned something bigger than themselves, something that would live on after they were no longer here. It was their dream to use their knowledge, their wealth, and their contacts for philanthropic purposes. And you all know what a great success they achieved."

Helen Hendrickson finally got her word in. "But that's the thing, Elaine. Zendy Industries is bigger and more successful than our fathers ever imagined. It's got holdings in every major market in the world. Just think about the good that can be done if we were to sell it."

Mrs. Campbell shook her head. "The good can only continue if Zendy remains under the charter upon which it was founded. Our fathers entrusted us to carry on their vision. If we sell now, what will we be doing to future generations?"

Volkov growled, "My children *are* the future generation. Seems to me our parents would want us to ensure their security."

"My dad told me that Zendy Industries was the best investment he ever made," she said softly. "He believed in its mission. And he made me promise never to sell."

The three others gasped.

Mrs. Campbell licked her lips. "I invited you all here tonight to tell you once and for all that I will *not* sell. Not before December fifteenth. Not ever."

Volkov bolted upward, upsetting his chair. For a moment I thought one of the agents would grab him, but he strode away from the First Lady. "Idiocy!" He threw his hands upward, gesturing to the ceiling as he paced.

"I had hoped to . . . wait," Mrs. Campbell continued. "To discuss this more fully at a later point in time, when everything settled down. Sean's death . . ." She bit her lip.

Cyan nudged me. "Getting an earful?"

I nodded.

Blanchard flexed his jaw, in an obvious attempt to keep himself in check. "Did you discuss this decision with your own children?" he asked.

"This is not their concern," she said. "Not now. Someday when it becomes their decision, I hope they'll see the wisdom of keeping Zendy Industries under family control."

Volkov, at the far end of the room, shouted, "Then buy us out. We can sell it and you can control it all."

Mrs. Campbell returned to her seat. "You know I don't have the means to do that, Nick," she said.

I glanced up at Jackson and tilted my head toward the door, asking if he was ready to serve dessert. Maybe a little sweetness would bring these people around.

While Jackson placed the peppermint ice cream at each diner's place, Volkov returned to his seat, grumbling. He stopped Jackson. Holding up his lowball glass, he swirled it briefly before lifting it to his lips and draining the last few drops. "Get me another one of these, would you?"

Jackson nodded wordlessly, but when he returned to the bar area of the pantry, I watched him prepare the drink differently.

"Won't he know the difference?" I asked when Jackson added a liberal dose of tonic water.

"He's lucky to know the difference between his hands and his feet at this point."

When Mrs. Campbell excused herself to take a phone call, the three others talked among themselves. I hoped for a tasty piece of information—for some discussion of the recently deceased Kirsten Zarzycki—but they spoke in hushed tones, and all I could make out was their intense disappointment at Mrs. Campbell's decision.

Helen heaved a great sigh. "I guess there's nothing left for us to do."

I peeked around the corner long enough to see Treyton Blanchard pat her hand. "Let me talk with her one more time," he said.

"Fat lot of good it will do," Volkov groused. He knocked his dessert plate away with a look of disgust and staggered to his feet. "There's got to be another way around this. And I'm going to find it."

By the time Mrs. Campbell returned, he'd left. The

Secret Service agents on hand were only too happy to guide the blitzed Mr. Volkov out of the White House. Helen made her apologies. "I can't tell you how disappointed I am with your choice, Elaine," she said. "We have a couple more weeks before a solid decision must be made. Just promise me you'll think about it."

"Helen," Mrs. Campbell said, warning in her voice.

"I know how much Sean's death has affected you. Perhaps it was wrong of us to push you so soon after he died. Just take your time. I believe you'll see our point if you just give it a little time."

"It isn't just Sean—"

"Please," Helen said. "Just promise me you'll think on this again."

I could tell Mrs. Campbell was torn. Stick to her convictions, or give her old friend some comfort? "I won't change my mind," she finally said.

Helen reacted as though given a great gift. "I know. I know. But as long as you give it more thought, I believe we have a chance to find agreement."

Helen said good-bye and was escorted out. Senator Blanchard remained. "A moment of your time, Elaine?"

They returned to their seats. A moment later, Jackson refilled both coffee cups and stood just outside the dining room. I was cleaning some of our utensils, and listening hard above the clatter from Cyan's dish washing.

"Volkov is a loose cannon," Blanchard said. "You need to be careful."

From what I could tell, Mrs. Campbell's voice sounded weary. "If I didn't believe I was following our fathers' wishes, I wouldn't be holding on so tight."

"You were the first child born to any of them and you're like the big sister to us all. It's only natural you feel a stronger bond to the company. You were there when Zendy was created."

She gave a light laugh. "Zendy was conceived when I was about five. Then Helen was born, then Nick, and then years later, you." A long pause. "Can't you see how wrong it is to give her up? Zendy Industries is like our sister. We can't just sell her to the highest bidder."

"Some of us have plans, Elaine."

"Like a run for the presidency?"

I couldn't hear Blanchard's answer, but I detected sarcasm in Mrs. Campbell's tone when she said, "Isn't that comforting?"

Cyan turned off the water and dried her hands. Thank goodness. Now I could hear.

Blanchard's next words were clear, and no longer held their customary friendly charm. "Let me be clear on this," he said. "You may believe that selling Zendy Industries is akin to cutting off a sibling. But by not selling, you will cut *us* off. You know as well as I do that Nick is about to blow. Helen is quiet, but she's unhappy with your decision. As for me, I cannot condone your decision. If you choose to keep Zendy, you thereby choose to dispose of my friendship."

Mrs. Campbell's sharp intake of breath preceded her question. "What are you saying, Treyton?"

I couldn't help myself; I had to peer in.

He stood, hands up. "You leave me no choice. Unless you change your mind. Unless you choose your flesh-and-blood friends over the pie-in-the-sky aspirations of our fathers' company, I will no longer support you." He licked his lips. "And I will no longer support your husband."

"That's blackmail."

"No, Elaine. That's how important this sale is to me."

When he glanced in my direction, I ducked away. But I'd heard enough. What pressure they were putting on the First Lady and at such a difficult time in her life. Had they no sense of honor, of decency?

Treyton Blanchard left, informing Mrs. Campbell that he would no longer consider himself a regular guest at the White House.

She pressed him, and I heard his parting words. "It has become apparent that my own aspirations conflict with your agenda. It no longer behooves me to keep company with you or with your husband."

He added: "With that in mind, my family and I will not be present at the opening ceremonies tomorrow."

"Treyton," Mrs. Campbell said.

"Good night, Elaine. I hope you sleep well believing your goals and dreams are superior to those of the rest of us."

Whispering, Cyan made a face. "Well, I guess we know what the next primary race will look like."

In a rush I could see it play out: Treyton Blanchard would indeed make a run for the presidency. And if I were any judge of character, I believed he'd start the process sooner rather than later.

The jerk. Whether he cared or not, Senator Blanchard had just lost my vote. Permanently.

THE RED ROOM WAS NOT DIRECTLY ON OUR way back downstairs, but I pulled Cyan with me to see how great the gingerbread house looked in its setting.

Kendra and her assistants were there, adding liquid to the champagne fountain.

Cyan stepped closer to the tall device, which sloshed

when two assistants inched it closer to the wall. "Is that champagne in it now?"

Kendra laughed. "No, just water. I added a couple of gallons for testing. The reception starts at noon sharp and we don't want anything to go wrong."

Cyan and I were about to leave when Kendra called us to wait. "This is the first time I'm using this fountain," she said. "We just took delivery on this one. Want to see it in motion?"

Since we were done for the night, I said, "Sure."

Kendra looked like a little kid ready to blow out birthday candles.

The two assistants had pushed the fountain into place and one stood aside, ready to turn it on. "Should we lower the lights?" I asked.

Before she could answer, the assistant plugged in the fountain and Kendra leaned forward, fingering the switch. "I'm excited," she said. "This one is bigger than the one we had before."

She turned it on.

A loud rumble heralded the upsurge.

With a screeching rush, water shot high toward the ceiling, like an erupting volcano.

"Aaaack!" we all cried at once, lifting our arms above our heads. Water fell down on us all, a hard and fast rain.

The assistants ducked. Cyan cried out and turned away. Mouth open, Kendra was aghast. And dripping wet.

"Turn it off," I said, reaching for the switch.

Kendra beat me to it. One second later, the rain ceased.

"What the hell was that?" she asked.

"Look at the drapes," I said. "Can we get someone in here to clean these up?"

Cyan's red hair looked like a shiny helmet. "I'll get housekeeping," she said. And she was off.

Kendra held a hand to her mouth, surveying the sad scene.

My next worry was for Marcel's gingerbread house. Fortunately, however, it was far enough away that it missed the sudden rain shower. "Thank goodness the fountain only had a couple of gallons in it," I said.

"What's wrong with this thing?" she asked.

I had no answer. "Good thing you tested it tonight."

With a forlorn look around the room, she nodded. "This could have been a whole lot worse tomorrow." She closed her eyes. "Champagne can get sticky."

"This really isn't too bad," I said. "I think we bore the brunt of it. Look, the furniture didn't even get winged."

"You're trying to make me feel better," she said. "But what am I going to do for a fountain? It's too late to get a new one at this juncture."

Manny showed up just then. "What's going on?" he asked.

Kendra explained and he seemed to take it all in stride. As I left them, I heard him say, "I'll get this fixed in no time."

CHAPTER 21

"TODAY'S THE BIG DAY," BUCKY SAID UNNECES-
sarily when he arrived the next morning at six. "What time
did you get in?"

"Four," I said.

He whistled. "I thought you said we were all caught up."

I gave a so-so motion with my head. "We are. In fact
we're in great shape. I just . . ." I shrugged, unwilling to
share my feelings with Bucky. Give him an inch and he'd
probably take the opportunity to ask if I'd come in early to
sniff for bombs. I wasn't in the mood for his special brand
of humor today. "I just like mornings here."

"Me, too," he said, surprising me with the sudden far-
away expression on his face. "There's something impossible to describe about this place, isn't there?" As he tied an
apron around his waist, he granted me one of his rare
smiles. "Like knowing there's endless potential here. Like
knowing we can make a difference."

Bucky never ceased to baffle me. One minute he would

crab at nothing, the next he'd echo the very same protec-
tiveness I felt about the White House.

"Exactly," I said.

He walked over to the computer and wiggled the mouse,
bringing the monitor back to life. "What's the final count
for today?"

I told him.

He whistled again. "What were they thinking when they
invited so many?"

"Remember, this is a combined event. Everyone from
Sunday's cancellation and all of today's invited guests as
well."

"Still," he said, annoyance edging back into his voice.
"We're going to be working our tails off to keep the food
going with that many hungry people."

"Thank goodness it's just finger food today."

"But you'll be upstairs for the photo-op, won't you?"

I'd almost forgotten about that. "Yeah. Marcel, too."

"Great," he said. "Just what we need—to be short-
handed down here when we're expecting a full house."

Ah . . . cranky Bucky. We were back to normal.

I didn't bother to respond, and minutes later the rest of
the crew trooped in. In short order, we were going full
force, producing attractive and delicious hors d'oeuvres for
today's crowd to enjoy. There was almost no sound in the
room as the clock struck the next hour . . . and the next.

After we sent Mrs. Campbell's breakfast to the residence, I stole up to the first floor with Marcel to get another
look at where the press conference would be held. "I do not
appreciate the way they have been moving my house
around," he said as we headed up the steps. "They can easily break it, and then where would we be?"

"They moved it?" I asked.

"Yes," he said. "They tell me this is a better location for crowd control." He sniffed.

"Maybe it would be better to display it in the State Dining Room after all," I said, trying to sound encouraging. "The photographers would have more room to maneuver and get better pictures."

"This, unfortunately, is not my decision."

"No matter where it's displayed, your gingerbread house will undoubtedly be the center of attention."

He acknowledged the compliment in his customary way. "Very true," he said, "but I still believe that the house should not be moved as often as it has been. We placed it properly and that is where it should remain."

When we made it to the Red Room, we were both surprised to find the gingerbread house against the east wall. "Where's the fountain?" I asked, turning in a circle to look for it.

Marcel wasn't paying me much attention. "Look at what they have done," he said, pointing to the house's back corner. "The clumsy fools!"

I rose to tiptoes to peer where he was pointing. "I don't see anything wrong."

"I took great care to cover the wiring with special décor," he said, huffing. Tugging his tunic, he straightened and informed me that he would see to repairs at once.

The moment he was gone, I looked again. A small green wire winding around the back of the structure had poked out from the white, snowy groundcover. Unless you were looking for it, it could easily go unnoticed. But Marcel was a perfectionist. As were we all around here.

I poked into the Blue Room and into the State Dining Room, but saw no sign of yesterday's gusher. I knew that was not my concern; I needed to worry about providing food for our guests, making sure whatever we served was properly hot or cold, and ready to go precisely when the guests were shown to the State Dining Room. Marcel would accept accolades for his gingerbread creation and I would be expected to discuss the items we planned to serve today and for all other events throughout the holidays.

This would be my first Christmas talk to the media. Henry had always handled these and he'd told me they were a piece of cake—sometimes literally. Just as sweet and easy to enjoy. But nervous flutters danced in my stomach and I doubted I could handle any sort of cake right now. Having it or eating it.

I hadn't noticed the gingerbread men when Marcel and I were in the Red Room, because I'd been first taken aback by the fact that the house had been moved, and then my attention had been further drawn by Marcel's concerns about the visible wire.

Yi-im was back, evidently having been dispatched to make Marcel's repairs. He nodded to me as I came in. "See?" he said, pointing to the three Blanchard gingerbread men. They were positioned on the wall just above the gingerbread house, each of them connected to the house by means of a stick that resembled the little poles on the structure's corners. I was amazed yet again by the quality of the workmanship.

"This looks great," I said. "Thank you."

Even though I'd asked Yi-im to make sure the kids' creations were placed properly, I was no longer sure it mattered that they sat in such a place of honor. With Blanchard's pronouncement that he would no longer visit the White House, the pretty little decorations weren't doing that much good now.

As I inched to take a closer look at the piece, Yi-im

moved me away. "Marcel say no one come close. Only me."

Annoyed, I stepped back, although I understood the mind-set. Fewer people messing with Marcel's handiwork meant fewer chances for things to go wrong. I stepped back, hands up. "You're the boss."

He grinned, showing teeth. "Yeah. I boss today."

Kendra's heels clipped at a brisk pace, and I heard her call out instructions to her staff even before she walked in from the adjacent Blue Room. "Ollie," she said. "Ready for the cameras?" A quick look at her watch. "Just a couple of hours away from the big unveiling."

"Ready as I can be," I said.

She pulled a tight breath in between her teeth and gave a mock shiver. "I always get so nervous right before a big event. Really, you'd think this was my first time doing this, wouldn't you? But what a feat we've pulled off, huh?"

"What happened to the fountain?" I asked.

"That electrician said he couldn't fix it where it was, so he took it downstairs to the shop. Last I heard there was nothing they could do to get it in place on time. I ordered a replacement, but that's not here yet either." Her smile wilted. "Looks like we're going fountainless, after all."

"What a shame," I said.

She leaned in toward me. "To be honest, I was having nightmares about splashing and spillage. This may be a blessing in disguise."

About an hour later, I was checking on early lunch preparation down in the staff cafeteria when I happened upon Curly working on the very fountain Kendra and I had discussed.

He was on his hands and knees looking up into the underside of the contraption, scowling, as usual. I thought he looked like a little boy sent to sit under a table for punishment.

"What are you doing?" I asked.

He didn't acknowledge me.

I crouched next to him. "I thought Manny was fixing this."

"You are a nosy thing, aren't you?" he asked, his voice breathless as he rearranged himself to sit. I saw why in a moment. The new position allowed him freedom to lift his hands over his head and access the fountain's inner workings.

Nonplussed, I scooted forward until I could see underneath as well. "I didn't realize this was all one piece," I said.

He brought his hands down. "What the hell do you want with me?"

"You really want to know?"

"You've been dancing around, pointing your finger at me since Gene got himself killed," he said. "You trying to get me to say it was my fault?"

"No, I—"

"Because it wasn't my fault."

"I never thought it was."

"You don't know a socket from a volt ohmmeter," he said. "How the hell can you come to me and start asking me about electrical problems? You think I'm glad Gene got killed? You think I wanted his job? You think I arranged that?" Spittle formed at the corners of his mouth and, despite being in a confined space, he gestured wildly.

"No, of course not," I said.

He mumbled to himself, looked away, and began working over his head again. Then as though he just thought of something, he tapped the fountain's underside. "You were there when this thing broke down, weren't you?"

"Yes," I said slowly.

"And you swear you saw this thing shoot water to the ceiling."

"Just short of the ceiling."

"But you swear you saw it."

"Yes, I saw it."

"Well, there ain't nothing wrong with this here fountain," he said. "What kind of game are you playing, anyway?" he asked. "What do you want from me?"

"All I ever wanted from you," I said in a clear voice, "was to answer one question. And before you shut me up again, here it is: A friend I trust has been an electrician for more than fifty years. He told me that more than one expert has been killed by floating neutrals. We had that storm the day of Gene's accident, remember? My friend just suggested I ask you to check to make sure the White House is safe. All I ever wanted from you was to make sure the house was safe. Okay?"

Angry now, I stood and didn't intend to look back before I left him sitting under the fountain. But I did look back and was immediately sorry. Though not directed at me, the intensity of his furious gaze nearly made me miss a step.

CHAPTER 22

BINDY WAS WAITING FOR ME IN THE KITCHEN when I arrived.

"Are they there?" she asked me.

I didn't understand. "Are who where?"

Behind her, Bucky rolled his eyes. "We have a lot of work to do here," he admonished. "I hope you're not planning to stay long."

Bindy's face reddened. "I'm sorry to bother you. I just felt as though I needed to make sure. They've closed off the upstairs to everyone until noon." She looked at her watch. "But I promised Treyton I'd double-check on the placement of his kids' gingerbread men."

Senator Blanchard had very clearly washed his hands of the White House—at least until he himself could call the place home. There was no mistaking that, after last night's arguments. Bindy was apparently far out of the loop. "Maybe there's something you ought to know," I said. "Give me a minute here and we'll talk, okay?"

I went around to the computer where I checked my schedule, to ensure we weren't running behind.

Bindy watched as I took turns to speak with each of the chefs. My first duty was to make sure that the kitchen produced the quality edibles we were known for, so I didn't skimp on any of my questions. Nor did I harbor any fondness for Bindy's boss. Let her wait.

"I'll be out in the hall," she said when Cyan pulled me back toward the storage area.

"Thank goodness," I said under my breath.

Agda smiled and asked us to move out of her way as she slid a tray of petit-fours into the large stainless steel refrigerator.

I kept my voice low. "Can you believe she's still bugging me about those gingerbread men?"

"Give it a rest, girl," Cyan said. "Did you tell her they're safe and sound in their place of honor?" She shook her head, then turned the subject back to our current concerns. "Whatever. I've got a slight change to the design we decided on for the lobster cake appetizer."

She was about to reach into the same refrigerator Agda was using when the taller woman tilted her head and closed the door. "Pretty men?" she asked us.

We both looked at her, not understanding.

The blonde bombshell pulled her lips in as though trying to decide how to word what she wanted to convey. She held up three fingers. "Gingerbread from box?" she asked.

I remembered that Agda had been there when we received the three additions from the Blanchard family. I nodded. "Yes."

"Very pretty," she said again.

With Bindy waiting for me out in the hall and several thousand appetizers waiting for my approval in the next room, I was eager to put an end to this not-so-scintillating conversation. "They truly are," I said, eager to see the change Cyan wanted to show me.

Agda put her hand on my arm. "They are broken?"

"No," I said. "Last I looked, they were upstairs."

She shook her head. "Yi-im," she said, pronouncing his name Yim instead of Yee-eem. "He is fixing them, no?"

Now I was totally confused. "No. No one is fixing them. They're upstairs." I asked Cyan, "When did you last see them?"

She thought about it. "This morning. Yeah. All three were there. They looked fine to me."

"And I saw them about an hour ago," I said. I'd hate to think that one of them fell off their little posts. I turned to Agda. "Did one of them fall?"

She held up her hands in the universal language of "I don't know." Biting her lip before she spoke again, she said, "Yi-im tell me to shh." She placed a finger over her lips. "He say he break it, he fix it."

"When was this?" I asked.

Her big eyes moved up and to the left. "Eight o'clock, at night."

"Yesterday?"

She nodded.

"Wow, that's pretty specific," I said.

She may not have understood my surprised reaction, but she must have understood my meaning. "I have couple minutes before I go home last night," she said. "I want to see White House upstairs. Yi-im say, 'Shhh.' "

"You asked him about it?"

"Yah. He say he fixing." She tilted her head. "Fixing all three."

With Agda and Yi-im and their combined broken English,

I couldn't begin to guess what either of them really meant. I rubbed my eyes. The last thing we needed was another loose end. "Maybe I should go check," I said.

Cyan gave me a look. "And what will you tell Bindy if one of her precious decorations is broken?"

I was already moving back into the main part of the kitchen with a plan to keep Bindy at bay. "Maybe she doesn't have to know."

She was pacing the Center Hall when I returned. "Took you long enough," she said.

I swallowed my annoyance at her snippy remark, deciding instead to go on the offensive. "I don't know why you even care about these gingerbread men anymore."

"I told you that Senator Blanchard was very eager to have his children's—"

"What difference does it make if he and his family aren't coming today?"

When her jaw dropped just a little, I realized she really hadn't been brought up to speed.

"Bindy," I said. "I am not one to tell stories out of school, but I have the distinct impression that Senator Blanchard is intent on severing his ties with the White House. And I have it on good authority that he is boycotting today's event. Or didn't you get the memo?"

That one struck a nerve. She pulled her shoulders back. "I spoke with Senator Blanchard just before I came here. And he told me to make sure everything was still in place for the photo-op. That's why I came. To make sure the kids' men are where they can be seen."

Blanchard must have had a change of heart, I thought. But he'd made things perfectly clear to Mrs. Campbell yesterday. I wondered what had changed, why his bitterness had suddenly made the leap to good sense.

I sighed. "I'll be the first to admit that plans change here faster than a collapsing soufflé. But I can't take you upstairs."

"Can you just go check and report back to me?"

Did she think I had nothing better to do than to double-check her boss's whims? I bit the sides of my cheeks to keep from a snappy retort. I knew the relationship between Mrs. Campbell and Senator Blanchard was on shaky ground today. Perhaps it wouldn't hurt for me to just take a peek and give her an update.

"Wait here."

I took the steps two at a time and turned left when I made it to the top. Crossing the Entrance Hall, I hurried past the tall pillars toward the Red Room, my soft-soled shoes making tiny squeaks on the shiny floor. There were photographers in all the public rooms. They'd been granted early access in order to set up. Big, shiny, white flash umbrellas decorated each corner, and bright spotlights were clicked on and off, as light meters were tested.

Despite the fact that I couldn't wait for Bindy to be gone and out of my hair, I stole a quick peek into the Blue Room where the Fraser fir stood, decked out in all its glory. Just like the rest of the house, the lights that decorated it were unlit. Everything had been tested as it had been installed. But the holiday season wouldn't begin until noon when the First Lady threw the switch.

In the Red Room, Marcel had an icing bag in his right hand, a tiny trowel in his left, and a panicked look on his face. "They have ruined it," he said.

"What?" I asked. "Where?"

"*Ici*," he said, pointing. "Again, I have found a piece that should not be open to the eye. This should have been covered earlier."

The flaw Marcel spoke of was another wire appearance. This time the wire was gray, and attached to the back of the structure. "Maybe when Yi-im was fixing the gingerbread men," I said, "he bumped it and the icing fell off?"

"Fixing what gingerbread men?"

The fear on Marcel's face made me sorry I'd said anything.

"Oh," I stammered. "Maybe I'm wrong. One of my chefs said . . ."

I purposely let the thought hang as I moved closer to inspect the three gingerbread men perched just above the cookie White House. Not one of them looked marred in any way. Perhaps Agda had been mistaken. Perhaps Yi-im had been working on other gingerbread men. They were all certainly fragile.

"I guess Agda meant different gingerbread men," I said. "She told me some were broken."

"And thank heaven for that," Marcel said with spirit. "Some of them were . . . *exécrable*, and I would be ashamed to show them to the public. Even if they are made by children in America, we must always strive for the best display we can manage."

Personally, I thought Marcel was missing the point of the exercise, but I kept quiet. Scrutinizing the decorations, I tried to see if I could find any evidence of them having been repaired.

Marcel was so intent on his own repairs that he no longer paid me any mind.

Each of the three men sat perched atop a pole. None of the poles had cracks or anything visibly wrong with them. I remembered being impressed with the gingerbread men because each held a tiny flag made out of sugar. Even these delicate details looked to be perfect.

"These are supposed to light up, too?" I asked, pointing to the three men.

Marcel gave me a brief glance. "No," he said. "Only the house is to light. And these poles." He pointed vaguely in the direction of a corner of the building. "You remember? The sparklers. We have added more for effect."

They certainly had. In addition to the three poles attached to the Blanchard gingerbread men, there were several additional ones along the side and back of the White House itself. I could only imagine what a beautiful background it would make for the house when the creation was officially lit this afternoon. I selfishly wished they'd had them in place when we'd tested it earlier.

But I would see it later. One of the nicest things about being executive chef was the fact that I was not only welcome, but featured, at many of these official events.

"Okay, thanks," I said. "Good luck with your repairs."

Marcel grunted.

WITH BINDY FINALLY GONE—PLEASED WITH the knowledge that her boss's kids' artwork was in place— and the last of the hors d'oeuvres complete, all we had to do now was wait. In twenty minutes, one of the assistants would come down to escort me upstairs for the media event.

I checked my watch for the fifteenth time in the space of twelve seconds.

"Nervous, Ollie?" Cyan asked.

I pretended not to hear her. The last thing I needed was to endure the well-intentioned jibes of my coworkers while I was fighting off butterflies in my gut.

"Agda," I said, trying to divert everyone's attention.

"I checked those gingerbread men upstairs. None of them were broken."

Her brows came together in a puzzled look. "Yah," she said. "All three broken."

"Not the ones from the Blanchard family," I said patiently.

Her perplexed frown grew tighter. "Yah," she said again, with feeling. "Three from box."

As luck would have it, Marcel walked in just then. "Ask him," I said to Agda. "He and I both checked the gingerbread men. There's nothing wrong with any of them."

She seemed so miserable to be wrong, that I added, brightly, "It must have been some of the others," I said.

"No." She gave me the most direct look she had since she'd begun working here. "I see him fix *två*." She stabbed three fingers into the air for emphasis.

"What is wrong?" Marcel asked, glancing from one of us to the other. "Something is amiss?"

I explained, but even as I began, Marcel shook his head. "Once we installed the three gingerbread men above the house, they were not to be moved," he said. "Yi-im knew this. He would not move them."

Agda's lips were tight and her entire being seemed to reverberate with tense frustration. I rested the tips of my fingers against her forearm. "I believe you saw him fixing gingerbread men," I said. "But the three from the Blanchard family—from the box—are looking great." I didn't reiterate that they'd never been broken. I just wanted to put this matter to rest. In the large scheme of things—with an event the size of which we would be working today—this was nothing. "What's important now is that there are only about ten minutes to go before the ceremonies begin, and everything is perfect."

The words hadn't left my mouth before one of the assistants, Faber, appeared in the doorway. "Five minutes."

Marcel and I didn't waste another moment. "Bucky, come on," I said, inviting him to join us. "I'd like you to be part of this, too."

Pleased, he hurried along with us to don clean jackets—crisp, white, recently pressed—and our tall toques. While we kept them here in the kitchen for occasional use, we *always* wore them for media events. I liked the fact that wearing one made me seem taller.

Marcel was repeating things to himself in a low voice.

"What are you doing?" I asked.

With an abashed look, he whispered, "I am trying to remember key words to respond when the First Lady asks me the questions."

He and I had been provided with scripts, ahead of time. Nothing in them was difficult or unusual, but I understood his discomposure. We were supposed to recite from our prepared scripts, but make it look conversational. Sure. Get in front of the cameras and all memorization, all practice, goes out the window.

I'd surprised Bucky by inviting him to participate with me. My intention was not to make him eat his words about being left shorthanded in the kitchen but to foster a sense of inclusion. Henry was my idol where that talent was concerned, and I was eager to prove myself a worthy pupil. As my second-in-command, Bucky wasn't likely to be called upon to answer any questions on camera. But you never could completely predict these things.

Bucky's eyes were wild as he straightened and re-straightened his white jacket. "Do I look okay?" he asked.

"You look great," I said. And it was true. Though he and I occasionally bumped heads and ideas in the kitchen, we had a mutual respect and I was, if not glad, then resigned to the fact that he would always be part of our crew. No doubt about it: In the kitchen, he was an asset. Unfortunately, he was also a pain in mine.

"Where's Yi-im?" I asked Marcel. "Didn't he want to be part of this? He's done so much lately."

Marcel wagged his head sadly. "He has taken ill."

I'd seen him this morning, and he'd looked fine to me. I said so.

Marcel gave a very French shrug. "What can I say? He tells me he is sick; I have to believe him. We do not want germs on our precious creations."

"That's true."

Faber led the three of us up, using the stairs closest to the usher's office. I felt the nervous jitters myself and I, too, started to rehearse my lines for when the First Lady would ask about menu preparations.

On our way up, we met Curly coming down. Looking a lot like an angry bulldog, he seemed not to even notice us until we passed him. But then he grabbed my arm and looked directly into my face. "You seen Manny?" he asked.

"No," I said wiggling my arm to dislodge his hand. But he held fast.

Faber cleared his throat. "We are on our way to the official opening—"

"I know where the hell you're headed," he said, his voice a growl that matched the bulldog visage to perfection. The long, pinched scar throbbed red. "But since you're always chasing after Manny and Vince, I figured you'd know where they are. It's the last minute before everything goes hot and they ain't anywhere."

Although he let go of my arm, he stood right in front of me, blocking my passage.

"So I'll ask you again," Curly said. "Where are they?"

Faber stood two steps higher than I did. "Ms. Paras," he said, meekly. "It's almost time."

"I don't know what your problem is, Curly," I said. "But I have a commitment and I believe in doing my job. Maybe it's time you started doing yours."

His face whitened even as his scar burned crimson. I stepped around him, shaken by the altercation. With Gene around all these years, I'd never had to deal with Curly directly before—at least, not so often. I sincerely hoped Paul would not see fit to promote him from "acting" to "permanent" chief electrician.

When we finally got upstairs, I was blown away by the number of people. Sure, we'd been given a list and a headcount, but it's one thing to expect a specific number of guests, and another to see them up close. On paper, and during planning, it's abstract. Here, it was very real. Warm, close, sweaty real. Hundreds of milling folks. Mostly Capitol Hill types, media moguls, and their families.

The holiday opening was, indeed, one of the more family-friendly events the White House threw each year and I was pleased to see so many little ones in attendance.

Camera crews behaved themselves, maintaining the decorum prescribed to them by social secretary, Marguerite Schumacher. She was on hand, of course, overseeing every minute detail. This was her moment, as well as Kendra's. The two had worked side-by-side with the First Lady to create the rich, warm, welcoming festival that was the official beginning of the White House holiday season.

Faber led us through a cordoned-off walkway where Marcel, Bucky, and I were directed to stand. He waited with us, one hand low, keeping us behind the ropes, until one of the other ushers nodded. Continuing along the cordoned-off path, we smiled at the reporters, who lobbed questions at us as we passed.

All three of us nodded, looking as happy and content as possible. We knew that we were not to answer any questions directly. The only time we were to speak to the reporters was in the Red Room, and only when we were addressed by the First Lady.

Marcel stood to the right of the gingerbread house. I stood to its left, with Bucky next to me. Had Yi-im been here, he would have taken my position, and Bucky and I would have stood a bit farther away. Photo-op-wise, however, it looked better to have the house flanked by two chefs. Symmetry and all that.

The crowd was currently enraptured by the show in the Blue Room behind us, while we waited, practically standing at attention. I twisted to peer into the next room, to watch the delight wash over the faces of the kids and the adults when the marvelous White House tree was lit.

I stifled a sigh. Marcel shifted his weight and adjusted his neckline.

We waited.

In the next room, the First Lady was answering questions. I could just make out her words, high and clear over the crowd sounds. The tree hadn't yet been lit, and she was explaining the logic behind this year's theme, and how she, Marguerite, and Kendra had worked together for nearly half a year, planning the celebration. Mrs. Campbell was effusive with praise for her social secretary and florist.

I let my gaze wander toward the First Lady.

In the doorway that connected the Red Room to the Blue Room, I spied a familiar face. Little Treyton Blanchard, the senator's oldest son, peeked around the corner.

He smiled when he saw me, and gave a quick wave. I waved back. His mother, with her back to us, didn't notice.

Bindy was right, after all. I guess the temptation of seeing her children's creations up close and personal when the world got its first look was too much for Mrs. Blanchard to pass up.

Little Trey broke away from his mother and made his way over, all smiles. He pointed. "Those are ours," he said, with more than a little pride.

"They sure are," I said in a soft voice as I bent down to talk with him. "I bet you're glad now that you made them."

He gave me a face that looked out of place in someone so young. Cynical and amused. "We didn't really make those," he said, inching closer. "But we helped a little bit. I helped the most."

"I had a feeling you did."

Mrs. Blanchard had turned around to look for her son. When she saw him talking with me, she came over, carrying the youngest Blanchard on her hip, the middle one toddling behind. "I'm so sorry," she said in a stage whisper. "I hope he hasn't been bothering you."

Her eyes raked the gingerbread house and her gaze settled on the three gingerbread men just above it.

"Not at all," I said.

The murmurs in the other room grew, perhaps in response to one of the First Lady's comments. Maryann Blanchard shot a nervous glance back to the Blue Room. "My husband didn't want us to come today," she said, with a guilty smile, "but I couldn't bear to miss this opportunity." She shifted little Leah in her arms and spoke to the children. "Do you see?" she asked them. "Look!"

Pointing with her free hand, she indicated the three

gingerbread men. "You made those, and now the president of the United States is using them to decorate his house for Christmas." The woman positively glowed. "Isn't that great?"

John, the middle child, stepped back to see better. "Can't we take them home to our house?"

Maryann Blanchard shook her head. "We made these as gifts. It's like giving your country a Christmas present."

John looked unimpressed. Leah sucked her thumb and rested her head on her mother's shoulder. Only the oldest, Trey, had anything to say. "I wish I would've worked harder on it."

She patted him on the head. "You did a wonderful job."

From the sounds of things, the tree in the Blue Room was about to be lit. "Come on," Maryann Blanchard said to her brood, "we don't want to miss this."

I smiled after them. The three kids were nowhere near as impressed with the White House as their mother was, but I supposed someday they could tell their own kids about being featured. Of course, if their father had any say in the matter, after the next election, they'd be living here themselves.

I would have loved to watch the tree-lighting ceremony, but it was my duty to stay put, to be ready for my turn to talk to the country about the small part I played in bringing the holidays to the president's home.

The next room quieted, and someone lowered the room's lights. A hush settled over the onlookers and even the reporters assigned to this room craned their necks to see.

I tried peering over the tops of the guests' heads but had no luck.

After a prolonged silence, the room next door lit up, and everyone broke into spontaneous applause.

My heart pounded. Both because it was our turn next and because I was so proud of all we'd accomplished. Not just Marcel and I, not just the crew in the kitchen, but all of us. The country had been under siege—both from terrorists and economically—for an extended period of time. Those on the right side of the Senate aisle and their counterparts on the left could not agree on even the simplest matters, and pundits were having a field day.

These few weeks in the White House gave us all a respite. A time when we could just be together as citizens of this great country. A time for all of us to take a moment and reflect on the goodness that we all share. Whether we celebrated Christmas, Hanukkah, Kwanzaa—all of them, or none of them—we were doing so together.

Bindy appeared at the doorway to the Red Room, her hair blown back from her face, and her cheeks bright red, looking as though she'd run all the way from the East Appointment Gate. She scanned the room, one hand gripping the door frame, as though it was difficult to hold herself up. When she saw me, her expression changed. I would have characterized it as panicked. "Ollie, where are they?"

I had no doubt who she meant. I pointed. "In the Blue—"

She didn't wait for me to finish. Bolting away, she spied little John Blanchard and grabbed him by the arm. He protested loudly.

Maryann Blanchard turned, as though to admonish her son, then saw Bindy standing there. "What are you—?"

"We have to go," Bindy said.

I'd left my position next to the gingerbread house to follow. "What's going on?"

Bindy ignored me.

Mrs. Blanchard shook her head and answered the assistant. "The tour isn't over yet." She tugged John closer.

"Your husband wants you home," Bindy said. "Now."

That got Maryann Blanchard's back up. I watched fire light her eyes. "Oh really? Well, you can tell him that no matter what his quarrel is with the White House, I am not giving up the chance to have my children photographed at this event."

Bindy shook her head, and pulled Mrs. Blanchard's elbow. She spoke softly. "You don't understand," she said, her nervous giggle making its appearance. This time it sounded almost like a hiccup. "It's an emergency."

Mrs. Blanchard's eyes clouded. "What happened?"

"Come with me. Please."

"Mommy, I don't want to go," Trey said. "We haven't got our pictures taken yet."

Bindy's gaze floated toward the three gingerbread men, then back to Mrs. Blanchard. "We have to go. Now." She squeezed John's arm and he cried out. "I'm not kidding. You've got to listen to me."

The crowd around Mrs. Blanchard had begun to notice the minor fracas, and Mrs. Blanchard noticed them. Reluctantly gathering her children and shushing their complaints, she followed Bindy out the door. As soon as they were gone, the onlookers returned their attention to the question-and-answer session going on under the Blue Room's spotlights.

I returned to my post, and tried to process what just happened.

"What was that all about?" Bucky asked.

Marcel snorted. "Who can understand such females as these? You remember how Bindy behaved when she worked here. Always too impressionable."

Marcel was right. She'd been an unpredictable and often

unstable staffer. I'd harbored hope that this new position, working for the senator, would have settled her down.

Senator Blanchard was apparently still angry enough at Mrs. Campbell that the very idea of his family being here appalled him. I didn't for one minute buy Bindy's excuse of an emergency. I'd seen the lie flit across her face as she grasped for a reason to persuade Mrs. Blanchard to leave the premises.

Bindy had been manic in her demeanor. Frantic, actually.

I looked up when Gav appeared in the doorway. Keeping one eye on the festivities next door, he sauntered over and spoke softly, close to my ear.

"This is not for public distribution," he said.

He waited till I leaned back and met his eyes. "Okay."

Bucky was close enough to listen in. At Gav's glare, he stepped a few feet away.

Gav whispered, "Sean Baxter didn't commit suicide."

I jerked away from him, looking again into his face. Although in my gut I'd known that to be true, it was far different to hear someone in authority say the words. "Who killed him?" I asked.

He shook his head. "We don't know yet."

"But they know for sure it wasn't suicide?"

He nodded. "And I checked that other rumor you asked me about."

"About Nick Volkov?"

"He didn't kill Mr. Sinclair," he said. "But someone has gone to a lot of trouble to make it look like he did."

"What does that mean?"

Gav gave a slight headshake. "Tell you more later. For now, just be aware."

Like a ghost, he slid away.

Be aware? Of what? I wondered.

Bucky moved to stand next to me again just as the group began to filter into the Red Room. This was it: my time to shine. But I couldn't feel the joy. Something was holding me back. A tight, annoying prickle told me something wasn't quite right.

Cameras were set up and the First Lady was led to her spot just in front of the gingerbread house. It was then I realized that I was standing next to the switch. Mrs. Campbell would have to get in close to me in order to turn it on. Which meant I would have to move when the time came. A perfect photo opportunity, with the pastry chef on one side and the First Lady on the other. Whoever had plotted this out had vision.

Too bad poor Yi-im had gone home sick. If he'd been standing right here, he'd have been in the picture, too.

A feeling prickled the back of my arms and creeped across my shoulder blades.

I stole a look at the three gingerbread men the Blanchard family had insisted we place prominently in this room. The three men that, according to Agda, Yi-im had supposedly been "fixing" late last night.

I'd convinced myself she'd been mistaken in her observation. But . . . why had I made that assumption? Agda had been the personification of precision since we'd hired her. And for some reason, I'd chosen to doubt her when it came to Yi-im.

Yi-im, a "lazy man" by Jackson's standards, who'd maneuvered his way into the pastry kitchen, even though he'd been hired as a butler.

I shook my head and paid attention to the ceremony.

Mrs. Campbell was wearing a black skirt suit, with no festive adornment whatsoever. Although she smiled as she took up her position next to Marcel, I knew from the look in her eyes that she couldn't wait for this tour to be over. But we'd all worked so hard, and I knew she wouldn't want to disappoint our nation's citizens.

I thought about the dysfunctional champagne fountain. I wondered if anyone even missed it.

My mind flashed—a quick recollection—Curly sitting under the fountain, proclaiming nothing wrong with the device.

And yet it had blown water to the ceiling when activated in this room.

Here.

I swallowed.

The gingerbread house was exactly where the champagne fountain once stood.

Marcel nodded in answer to a question Mrs. Campbell posed. I hadn't paid attention, but forced myself to refocus.

"And this only took you two weeks?" Mrs. Campbell said. "I don't think I could create something this beautiful in a year."

A titter of polite laughter from the audience. Marcel nodded again. "Thank you."

I leaned back and peeked behind the skirted table, hoping no one would notice me. In order to get the gingerbread house to light up at just the perfect time, it had been plugged in—into two separate outlets that would work together, to light up both the inside and the outside of the structure.

These were the same two outlets the fountain had been plugged into before. Two outlets. Just like the two sockets that Stanley had shown me.

Blood rushed from my face to my feet. Bucky sidled closer. "Hang in there."

I caught sight of Gav, watching everything from a far corner of the room, and thought about the real bomb that only he and I knew about. He gave me a funny look and I remembered, suddenly, Tom's one-on-one lesson. He'd told me that explosives could take almost any shape. He'd shown me pictures. I thought about Gav's training session with the simulated bomb in the presidential seal. I'd screwed that up because I hadn't noticed the wires. If only I'd seen . . .

The wires.

I twisted my head. The Blanchard gingerbread men.

"My God," I said, finally piecing everything together.

Mrs. Campbell started toward me—toward the switch.

Frozen by wild terror, I couldn't move. Bucky tugged at my elbow, urging me to step away.

"No," I said to him. "I think . . ."

It couldn't be. Could it? I stared at the gingerbread men again.

Bucky's teeth were clenched. "Ollie, come on."

Mrs. Campbell gave me an uncomfortable smile as she shoehorned her way between me and the house.

"And our theme this year wouldn't be complete without Marcel's masterpiece, an absolutely magnificent reproduction of the White House." Mrs. Campbell smiled, shooting me a look of confusion. I still hadn't moved. "I give you our holiday theme and invite you all to enjoy . . . 'Together we celebrate—Welcome Home.' " Her finger skimmed the switch.

"No!" I shouted, pushing her away from the table. I dove beneath the skirting and grabbed at the cords—one in each hand. They pulled free from the outlet with more ease than I expected, which sent me tumbling backward, dragging the tabletop with me.

Its base upset, the gingerbread house tilted for a crazed, breathless moment, then slid away, crashing onto the floor behind me, into a million tiny crumbles.

"*Sacre bleu!*" Marcel screamed. "Olivia, what have you done?" I peered out from under the skirting, flipping the fabric up to see him holding his head in his hands, a disbelieving, furious expression on his face.

I sat on the floor, looking up at Mrs. Campbell, who stared down at me for a long moment, her hands over her mouth.

I was vaguely aware of incessant clicking, of hundreds of flashes, as the photographers captured my moment of shame for all posterity.

Gav had moved in, as had a crew of Secret Service personnel. "That's enough. Everyone out."

As reporters and others plied them with questions, I heard the repeated refrain: "We will issue a statement later. No questions now."

I hung my head and sat under the table, with Marcel sobbing behind me, and Bucky shuffling through the broken pieces of house that littered the floor. "You sure did it this time, Ace," he said.

I looked up. "Thanks."

Mrs. Campbell had been whisked away by her protection detail, and I was surrounded by Secret Service who didn't wear happy-to-see-me looks.

Gav broke through their perimeter. "What happened?"

Now that I needed to put it into words, I hesitated. What if I was wrong?

I pointed to the gingerbread men that had tumbled to the ground along with the house. Not one of them had broken. "I think there might be plastic explosives in those," I said.

One of the agents behind Gav rolled his eyes, but Gav picked one up.

I bit my bottom lip. "And I think those two outlets have a floating neutral."

"A what?"

I explained, realizing how ridiculous everything sounded when spoken aloud. "If there is a floating neutral, then the gingerbread house would have gotten too much voltage," I said. "There are sparklers—little pyrotechnic things that Marcel added—but I think his assistant added more." I licked my lips, my voice cracking under the pressure. "If the voltage would have hit . . . Well, I don't know what would have happened."

Before I'd finished my explanation, Gav had picked up one of the three Blanchard gingerbread men. His brow furrowed as he examined the back of the decoration. "I don't see anything—"

My heart dropped. I'd be sacked for sure this time.

"Wait," he said, turning the design around to the front. To one of the other agents, he said, "Get Morton up here."

"What is it?" I asked.

The agents around me had relaxed their positions a little. They'd taken the weeping Marcel away. Bucky had asked to stay but had been sent back downstairs.

Gav shook his head. Within moments a burly man wearing body armor arrived. Morton. Gav handed him all three gingerbread men to examine.

"Don't feel like standing up yet, do you?" Gav asked me.

I knew my legs wouldn't handle it. "No."

He sat on the floor next to me, and released the collection of agents whose very presence crowded the room more than all the reporters, visitors, and photographers had, combined.

"You're going to get crumbs all over your suit pants," I said.

"Hazard of the job."

"What did I do?" I asked.

"One of two things," he said. "You either gave the media a whopper of a story to ruin you with . . ."

I moaned and put my head down.

"Or you saved a lot of lives, including the First Lady's."

Morton spoke. "Special Agent-in-Charge?"

Gavin looked up. "Yes?"

"Clear the building."

CHAPTER 23

"WHERE'S THE FIRST LADY?" I ASKED AS GAV rushed me from the room.

Two Secret Service agents accompanied us, Patricia Berland and Kevin Martin. Agent Martin shook his head, refusing to answer.

I'd expected to be led outside, as we had when I'd shouted the alarm Saturday, but to my surprise, I was herded into the East Wing and down the now-familiar set of stairs. "The bunker?" I asked.

Gav kept his lips tight and never broke stride. When the agents ushered us into the first door on the right, I was visited with a peculiar sense of déjà vu. This is where it all had begun, just days ago, when the fake bomb had been found . . . when Sean was still alive.

My sense of repeating past events was heightened when I walked in to see the First Lady sitting at the table where the three of us had shared our lunch.

She stood. "Ollie, I just heard what you did."

The enormity of the experience was making my legs heavy, my head tight. I made it to one of the chairs and didn't even think twice about etiquette. I sat down and blew out a shaky breath.

Gav and the two agents sat with us while we went over details. I explained again why I suspected an explosive, and a misfire in the electrical system that would trigger it. When I told them that this unusual phenomena could be purposely engineered, Agent Martin said, "Then they had to have had help from the inside."

"Curly!" I sat up, startled by my own realization. "The electrician who took over when Gene was killed. He's been fighting me the whole way. I tried to get him to look at the problem, but he refused." I spoke very quickly, gauging the three agents watching me, trying hard not to be stalled by their solemn expressions. "I think he might have set all this up. He was impossible to deal with. And . . ." I was grasping at straws, but I couldn't stop myself. "He might have even been the one who had me attacked."

Mrs. Campbell had been silent for most of this. When she spoke, she did so very quietly. "I can't believe that anyone would want to harm me," she said. "I know the gingerbread men were contributed by the Blanchard family. But how can you be sure that Treyton Blanchard is behind this? Couldn't it have been someone else?"

I looked to Gav. He answered, "We're rounding up a number of people for questioning right now. We'd been operating under the assumption that the president was the bomber's target, but with the information we have now, we believe that you may have been the target all along."

Mrs. Campbell looked away.

Agent Martin held a hand up. He held tight to his earpiece and listened closely. "We're needed back upstairs," he said, and started for the door. Agent Berland followed him.

Gav started to leave, too. "Will you be all right for a little while?" he asked.

The prickle at my shoulders was back. I was missing something.

He was just about out the door, when I said, "Wait."

Motioning for the two agents to go on ahead without him, Gav stopped. "What is it?"

When Tom had taken me through his version of Explosives 101, he'd been adamant on one point. In fact, he'd pounded the concept into my brain by making me repeat a mantra, over and over. "Always assume there's a secondary device."

"I think," I said, standing, pulling my thoughts together and attempting to make sense of them. "I think we need to go back to the kitchen."

GAV WANTED TO SEQUESTER ME IN THE BUNKER with Mrs. Campbell while he called the bomb squad back for a look, but I balked. "I could be wrong," I said.

He shot me an intense look. "You haven't been wrong yet."

I opened my mouth, but he interrupted.

"You cannot go traipsing around the White House when there might be a second bomb ready to go off," he said.

"You'll never find it without me."

"Wanna bet?"

The idea of going bomb-hunting was not high on my list of healthy activities, but the truth was, if I was right, they wouldn't find the second bomb for a long time. And by then it could be too late. I swallowed, unable to find the words to convey my need to protect the White House, but I saw that need reflected in all the agents' eyes. I knew they saw it in mine.

After a brief discussion on the possibility of setting up a camera for me to direct Gav and his agents from a safe distance, they decided there just wasn't enough time to arrange for that. "Putting your life in danger is not an option," Gav said. "We'll just have to do our best without you."

"Nobody knows the kitchen like I do," I said. "And the clock is ticking."

They knew it. I knew it.

I grabbed Gav's arm. "Literally."

The bomb squad took over our area of the bunker and outfitted me in protective gear. Just as they hustled me out, Mrs. Campbell asked, "Are you sure you know what you're doing?"

Covered by a helmet and a clear plastic face guard, I couldn't be certain she heard me assure her I did. Not that it mattered. I wasn't quite sure myself.

Walking with body armor was harder than I anticipated. Covered from head to toe, I felt as though I weighed six hundred pounds. Within moments of leaving the bunker, I was wet around my waist and collar, and rivulets of sweat dripped around my ears.

Gav, similarly outfitted, remained silent as we made our way through the hall and into the kitchen. Like I'd told them, I knew my kitchen like I would know my own children, if I had any. But to explain where to find something to a person unfamiliar with the area would be an exercise in futility. And the last thing I needed was for an army of military bomb experts to toss my pristine kitchen in an attempt to find an explosive device that I could put my hand on in moments.

Yeah, I was nervous. But more than that, I was determined.

Once in the kitchen, though, I faltered. My heart slammed so hard in my chest I could almost hear it clang against the body armor. If I was right, this entire room—the place I considered home even more so than my apartment—could be vaporized. Me with it.

I bit my lips, but it was hard to do since they were slippery with perspiration. My voice was hoarse. "Okay, here," I said, even though I wasn't sure they could hear me. I made my way to the far end of the room, bomb squad in tow. With the sinks to my left, I yanked up the drop-side of the center stainless steel countertop. "This is why you'd never find it." Once the side was secure, I crouched and reached beneath it to reveal a hidden cabinet door. Because of its inaccessibility, we rarely used this storage space except to shove junk we hoped never to see again.

I thought I heard them all gasp as I lost my footing, but it was just a quick stumble, and within seconds I'd righted myself, ready to root through the collection of useless items we'd retired here. I'd tucked this thing deep, hoping to forget about it until the time came for a seasonal clean-up.

Gav placed a hand on my padded shoulder. "I'll take over from here." His voice sounded far away. Blunted.

"But it's right—"

He silenced me with a look. "Think back to the Briefing Room, Ollie."

He was right. I remembered my mistake snatching the

fake IED from its perch, risking setting off a bomb. Finding this device was one thing. Handling it was something else.

Gav pointed to the door. "And get out."

I scooted backward, but panic gripped when I realized I'd have to cross the kitchen again to escape. As brave as I'd been coming down here, the terror I felt now, knowing that any movement in Gav's peripheral vision could affect the outcome, froze me in place. His focus right now was inside that cabinet door and he couldn't see me huddled in a corner behind him. All *my* focus was on him as he took a breath and steeled himself.

Twisting, Gav pushed his arm deep into the cabinet's recesses, his fingers working along objects I could picture even though I couldn't see. "Careful," I breathed, clouding my face mask.

"Hang on," he said to himself.

Very slowly, Gav eased backward, his hands cradling the familiar, ugly clock.

"That's it!" I said.

Other bomb squad technicians rushed forward and gently removed the clock from Gav's hands, placing it into a thick, insulated box. With a nod of acknowledgment, they hurried out.

The moment they were gone, I pulled the helmet off. So did Gav.

"What now?" I asked.

He shot me a skeptical look. "Haven't you had enough?"

WITH THE GINGERBREAD HOUSE DESTROYED, the official opening celebration abandoned, the First Lady relocated from the bunker to the residence, and reporters trampling over one another to try to get the scoop, it was a wild day, even by White House standards.

Not for the first time did I find myself the center of attention of a bunch of serious-faced males. This time we were back in the Red Room, and I was walking five men—all agents and security personnel—through my thought processes when I'd been waiting for Mrs. Campbell to throw the switch.

Though Gav was present, he didn't participate. He stood back as I fielded questions from the group, explaining what I could about floating neutrals. "I don't know how to test for them," I began, "and I don't even know if one was present. . . ."

"There was." The voice came from the back of the room, and I was surprised to see Curly Sheridan escorted in by two more agents. He looked as grumpy as ever, but to my surprise, he wasn't handcuffed, or in any way restrained.

I took an instinctive step back.

"It's okay," one of the agents said. "This is the guy who disabled the voltage problem."

I didn't understand.

"Damn Manny," Curly said. When he looked at me, his eyes narrowed. "When you found me working on the fountain, I thought you were talking out your a—your backside. But what you said made sense." He rubbed a finger along his scar, which made me feel guilty even though I hadn't done anything wrong. "I started looking into what you were talking about."

"The floating neutral?"

"Yeah," he said. "Looks like Manny, or Vince—or both of them—rigged one up to set those outlets to blow 240." He nodded toward the wall.

He didn't admit that he should have listened to me earlier,

but regret radiated off him like waves of heat. And that was good enough for me.

"They took off," said Gav from the back of the room. "We're picking them up now for questioning."

"Yi-im," I said suddenly.

"We're after him, too."

CHAPTER 24

MARCEL WAS STILL MOURNING HIS LOST GIN-
gerbread house the next day. "There are not even photos of
it other than those I took myself," he said. "All the photographers waited until the lighting ceremony." He heaved a
great sigh. "So much work. All lost."

We stood in the kitchen, having just finished preparing
breakfast for the president and First Lady. Other than the
fact that the upstairs was still being processed as a crime
scene, life was back to normal. After the excitement yesterday, the president had come home to be with his wife. Tom
had come back last night, too—in fact he'd picked me up
inside the grounds, sparing me having to run the gauntlet
of reporters that swarmed the place. Thank goodness. I'd
needed to vent and he was only too willing to listen.

"There are plenty of pictures of Ollie in today's paper,"
Cyan said, pushing the front page across the countertop.

I'd seen them. Crisp color pictures of me sitting under a

table amid gingerbread detritus graced the first page, under the headline "That's the Way the Cookie Crumbles." I turned away, groaning. "Can't we just forget yesterday ever happened?"

"The ace executive chef does it again," Bucky said, with more than a hint of sarcasm. "Olivia Paras, always in the middle of everything."

"Back off, Buckaroo," Cyan said. "She saved your life. All of ours, probably."

His mouth puckered and he glanced at Cyan, before turning to me. "I guess I never thanked you, did I?" He lifted his chin. "Thanks."

"No problem," I said, wanting to keep the mood light. "All in a day's work."

"You sound like James Bond," Cyan said. "Or . . . Jane Bond!"

Agda's eyes lit up, as she joined in on the banter. "Maybe she spy!"

Rafe nodded. "A Russian spy!"

"Russians are out," I said, laughing. "They're not the bad guys anymore."

Bucky wasn't being particularly unpleasant, but his words had more of a bite than anyone else's when he asked, "I still don't get it. How do you always get in the middle of all the intrigue around here?"

"Bad luck, I guess."

Gav leaned in the doorway. "Or good luck, depending on how you want to look at it." He greeted the staff and reminded them that even though recent events had thrown the schedule off, security classes would resume the next day. To me, he said, "Do you have a minute?"

I followed him to the China Room, thinking sadly about

Marcel's weeks of planning and preparation and of all the time he'd spent in here creating his now-trashed masterpiece.

Gav closed the door and motioned for me to sit in one of the upholstered chairs. "There will be a press conference later this morning."

"I'm not going to have to say anything, am I?"

He sat across from me, shaking his head, elbows on his knees as he studied the floor. The stress of the job obviously took its toll. He seemed to have aged since I'd met him. "No. In fact we'd prefer that you say nothing."

"Can you tell me what's going on?"

He sat back. "You probably know it all anyway."

"I don't. Really. I've just been guessing. Trying to fill in the blanks."

One eye narrowed. "I told you I believed in your instincts. And I'm glad you trusted your gut." Leaning forward again, but this time staring at me, he continued. "I'll tell you what I can. Fair enough?"

I nodded.

"The Blanchard gingerbread men were outfitted with a sophisticated type of explosive," he said slowly. "We haven't seen much of this stuff because it's so new. It's very malleable." He pantomimed, rubbing his thumbs and forefingers together. "Just like C-4, but this stuff is so advanced, they were able to use it as decoration on the cookies and not have anyone notice. Plus, it's stable enough for transport. Powerful stuff. Had it been ignited by a straight 120 volt, it would've been bad." He stared at me. "Very bad. It probably would have taken out everyone within ten feet of the explosion."

I didn't know if he was exaggerating to make me feel better, but I actually felt a little bit worse. Shivering, I tried hard not to imagine what might have happened if Mrs. Campbell had flipped that switch.

Gav must have read my mind because he added, "With the additional surge from the floating neutral, those three gingerbread men would have taken out the back half of the White House."

"Oh, God."

"Yeah," he said.

"And Blanchard arranged everything? But how and why? And what about Sean?"

Gav held up a hand. "Slow down. We've got Blanchard in custody. Your electrician Manny Fortunato, too. He rigged everything from the inside."

"But it was Blanchard behind it all?"

"Not according to Blanchard. He's trying to point the finger at his overzealous assistant."

"Bindy?"

Gav nodded. "Said she came up with all this on her own."

"No way."

With a shrug, Gav continued. "Blanchard claims he knew nothing about any of this. He's running real hard, trying to distance himself from the girl. Maintains he's completely innocent and seems just a little too eager to dump all the blame on her."

"What about her?"

For the first time all day, Gav smiled. "She's giving her statement now. Blanchard doesn't know, but she rolled right over now that he's pointing the finger at her. Oldest story in the book. Young, impressionable woman taken in by a powerful man. She was in it for love. He was in it for power." Gav added, "She's giving up every little detail in the hopes of getting off easy."

"Will she?"

"She was involved in trying to blow up the White House. What do you think?"

I grimaced. "What about Sean?"

Gav sobered again. "Blanchard again."

I sucked in a breath.

"Your friend Kirsten . . ." Gav began.

"I only met her once."

He dismissed my correction. "She was heading down the wrong path, but she was close. Turns out Sean was killed using Volkov's gun."

"What?"

"Crime scene investigators were able to prove that Sean didn't pull the trigger. That the note was planted, making the death a homicide. But." He bit the corner of his mouth. "The gun's serial number was mutilated. Not completely. Just enough to slow down its identification. When we figured it out, we realized the gun belonged to Volkov. He was brought in for questioning."

"That's probably what Kirsten heard about."

"Could be," he said. "Volkov admitted to it being his, but was as surprised as we were to discover how it had been used. He couldn't imagine how it could have gotten out of his house—until yesterday. He called the Metropolitan Police because he remembered that the last time he'd seen it, he'd been showing it to Blanchard." Gav placed a finger over his lips. "We asked him to keep that to himself, and told him that we'd be in touch."

"So it looks like Blanchard killed Sean and was trying to frame Volkov for it?"

"That's the premise we're working under." Gav licked his lips. "But he didn't do the messy work himself. According to Bindy there were a couple of other people involved."

I thought about the two guys who'd accosted me. "Who are they?"

He shook his head. "She didn't know their names. Just knew that Blanchard handled parts of the plan himself. He, or one of his operatives, may have fed the information to Kirsten. In fact, we believe they killed her, too."

My heart broke for the poor kid. She'd been trying so hard to make a name for herself and had instead been used and discarded by a powerful senator who was bent on a run at the White House. "How did Blanchard get to Manny, or to Yi-im?"

"His girl Bindy. She had all the connections from her days working here. In Manny's case, it was pure greed. Yi-im and Blanchard go way back to the senator's days as an army intelligence officer in Seoul." He gave me a look. "Yi-im was in the Korean CIA, although under a different name, of course."

"How did he pass the background check here?"

"Blanchard sponsored Yi-im into the United States. If he's who we think he is, your friend Yi-im and his brother were Korean operatives who may have been involved in the assassination of Park Chung-hee back in 1979."

My mind was having a hard time assimilating all this. "Then he's a dangerous guy."

"You think?"

"Have you arrested him yet?"

"We're working on it, but he's slippery."

This was too much for me. "And all this was so that Blanchard could sell Zendy Industries?"

"That's only part of it. The senator is an ambitious man. For a successful run at the presidency he needed the money from Zendy and spies inside the White House. And he wanted all that enough to kill. He might have had a hand in killing Mr. Sinclair; we're looking into that now."

I gasped.

"There are bad people in this world, Ollie," he said.

"I know. I just can't imagine. . . ."

"There's something else," he said.

By the look on his face, I knew it wasn't good news. "Go ahead," I said.

"When your chief electrician was killed . . ."

"Gene."

"Yes, Gene. When he was killed, he was felled by that phenomena you talked about—the floating neutral. But it looks as though it occurred naturally."

My stomach clenched. I knew what Gav was about to say, so I beat him to it. Maybe it would hurt less that way. "And I brought the idea to their attention?"

"You did," he said. "Blanchard's team had placed a bomb in the White House, in an effort to target the First Lady, but their attempts were crude and unsuccessful. Bindy kept in regular contact with Manny. He tossed out the idea of rigging a floating neutral after you kept badgering him about it. He said he thought he could make the blast look like a natural occurrence."

My head was spinning. "So I played a part in almost getting the White House destroyed."

"No almost about it. The White House is gone." Gav smiled. "The *gingerbread* White House, that is. Completely decimated, thanks to you." His eyebrows rose and the gray eyes sparkled. "But also thanks to you, the real White House is still standing."

MARCEL'S GINGERBREAD MASTERPIECE WOULD be the first one to go down in history as a casualty of political warfare. But some good had come of it. In the First

Lady's press conference later that night, she'd chosen not to dwell on what was lost, but on what remained. She'd reminded everyone in the televised event that all the gingerbread men sent in by the nation's children had survived intact.

She said: "That our children's contributions are still with us—that each one is still just as beautiful as it was when we received it—is really what's important. Thanks to our fine staff and American gutsiness, our White House is still standing, and we are still together to enjoy it. Our holiday theme has special meaning for us tonight because . . . together we do celebrate. Welcome home." At that she'd opened her arms, inviting the cameras into the residence for their much-belated Decorator Tour.

As I watched her, I realized that for the first time since she'd received the news of Sean's death, Mrs. Campbell was at peace.

CHAPTER 25

A WEEK LATER THERE WERE STILL A HUNDRED questions I hadn't gotten answers to, but knowing the tight-lipped nature of the White House security personnel, I counted my blessings for having gotten as much as I had out of Gav.

I thought about this as I sat in the kitchen, today's *Washington Post* on the countertop in front of me. It was quiet and I appreciated the solitude. I'd sent everyone home early tonight. Dinner was done, and with no big events scheduled till next week, I decided we all needed some time off. Agda smiled and promised to be in early the next day. Bucky actually thanked me again, and I was surprised to notice Rafe helping Cyan into her coat as the two of them made plans for spending the evening together.

The front page of the *Post* caught me up on the latest in the Blanchard Blowup, as they were calling it. There was yet another picture of Bindy, who, in every shot, seemed to be running past cameras, face covered, hopping into a waiting car or being hustled into the police station. Charges against her were still pending. Next to her photo was one of a smiling Senator Blanchard, who'd been indicted along with Manny and Yi-im.

Blanchard held his head high and gripped a microphone with both hands. The caption below the picture quoted: "I am innocent of these ridiculous allegations." His wife stood behind him, looking stricken and gaunt. The kids were nowhere to be seen.

I scanned for updates, but it was mostly just rehash. I turned to page five to finish the article.

The Blowup was hot stuff—real news—and I was thankful for the shift in attention away from me. Even though all the articles still made mention of my leap under the table to prevent the explosion—after all, that's where the Blanchard Blowup story started—my name was being mentioned less often. For that, I was grateful.

Secret Service personnel had been my constant companions. Two agents shuttled me back and forth to work since the big holiday commotion to keep me out of reach of the mob of reporters. Hordes of them camped outside the White House gates, every one of them eager to get an exclusive interview with the chef who had literally brought down the house—the gingerbread house. I didn't complain about my escort service—instead of taking the Metro, I'd been riding in the back of a luxury sedan, with door-to-door attention. Tom had at first offered to take over bodyguarding duties, but his schedule kept him busy until late in the evening almost every night. After all, his first duty was to the president. At least in the daytime. But he was always happy to do some extra undercover work with me.

Tonight, exactly one week after the fracas, I was on my own again. My personal Secret Service detail had informed me they deemed it safe for me to resume my normal commute. Thank goodness. As much as I'd miss the cushy comfort of the chauffeured car, I was happy to be free of constant surveillance. I wondered how the president and his family tolerated the never-ending attention.

I was about to close the newspaper when a related sidebar headline caught my eye: "Zendy Industries Sold." The sidebar directed me to the business section—E, which I turned to as quickly as I could.

It can't be true, I thought, as I pulled out the section to search for the article. Mrs. Campbell was adamant. What could have caused her to change her mind?

I didn't have to search far. On the first page of the section, the Zendy headline was repeated and a lengthy update appeared below. I scanned, then realized I wasn't comprehending. Starting from the top, I began again, trying to absorb this late-breaking news update.

Mrs. Campbell had, indeed, announced an agreement to sell Zendy Industries. But she'd done so in a spectacularly intriguing way. She was quoted: "With the recent developments of which we're all aware, I have decided not to continue my association with my former colleagues. While Treyton Blanchard and Nick Volkov are occupied with their own personal issues, I have come to understand that they have neither the time nor the inclination to see to the best interests of Zendy. With that in mind, I have taken Nick Volkov's offhand advice. He may have been joking, but I am quite serious.

"Although I am unable to finance an entire buyout, I do have sufficient resources to allow me a 51 percent share. The remaining 49 percent will be acquired by other investors."

When pressed to name these other investors, Mrs. Campbell was further quoted as saying, "I don't care to divulge that to the press, at this time. But I can tell you that it is refreshing to work with investors I can trust."

Good for her. I smiled as I pulled the newspaper back together, and dropped it into the recycle bin. After taking a moment to disinfect the countertop, I headed home.

CHAPTER 26

NO REPORTERS WAITED FOR ME AT THE GATE. No camera crews stalked me on my short walk to the MacPherson Square station. And yet . . .

That prickling feeling was back.

The evening was dark, as it usually is after eight at night in early December, but the cold, snappy air held a hint of electricity I couldn't put my finger on. I turned to see if anyone followed, but the street was mostly quiet. A male-female couple walked a prancing Pekinese, which wore little leather boots on each paw.

Across the street a few other pedestrians ambled, scurried, and strode, but no one paid me any attention.

Once at the station, I slid my new Metro pass into the machine, and picked it up when it popped out of the slot on the top of the turnstile. Over the past week I'd been able to replace almost everything that had been stolen, including credit cards. Replacement cards showed up in my apartment's mailbox with blazing speed. I guess they didn't want me to miss even one day of holiday shopping. I always kept my cell phone in my back pocket, so that was one headache I didn't have to deal with. My personal stuff, like the few pictures I carried, a little cash, and some recent receipts, were gone for good.

As I returned the Metro pass to my purse, my fingers sought and found the pepper spray. Just wrapping my hand around the little canister made me feel more secure. Still, the uncomfortable feeling of being watched stayed with me until the train arrived. I paid careful attention to those who boarded the same time I did, but saw no one suspicious.

Once settled in my seat, the feeling disappeared, and I attributed my paranoia to having gotten used to being followed by Secret Service agents every day for the past week. I'd get over it.

At my stop, I took care to take note of the folks who got off with me. A woman with a baby, an elderly gentleman, and two young men with Mohawks. So far, so good.

When I made it outside, however, the oppressive sense of being watched was back. I twisted, making a complete 360, but I saw no one of interest.

Keeping my head down to fight off the wind, I hurried to make the quick trek from the station to my apartment building. I'd just gotten past the very spot I'd been accosted when I heard it.

Double-tap footsteps behind me.

I spun. My hand dug straight for my pepper spray.

Nobody there.

The footsteps stopped.

I stole a quick glance in the direction of my building, gauging how fast I could get there, and how best to outpace the big guy, for I had no doubt he was back. In that instant

I knew with certainty that the little Asian guy and his bulky cohort had been in league with Yi-im, and, it followed, with Blanchard.

I scanned the area, knowing they would be bent on revenge.

A rustle to my left.

Shan-Yu, my would-be abductor, stepped from the shadows.

I jumped backward as my heart thudded—crazed, like a gong in my chest.

"You not smart woman," he said. Behind him, Mr. Tap Shoes emerged, arms at his sides, his stance telling me he was ready to tackle me if I tried to move. I inched backward, my cold-sweaty hands fighting for a better grip on my pepper spray.

"I'm not?" I asked, buying myself precious seconds. My hand still tucked inside my purse, I needed to get my index finger and thumb into position. There. I released the safety catch.

Shan-Yu's eyes caught the streetlight's beam, glittering as he stepped closer.

"You think you so smart," he said, again. "But you not."

"Oh yeah?" I said, knowing I needed a distraction. "Then how come you didn't notice the Secret Service agents following me?"

Instinctively, they both looked up. I leaped forward, dragging out the spray, holding my breath as I shot them both in the face. I held down the plunger as long as I could before backing up fast and averting my eyes.

The two yelped, coughing and waving their hands as I bolted away from them, squinting to keep the chemical from burning my own eyes.

I'd gone only two steps when I slammed into something

hard. My first thought was that I'd hit a wall, or a tree, but when the limbs reached out to grab me, I knew better. I screamed, scratched, and tried to bite.

"Ollie!"

At the familiarity I stopped fighting. I looked up. "Gav?"

He pushed me behind him and moved toward Shan-Yu and Mr. Tap Shoes, who were already being cuffed by two other agents. Seconds later, an unmarked car eased around the corner and the agents hustled the coughing creeps inside.

"What's going on?" I asked. "How did you know?"

Gav conferred with the men before turning to answer me. "We didn't."

Realization was beginning to dawn. "You suspected these guys were part of Blanchard's army."

He made a so-so motion. "We assumed."

"But you couldn't find them."

"No."

"So you hung me out as bait?"

Gav winced. "Something like that."

The two agents who'd corralled my attackers were finished loading them into the car. A second later they pulled away from the curb, and the agent in the passenger seat waved. I watched them for a long moment before I could speak again. "Well, thanks for letting me know."

"When you shouted about being protected by the Secret Service, I actually thought our cover had been blown," he said. His mouth twitched—an almost smile. "Did you *know* we were tailing you?"

"No."

"Well, you seemed to be doing just fine on your own. I don't think you even needed us."

I tried to smile, but I was shaking too much. Gav noticed.

He walked me to my door, one hand on my elbow. "We're packing it in, you know. We completed the staff training. Time to take the explosive show on the road."

"You're not coming back?"

"Not until we're needed again."

I was surprised to realize I was sorry to see him go. I said as much, then added, "But for the president's sake, I hope your team isn't called back for a long time."

He held open the building's front door. "Until then, Ollie," he said, "I'm counting on you being our eyes and ears."

I scooted inside, then turned back. But I didn't know what to say.

Gav gave a quick two-fingered salute, and was gone.

AN ADORABLE
ASSEMBLY OF APPETIZERS

FORGIVE THE TITLE—I CAN'T RESIST A GOOD alliteration. But it's true that there's nothing better to have in your cooking repertoire than a bunch of appetizer recipes. Most appetizers are fabulously tasty, and many are good for you, too (though not all; the cheese straws, brownies, and cookies below are pure sin). When you want to throw a fancy reception or a party and you don't want to drag in waiters and bartenders to lend a hand, whipping together a big bunch of appetizers is a surefire way to feed a crowd and keep them happy without having to go through the trauma of a big sit-down dinner. Even at the White House, the number of affairs where we field a wide assortment of appetizers for guests to nibble on far exceeds the number of big State dinners we host each year. One real advantage of this kind of spread is that it makes it so much easier for people to mingle and talk. Washington really is a fairly small town, so the guests at most White House receptions are likely to have met one another before. But even when they haven't, conversations always start at the appetizer tables. Usually it's just advice not to miss a particularly succulent item in the array; but from such simple beginnings, real conversations grow.

And if you put out the right kind of appetizer spread, people can truly make a meal out of it. The recipes below, some of which Mrs. Campbell chose for her receptions this year, are easy to make, easy to eat, and work well together as a display. With a wide variety of colors, textures, and tastes, these items create a wonderful appetizer party. All are made with ingredients easily available at any supermarket. (Though I have to say, it's nice to grow your own herbs. If you have a sunny window, a few pots overflowing with chives, basil, sage, and parsley can really punch up your cooking. And they're very easy to grow.) Most of these recipes can be prepared ahead of time, so you can enjoy your own party. Even the ones that need to be prepared right before the party are fast. Each recipe also stands well on its own, so you can also add them to your regular meal rotations if they strike your fancy.

Enjoy the party—and happy noshing!

Ollie

APPETIZER PARTY MENU

Blue-Cheese Straws

Stuffed Cherry Tomatoes

Asparagus Spears and Lemon Butter

Garlic–Green Bean Bundles

Mini Red Potatoes with Sour Cream, Cheddar, and Chives

Bacon-and-Cornbread Muffins

Little White Rolls

Sugar-Cured Ham with White-Wine Honey Mustard

Chicken-Fried Beef Tenderloin with White Onion Gravy

Brownie Bites

Gingerbread Men

BLUE-CHEESE STRAWS

½ pound blue cheese, softened
½ cup (1 stick) butter, softened
3 ounces cream cheese, softened
2 tablespoons heavy cream
¼ teaspoon red pepper flakes
¼ teaspoon kosher salt
3 cups flour, sifted
½ cup finely chopped smoked almonds (optional)

Preheat oven to 400°F.

Place blue cheese, butter, and cream cheese in bowl or mixer. Cream them together. Mixing by hand, add the rest of the ingredients, one at a time, until fully incorporated.

Turn the dough out on a floured board. Roll out to a medium-thin dough (about ¼-inch thick). With a sharp knife, cut the dough into ½-inch-wide strips. Twist each strip until it is a loose spiral from top to bottom and lay the spirals on an ungreased cookie sheet, not touching their neighbors.

Bake until strips are golden brown, 5–10 minutes. Remove to wire racks and let cool.

Store in tightly covered tins lined with wax paper until ready to serve.

STUFFED CHERRY TOMATOES

1 8-ounce block cream cheese, softened
¼ cup sour cream
1 small bunch chives, washed and chopped, about 3–4
  tablespoons (Reserve 1 tablespoon for garnish.)
2 cloves garlic, cleaned and minced
20 fresh basil leaves, washed and cut into thin strips
Pinch kosher or sea salt, to taste
1 pint cherry tomatoes, washed and dried

Make the filling by combining the first six ingredients in a bowl and stirring well. Place in a pastry bag fitted with a large star point, if desired. Otherwise, the filling can be spooned into the tomatoes. Set filling aside.

Using a sharp paring knife, cut a small slice off the bottom of a cherry tomato so that it will sit firmly on its tray without rolling around. Cut an *X* into the top of the cherry tomato with the same knife. Either use a watermelon baller to remove the pulp from the tomato, or squeeze it gently over a waste bowl to get the pulp out. Repeat with all the cherry tomatoes, laying them out in rows on the serving tray, ready to be filled.

Pipe the cream-cheese mixture into the prepared tomatoes, or spoon it, for a more rustic look.

Sprinkle finished dish with reserved chopped chives. Serve chilled.

ASPARAGUS SPEARS AND LEMON BUTTER

1 pound fresh asparagus stalks, washed, tough
  stems cut away
¼ pound butter (if unsalted, add ¼ teaspoon salt)
Fresh cracked pepper, to taste
1 tablespoon fresh chopped parsley
Juice of one medium lemon

Place asparagus in a steamer basket. Place steamer basket into a large pot with about a half inch of boiling water in the bottom, and cover. Steam asparagus until bright green, but still a bit crisp, about 3–7 minutes, depending on the size of the asparagus.

While asparagus is steaming, melt butter in a small saucepan. Add salt, pepper, parsley, and lemon juice and whisk well. Pour into serving bowl.

Remove steamed asparagus. Place on oblong platter. Place the bowl of butter on one end of the platter with a small ladle for guests to pour it over their asparagus as they serve themselves.

Serve warm.

GARLIC–GREEN BEAN BUNDLES

*Two pounds fresh green beans, washed, ends and
    strings removed
1 pound good-quality smoked bacon, sliced
½ cup olive oil
3 cloves garlic, cleaned and minced*

Preheat oven to 350° F.

On a sheet pan, cookie sheet, or jelly-roll pan (a large, flat
pan with an edge sufficient to prevent the grease you're
about to make from running all over your nice, clean oven),
divide the green beans in bundles of roughly 10–12 beans,
with beans bundles laid out in parallel formation.

Wrap each bundle loosely with a slice of bacon, tying it on
top with a simple knot and arranging the loose ends artistically.

In a bowl, whisk the olive oil and the garlic. Brush oil lib-
erally over the green-bean bundles.

Bake until the bacon is cooked to taste and the green beans
are warmed through, approximately 15 minutes.

Remove bundles to a serving platter, using a spatula. Serve
warm.

MINI RED POTATOES WITH SOUR CREAM, CHEDDAR, AND CHIVES

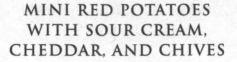

> 2 pounds small red new potatoes, scrubbed, peels
>   still on
> 1 cup sour cream
> 1 small bundle fresh chives, washed and chopped
>   (about 4 tablespoons)
> 6 slices precooked bacon, crumbled
> Kosher salt, to taste
> Fresh ground black pepper, to taste
> 3 ounces good sharp Cheddar cheese, finely grated

Boil the red potatoes in enough water to cover until they are fork-tender, about 15–20 minutes. Drain the potatoes, and let cool enough that they are easy to handle.

Cut each potato in half. On the uncut end of each half, slice away a small amount of peel and flesh so the potato half will sit flat and securely on a platter. Using a melon baller or a spoon, scoop out the middle of the potato. Arrange the prepared halves on a broiler-safe serving tray.

Make the filling by mixing the sour cream, chives, bacon, and salt and pepper to taste. If the bacon is very salty, I often don't add additional salt. Spoon filling into potato halves. Sprinkle with grated Cheddar cheese. At this point the tray can be set aside, or even refrigerated, until ready to cook.

Place under broiler until cheese begins to melt and filling begins to bubble, about 3–5 minutes.

Serve warm.

 # BACON-AND-CORNBREAD MUFFINS

1/2 cup canola oil

3/4 cup cornmeal (preferably stone-ground, but regular will work if you can't find the good stuff)

1 cup flour

1 teaspoon baking soda

1 tablespoon baking powder

1/2 teaspoon salt

1 tablespoon sugar

3 tablespoons cold butter

1 cup buttermilk

2 large eggs, beaten

1/2 cup grated Cheddar cheese (Sharp is what I prefer, but use a cheese you like eating.)

1 bunch chives, washed and chopped (about 4 tablespoons)

8 slices precooked smoked bacon, chopped into 1/4-inch strips

Preheat oven to 400° F.

Put 1 tablespoon of canola oil into each well of a standard 12-cup muffin pan, and place muffin pan into oven to heat the oil.

Meanwhile, working quickly, sift flour, baking soda, baking powder, salt, and sugar together into a large mixing bowl. Cut in the butter until the butter is blended in. Add buttermilk and eggs all at once, and stir just until ingredients are barely blended. A few lumps are fine; this batter gets tough if you overwork it. Add the cheese, chives, and bacon, stirring only until the ingredients are roughly mixed in.

Pull hot muffin tin from oven. Drop batter into the muffin cups, filling each roughly three-quarters full. The hot oil should make the batter bubble and brown on the sides. Place pan into oven and cook until muffins are done and golden, roughly 20–25 minutes.

I like to serve them hot, but they're great at room temperature, too.

LITTLE WHITE ROLLS

I have to make an admission here: When it comes to bread making, I cheat. The pastry chefs at the White House do most of the baking, so it isn't a problem at work. But at home, I use a bread machine. I set it on the dough setting and let the machine handle the kneading. Then I shape the dough by hand and let it do a final rise in the pan or pans of my choice. I actually like kneading bread by hand, but I'm busy, so I sacrifice the fun of kneading for the time I save by letting the machine handle it. The instructions here are for any standard bread machine.

> 2½ tablespoons (1 standard packet) granulated
>   dry yeast
> 4–4½ cups bread flour
> 2 tablespoons sugar
> 1 teaspoon salt
> ¼ cup nonfat dried milk
> 1 egg, beaten
> 1–1½ cups lukewarm water
> ⅓ cup olive oil

Set your bread machine to the dough setting. Add the yeast, 4 cups flour, sugar, salt, milk, egg, 1 cup water, and the oil to the bread machine vessel. Turn on bread machine. After 4 minutes, look at the dough. If it's too floury, add water a few drops at a time, until the dough looks right. If it's too runny, add flour 1 tablespoon at a time, until the dough looks right. The dough should look smooth and have a texture that feels roughly like the lobe of your ear when you pinch it— yielding but resilient. Balance the flour and water additions until you reach that middle point where the dough comes together nicely in a ball without being too watery or too stiff. Then walk away and let the machine do its thing. Most machines take around 1 hour and 20 minutes to 1½ hours to run the dough cycle. The machine will usually beep when it's finished.

When the dough is done, unplug the machine. Grease the wells of two standard muffin tins with a spray-on like Pam or Baker's Choice, or rub with shortening. Pinch off balls of dough roughly the size of golf balls, and place a ball in each muffin-tin well. When manipulating the dough, it makes the resulting bread prettier if you stretch the pinched dough ends to the back of the ball, and put that side bottom down in the tin, leaving a smooth, rounded surface at the top of each roll.

Cover the tins with a damp dish towel and set aside to let rise until doubled in size. This time can vary enormously, depending on the temperature of the site where you are resting the dough. The warmer it is, the faster the dough will rise. In a busy commercial kitchen, where the temperature often hovers around the 100° mark, it generally takes about 30 minutes—but if it gets much hotter than that, the yeast will start to die and the bread will start to cook, so don't let the air temperature get over 100°. In a 70° home kitchen, it can take as long as two hours. A long, slow rise time often imparts more flavor to the bread. I find that putting the tins in a cool oven over a pan filled with hot water is just about perfect. The heat from the water warms the space, and the steam keeps the dough from drying out.

Preheat oven to 350° F.

Place the muffin tins in oven. Bake until rolls are golden, roughly 15–20 minutes.

Remove from oven. Let stand until rolls are cool enough to handle—usually about 5 minutes—then pluck them out of the muffin tins.

Serve warm.

For all you purists, if you prefer working this dough by hand, feel free to do it. The only thing that's different is that you'll need to proof the yeast—that is, dissolve it in the warm water along with the sugar, and let it get bubbly—before you mix the ingredients. Then knead until smooth, let it rise, punch it down, let it rise again, punch it down again, put it in the pans, and continue as the recipe indicates.

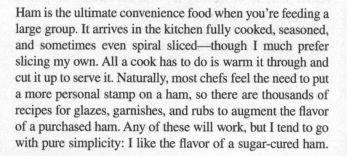

SUGAR-CURED HAM WITH WHITE-WINE HONEY MUSTARD

Ham is the ultimate convenience food when you're feeding a large group. It arrives in the kitchen fully cooked, seasoned, and sometimes even spiral sliced—though I much prefer slicing my own. All a cook has to do is warm it through and cut it up to serve it. Naturally, most chefs feel the need to put a more personal stamp on a ham, so there are thousands of recipes for glazes, garnishes, and rubs to augment the flavor of a purchased ham. Any of these will work, but I tend to go with pure simplicity: I like the flavor of a sugar-cured ham.

And I find that a thin coating of plain old molasses augments the flavor perfectly. But if you don't like molasses, feel free to glaze your ham any way you see fit. (I've got a friend who swears by dumping a can of ginger ale on the ham when he puts it in the oven. I've tried it. Surprisingly, it's good.) The most important thing when serving this dish is to pick a good ham to begin with.

> *1 good-quality sugar-cured ham, sized to fit the*
> *crowd of people you're feeding (I generally go*
> *with 3–5 pounds for home use, but any size*
> *will do.)*
> *1 cup molasses*

Preheat oven to 300° F. (Ham needs a slow cooking process to keep it from drying out and the sugar glaze from burning.)

Wash ham well in cold water. Place ham, fat side up, in a roasting pan on a rack, and place in oven. Cook 15–20 minutes per pound. Pull ham out of oven and carve off any excess fat, leaving about ¼-inch fat layer on the meat. Carve into the remaining fat with any decorative pattern desired—I usually go with 1-inch crosshatches. Brush ham with molasses. Put back into oven for 20 minutes, until glaze begins to bubble and brown.

Remove from oven. Place on serving platter. Slice into serving-size portions. Serve warm with White-Wine Honey Mustard on the side, and rolls and corn muffins handy, in case any guest feels like making a sandwich. Most of them will—you can trust me on this.

WHITE-WINE HONEY MUSTARD

1 cup good Dijon mustard
2 tablespoons white wine
2 tablespoons honey

Mix ingredients and chill. Serve with ham.

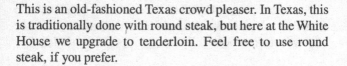

CHICKEN-FRIED BEEF TENDERLOIN WITH WHITE ONION GRAVY

This is an old-fashioned Texas crowd pleaser. In Texas, this is traditionally done with round steak, but here at the White House we upgrade to tenderloin. Feel free to use round steak, if you prefer.

Canola oil, for frying
2 pounds (roughly) beef tenderloin, cut crosswise
*   into ½-inch steaks*
1½ cups flour
1 tablespoon garlic powder
1 teaspoon onion powder
1 teaspoon salt
Fresh cracked pepper, to taste (I use about
*   ½ teaspoon.)*
2 cups buttermilk

WHITE ONION GRAVY

3 small onions, cleaned and sliced into thin rings,
*   rings teased apart*
2 tablespoons flour
2 cups milk
Salt and fresh cracked pepper, to taste

Preheat oven to 200° F.

This is a stovetop recipe, and you'll need a big, sturdy skillet, preferably cast iron, though any heavy-bottomed metal pan will do. Place about ½ inch canola oil in the pan, and set over medium heat. The oil should be at about 300°, or hot enough to make a drop of water dropped in it dance and sizzle, to fry the steaks.

While the oil is heating, place each steak between two sheets of good plastic wrap. Pound the steaks with a meat mallet to tenderize and to make them thinner. This ensures that the beef will cook through fully when it's put in the skillet.

In a large resealable bag, pour in the flour, garlic powder, onion powder, salt, and pepper. Close the bag and shake to mix.

Put the buttermilk in a bowl.

Place a steak in the bag of seasoned flour and shake to coat. Remove the steak and dip it in the buttermilk, then put it back in the seasoned flour and shake to coat again. Once all the steaks are coated, it's time to fry them.

Place a few of the steaks in the hot oil—you want the steaks to fit easily, with room to move around and not touch. I find frying 3 at a time works well for me. Fry until golden brown, about 3 minutes, then turn over and fry until golden brown on the other side. Remove cooked steaks to a warmed plate, and continue frying the rest of the coated steaks until done. Place the steaks in the oven to keep them warm while you make the gravy.

To make the gravy, pour off some of the oil in the frying pan. Leave a layer of oil sufficient to cover the bottom of the pan lightly. Add onions, and fry until brown and tender, stirring occasionally, 6–8 minutes. Gently scatter the flour over the cooked onions, stirring constantly until flour begins to brown and turns into a thick paste, about 3 minutes. Slowly add milk, stirring constantly. Gravy will thicken. Taste, and add salt and pepper to taste. Serve the steaks on the warmed platter, with a big bowl of gravy next to them, or plate the steaks individually, ladling a nice scoop of gravy over each.

 BROWNIE BITES

¾ cup good-quality cocoa
¾ cup canola oil
2 cups sugar
4 eggs, beaten
1 tablespoon vanilla extract
1½ cups flour

1 teaspoon baking powder
½ teaspoon salt
24 pecan halves, for garnish (optional)

FROSTING

¼ cup butter, softened
½ cup cocoa
1½ cups confectioner's sugar
1 teaspoon vanilla extract
⅓ cup milk

Preheat oven to 350°F.

Place the cocoa, oil, sugar, eggs, and vanilla into a large mixing bowl and stir until the cocoa is fully incorporated, and the mixture is smooth and glossy. Add dry ingredients all at once and gently fold the wet and dry ingredients together. Stir just until the ingredients are mixed. Too much stirring makes the brownies tough.

Place foil (paper cups will shred, so using foil is important) baking cups into 2 12-cup muffin tins. Spray with cooking spray or grease with shortening. Fill the cups two-thirds full with the brownie mixture.

Place in oven and bake until the mixture is just set, and lovely cracks appear on the surface of the brownie bites, about 15–20 minutes. Remove cups from tins and let brownie bites cool.

To prepare the frosting, place the softened butter in a large mixing bowl. Add cocoa, confectioner's sugar, and vanilla, and blend until the mixture is fully mixed. Add the milk, 1 tablespoonful at a time, and continue beating the frosting. When the frosting looks glossy and forms soft peaks, it's ready to use.

Frost the brownies in their foil cups. Garnish with pecan halves, or the garnish of your choice. Serve.

Other options for garnishes include everything from mini–chocolate chips to a sprinkle of coconut to a fan of candy corn–cute in the fall—to white chocolate curls to chocolate–covered coffee beans to peanut butter cups to peppermint patties to other chocolates. Tailor your garnish to your anticipated diners. If you're feeding mostly adults, go for sophistication. If you're feeding lots of kids, raid the candy store. The pecan halves are a compromise—both adults and kids like them, and the people who don't like nuts can easily remove them. But the sky's the limit as far as garnishing these goes.

 # GINGERBREAD MEN

3 cups flour
2 teaspoons ground ginger
2 teaspoons ground cinnamon
½ teaspoon ground cloves
¼ teaspoon fresh ground nutmeg
½ teaspoon salt
1 pinch ground pepper (optional, but it gives the
    cookies a little bite)

Scant 1 teaspoon baking soda
¾ cup butter, softened
½ cup brown sugar, well packed
¼ cup white sugar
1 large egg
½ cup molasses
Raisins (optional)

ROYAL ICING

2 tablespoons meringue powder
Fresh lemon juice from 1 lemon
Roughly 2 cups sifted powdered (confectioner's)
    sugar

In a large bowl, sift together flour, baking soda, salt, and spices. Set aside.

In the bowl of an electric mixer, blend the softened butter, then add the sugars, and cream at medium speed until smooth and fluffy. Add in egg and molasses. Reduce speed to low. Gradually add in flour. Batter will be stiff. Divide batter into workable batches (I usually divide it in thirds), wrap each batch tightly in plastic wrap, and refrigerate overnight.

Preheat oven to 350° F.

Pull the first batch of dough from the refrigerator. Roll out on a floured board until dough ¼- to ⅛-inch thick. I aim for a roll of dough about 8 inches wide. That makes cutting out 8-inch gingerbread men really easy. I then cut out gingerbread men freehand from the dough using a very sharp paring knife. Luckily, a gingerbread man is easy to draw, even for the artistically challenged. You can also use cookie cutters, if you have them. Remove the dough that isn't part of the cookies, then gently lift the gingerbread men with a long spatula, and place them on ungreased cookie sheets. If desired, add raisins for eyes and mouth. Otherwise, these can be piped on after baking. Continue rolling out gingerbread men until all cookies are shaped. The unused dough can be kneaded together and rolled out at the end. If you plan to hang these cookies as decorations, be sure to cut a large hole where you want to insert the hanging ribbon. I find a sturdy drinking straw is the perfect tool to get a nice-sized hole, but canapé cutters or a toothpick can function equally well.

Bake cookies until gently browned on bottom, about 8–12 minutes. Remove from oven. Let cool for 5 minutes. (This makes the cookie stronger and less prone to breakage.) Remove gently from cookie sheets with a long spatula, and set on a wire rack to cool.

To prepare royal icing, mix the meringue powder with the lemon juice in the bowl of an electric mixer. Gradually add the powdered sugar. Stop adding sugar when the mixture holds stiff peaks and is of good piping consistency.

Load icing into large piping bag fitted with a small circular tip. Pipe clothes and features on the finished cookies. Lay the cookies out flat for the icing to dry. Once they are very, very dry, serve them, or store the finished cookies packed in a tin in layers separated by waxed or parchment paper.

The better the spices, the better the cookies. I get my spices online at The Spice House, which has outlets in Milwaukee and

Chicago, as well as an excellent mail-order site at www .thespicehouse.com. I've found the spices I get there are simply the best available.

Piped royal icing makes for beautiful cookies. But kids much prefer these iced with buttercream icing and decorated with chocolate chips for the eyes, nose, mouth, and buttons. That's also faster. But since these cookies are wearing their party clothes, I'm giving the royal icing version here.